ToyShelf Publishing Presents

Dimes, Profiles, and Wives Book One©

Today's Proverbs 31 Woman

By

Toya Raylonn Vickers

Copyright © 2010, 2020 by Toya Raylonn Vickers

ISBN   Softcover   9798565606683

All rights reserved. No part of this book may be reproduced or transmitted in any form or by any means, electronic or mechanical, including photocopying, recording, or by any information storage or retrieval system, without permission in writing from the copyright owner.

This is a work of fiction. Names, characters, places and incidents either are a product of the author's imagination or are used fictitiously, and any resemblance to any actual persons living or dead, events, or locales is entirely coincidental.

ToyShelf Publishing

Acknowledgements

First I have to give all honor and glory to God for giving me the talent and umption to even write the words of this work some ten years ago and then to have the courage to go back and rework it to make it the best it could be. Since 2010 I have been through so much, married, divorced but yet and still standing on the promises of God. I will say this, being a true Proverbs 31 woman of God is something that is a daily walk that any woman can do, if she truly desires to do it. But it is not easy, yet it is so fulfilling.

As a daughter of the most high and believer in Christ Jesus, I have been privileged not to be totally dismayed by all the things that have been going on in this world. As we are called to be not of the world, I have learned to lean on my heavenly Father in my time of need and remember that He is my first love. That alone gets me through the days.

I have to say thank you to my prayer partner and friend Sister Yolanda Eclind and my church family at New Birth Christian Ministries where Bishop Kenneth Moore Sr. is our pastor. A special thank you to my mother, Raylonn Smith, sister Zoe Vickers, best friends Marisa Sherrod Gillium and Senora Jelks as well as Ashley Famara Manneh. I cannot forget my favorite auntie Delores Cox, cousin Therza Douglas and a special shout out to my ex husband who taught me just how strong of a woman I can be. Everyone of you had a special way that helped me during these past 10 years and I am forever grateful.

Prologue

Our love lives were full of surprises. No one could seem to get it right. It was not that we didn't have men out there who were interested in us. It was more like we didn't know how to get ourselves together. Most times we got in our own way, or we just wouldn't let God take the lead. Even now as we were starting a new year, the likelihood of any of us finally making it down the aisle anytime soon was slim to none. All I knew was that one day I would no longer be Destiny Karen Price, a single woman of God. I would be a man's wife. I would be a Proverbs 31 woman who knew her worth and was delighted at being her husband's help mate.

None of us could say that we knew what being a Proverbs 31 woman meant in this day and age, but I thought I was doing everything I needed to do in order to be the type of woman Stanley would be proud to have on his arm. He was the kind of man that I could only dream about. Since he finally proposed I had been planning our big day. My best friends had various issues in the romance department though.

If only Sharon could be open enough to let the right man find her and stop trying to control everything, she would be alright. She had to be in control of everything, but sometimes being in control could be detrimental to the natural order of things. I loved her to death, but my sorority sister knew how to play the part of both the man and the woman in the relationship.

Then there was Tracey. She knew she was the finest woman in the world and that every man wanted her. She felt she was a dime piece but didn't realize what God had for her had been staring her right in her face. Sometimes being in denial with reality could take you places you knew in your right mind you would never go. I didn't know how any of our lives were going to turn out now. I just hoped Jesus would fix it.

One
Dimes: Tracey
Winter

It was another Friday in a new year for my hair salon, Ooo-La-La Inc., and I couldn't wait to see how we would make out this year. I had some new products coming in from France that would give our clients more options. Now, they used products other shops didn't have any access to which could grow their hair longer and healthier. If we could sell those products, it would bring in more revenue. Since we had been getting them in, we've had a higher number of celebrity clients asking about the salon. I already had two celebrities lined up for appointments next week which was sure to keep the salon's name on everyone's lips.

I was all about how I was going to grow my business right now. Things were all going well. My shop was my life. I tried to make sure it was always on the forefront of my mind by always looking for ways to improve. Whether it was by buying new products, hiring the best stylists, or just making sure our salon experience was the best in the area, I was determined to work hard. As far as my personal life, I had Chucky wrapped around my little finger. Rob, on the other hand, was another pill to swallow. Most times I already knew what he was going to do but then he would just do something out of the blue and I would have to look at him from another angle.

I had been dating two men at once for about six months. Rob's the guy I had on the side to give my love life some much needed spice. My main squeeze, Chucky, was a no brainer. I loved the security I found in Chucky, also known as Charles Alexander Pryor, Jr. He was marriage potential, but this Robert Thrasher was off the hook. He was straight from the streets of southeast

D.C. where any and everything went down. I was sure Chucky was gonna propose by the end of summer. I always got my man, even if half the time I didn't want him.

Love was the one thing I could not maintain. My son would have been fifteen this year if I hadn't lost him in a miscarriage while I was in college. I learned a long time ago that love didn't mean a thing. I could remember like it was yesterday how it all happened.

When I was studying for my business degree at Howard University, I came home early from school one day. A new Chevy truck was parked in my spot. I figured it was one of Eric's new incentives. Eric was the love of my life in college and I was sure I would be his wife one day. He was Howard's star basketball player. We had been dating for almost a year. I was the most popular dancer on our dance team, and he was the most valuable player on the basketball team. Together we were the university's power couple. I thought it would be just another regular night for us at home.

When I opened the front door of the apartment there was a young woman sitting in our living room, mindlessly popping bubble gum. She had on a short halter dress that couldn't have cost her more than thirty dollars. Her hair was in box braids, and she had on loud red lipstick.

I was a little shocked to see her sitting there. Just to make sure I wouldn't fly off the handle on a heffa, I started counting to ten. One Mississippi, two Mississippi, three Mississippi.

"Hello." The mystery girl grinned.

"Hi, where's Eric?" I asked, perplexed. She was already on my nerves with her squeaky voice.

"Oh, Ricky. He will be down in a minute. You must be his sister. I'm Fatima. When are you due?" the girl asked, looking at my big belly and trying to reach out to touch it. I tried to get out of her reach. One of my pet peeves was people trying to touch my belly just because I was pregnant.

"Ricky? Sister? I am Eric's fiancée! Where is he?" I shouted. I left the door open, put my bags on the couch, and started to look for him. Then the girl said something that got all under my skin.

"Hold-up, you can't be his fiancée because I've been dating him all semester," Fatima said. She snapped her head back and forth while flinging her braids over her shoulder and rolling her eyes at me. Then she stood, put her hand on hip, and stared at me with no resolve. Still popping her gum, she blew a bubble and sized me up.

"Wait a minute. You go to H.U.?" I asked.

"The original," Fatima said smugly.

"And you don't know who I am?" I asked with my hand on my hip now moving towards her.

"No, am I supposed to?" she said, standing in a counter stance. Now she was face to face with me. The smell of her Juicy Fruit breath made me want to go off. Immediately, I threw my purse across the room. I was ready to fight for my man. She had to be a freshman. She wanted to test me, but I was sure I was going to win by any means necessary. We bantered back and forth until finally I slapped the girl in the face. She countered with a right punch to my jaw.

Finally, I heard Eric coming downstairs. "What in the world? Tima!" Eric yelled. He wore shorts and smelled of sex which made me angrier. Seeing Fatima preparing to hit me again, he used himself as a shield. I kicked off my shoes and charged toward the girl. He tried to hold me back, "Stop Tracey, hold up stop girl!" he yelled. He laughed under his breath. Still though, he grabbed a hold of me by the waist and held on for dear life. His eyes watered while he tried not to move. The baby was due in less than eight weeks and would be his first child.

"Tracey, no the baby," he pleaded with me.

"The baby, the baby, bastard the baby. F you Eric!" I screamed as I twisted out of his grasp and then lunged at him. I was wind milling, crying, and screaming obscenities. Tears ran down my face as my body shook. I charged at him because he was cheating on me. We moved closer to the door.

Out of nowhere Fatima grabbed my arm. She fell off balance, pulling me out the front door with her. We got tangled together and tripped down the steps. I fell hard on my belly. I could feel a sharp pain go straight through me. My head also hit the ground and a small knot started to form immediately. Fatima fell to the right of me landing on her side. She hit her head too and shouted out in pain. Our feet were still on the bottom step as Eric ran outside to help me.

"Oh, my God! No!" Eric screamed in panic. He pushed Fatima out of the way and pulled me to him.

"Get away from me. Let me go!" I yelled at Eric, trying to escape so I could pounce on the girl again.

"Tracey. No, sweetie. Remember the baby," Eric begged, holding on to me in desperation. Fatima had stood up and was standing there with her arms crossed. The tramp started to huff and puff then tried to reach for Eric.

"Oh, no. Forget this. Ricky, take me home. Take me home right now!" she demanded. "Why you didn't tell her about me, Ricky? Why you lie to me?" Fatima whined, bending down to touch him.

"You dumb whore, you ain't nothing but another groupie. Move!" he pushed her aside and ran inside. "I gotta call 911." He said running through the door.

"Oh, forget this!" Fatima yelled, walking after him.

"Oww! You stupid freshmen, you ain't nothing but a stupid slut!" I yelled while holding my stomach in agony. My heart raced, and I began to worry about the baby.

"Stupid? Look who's talking. He told me he loves me, and we make love all the time," Fatima said, pushing her chest out as she smiled.

"And! So? I'm the one he's going to marry, wench. Oww! Oh my God. Hurry E!" I shouted, feeling sharp pains coming from deep inside. It felt like my abdomen was on fire. Fear consumed me as the pains got worse and worse. My baby was in danger. Tears started to stream down my face.

"E, you would be all prim and proper. Too cute to really get down and dirty with me, you old high yellow trick. And you gotta weak slap. That's why I socked you dead in your mouth," Fatima said, standing right behind me.

I turned and grabbed her legs causing her to fall. The thud of her body weight hitting the ground put a smirk on my face. She screamed in pain. Eric ran back outside and pulled me away from the girl, making enough space between us where I couldn't get to her. I panted hard. Ten minutes later I could hear the sirens coming. Still screaming obscenities at the each other, we struggled to try to fight again while Eric stood watching. Fatima retreated to the porch when she realized Eric had started helping me and not paying her any attention. He sat me up finally and stood behind me putting more distance between us.

"No, baby. Don't move. The ambulance is on its way. Please, Tracey. Don't move." Eric flicked his wrist at Fatima as if he was shooing away a house-fly. "Tima, take your dumb butt back in the house and call yourself a cab."

"Wait just one minute. That whore is not going back into my house." I couldn't catch my breath. Still protesting, I winced trying to get comfortable on the grass.

"How many times you think I've been in there? I already know where everything is," Fatima scoffed.

"What!" My eyes widened at the thought of him cheating. A dumb look on his face made me angrier while he just stood there.

"Shut up, Fatima." Eric shrugged impatiently. I could hear the sirens getting closer. The sun pierced through the sky and beads of sweat rolled down my face. I couldn't catch my breath as Eric got on his knees behind me and rubbed my back trying to calm me down. Some of the neighbors had come outside. They witnessed everything and started pointing and shaking their heads. The ambulance pulled up to the scene behind my Camry. Two EMTs jumped out of the ambulance and ran toward me then started immediately caring for me. One started to check my pulse while the other took my blood pressure.

"How did she fall?" the EMT questioned.

Fatima said, "I beat her tail." She put on a front like she was Hercules or somebody holding her arm up and flexing her muscles. She was only about one hundred and twenty pounds but that right punch was a knock out for sure.

"Shut up, Fatima," Eric snapped. He then turned his attention to the EMT. "Ignore her, please, sir. She fell coming up the steps."

"Ma'am, is that how it happened? Did you fall?" The EMT checked my temperature. I looked at Fatima and rolled my eyes. Then I looked at Eric. He winked at me and squeezed my hand. He was nodding, pleading for me to agree to the lie he just told him. Then I remembered what he said about Fatima just being a groupie. Eric was the star player of Howard's basketball team and being scouted by the NBA. I had had many run-ins with whores trying to take my place and gain his attention. She was just like all the others. I needed to show him that I still believed in our love no matter who was trying to come between us. I knew that if God was for us, who could be against us.

"Uh, yeah. Yes, sir. That's what happened. I was startled and I fell." I lied to impress my boyfriend. Shoot, he was going to be an NBA player. Once I had his baby, I would never want for anything. He loved me. Fatima didn't mean a thing to him. I could tell. I already knew that our love was meant to be because God answered my prayers about us having a baby.

"Are you having any cramping or pain in your abdomen?" he asked.

"Yes, and I'm having a hard time catching my breath," I said.

"Well, both you and the baby have an elevated heart rate. So we are going to take you to the ER just to make sure everything is okay," the EMT said.

"Okay," I said, worried. They put me on a stretcher and into the back of the ambulance. Eric climbed in after them. I hoped he was going to go with me to the hospital.

"I'm going to call her a cab, then get the delivery bag. I'll meet you at the hospital," he said, trying to bend over to kiss me on the forehead. "I love you, baby."

"Really? Really, E. Or is it Ricky?" I pushed him away. Now, I recognized I was being played. "Get out! Just get out, Eric!" I screamed more obscenities. I cried harder, feeling disappointed and distraught. Even worse, I had allowed it to happen. Now, my child's life was in danger. Eric was more concerned with one of his whores making it home okay to even come to the hospital with me. I couldn't believe I had been so stupid. God had let me down. I did everything I thought I needed to do, even changing my major, to keep this man in my life. God didn't love me the way everybody said that He did.

I kept hearing from everyone that God loved me and no matter what I did, He would not let me go. Well, He did let me down then. How much did I have to lose in order for him to care about me? Did God really love me just as I am?
Eric smirked. "I'll see you at the hospital, boo." He jumped out of the ambulance, knowing he'd just gotten away with breaking my heart. He had been cheating on me since I was two months pregnant and started gaining weight. Even though he was busted red handed, he thought I was just emotional and would take him back with open arms. As a future NBA star, he was so sure that every girl wanted to be with him. He didn't care about any of us as long as he got whatever he wanted from us whenever he wanted it.

My mind came back to the present. "Today, men grovel at my feet. Hmm, yeah. I was such a fool back then." I whimpered as memories flooded my mind. At the tender age of twenty-one, I learned the harsh reality that love didn't have anything to do with keeping a man.
A couple of weeks later, I lost the baby. Two months after that, Eric got drafted by the Bulls and broke up with me. When I dropped out of Howard, my father found out. He was furious. He never forgave me for lying and blemishing the family name, not to mention almost bringing a bastard into the world with a boy he believed to be so beneath me. Still though, I decided to go to cosmetology school because styling hair came natural for me.

That was in the past. Today was a new day and now all

I had to do was concentrate on keeping the shop on the list of Who's Who of top salons in the country. I was in no hurry to get married. Even though I loved Chucky, he was a pain. Rob was the man who made me climb the walls, and he knew how to show me a good time. I would let my friends Sharon and Destiny deal with that marriage thing. If God wanted me to get married and be this Proverbs 31 woman that everyone kept talking about, He was definitely going to have to show me.

Two
Profiles: Sharon

Mr. Wynd had been calling me a lot lately. Maybe I would take him up on his offer
for a date or two, maybe even three. Then a year later, we would have the wedding of the century. Followed by a baby two years after that. I should be able to get a proposal out of him by the end of the year. My sources reported that he was looking for someone to settle down with and be his trophy wife. I could handle that and then some. As my girl Tina Turner would say, "What's love got to do with it?" If there was one thing I knew, this year was going to be extraordinary.

Mama had been on me about getting married. Well, I had been working on a plan. I was determined to have the quintessential love life that all the naysayers believed could not be reached by successful African American women. Now if only the Lord would just do me this one favor and help me put something on this candidate, everything would come together as it should be.

I still couldn't believe what happened to my best friend Destiny, though. I should have known that man was up to no good when I saw him with that boy at the grocery store. They were a little bit too chummy for me, but who could tell today. In today's society, it was okay to be a feminine man and dressed to kill. Men wore tight pants and sometimes even high heels. Back in the day, though, being like my daddy, Big George, was the way to show manhood in our community. I was glad times changed, but at what cost? Why does everything have to be so extreme? Is there any normal men out there? Yes, there is and his name is Cornelius Eugene Wynd.

At this point in my life, my main goal was to find the

right kind of man to be my husband and create the picture perfect family. I attended Howard University because teachers said I never would. Then I pledged Delta Sigma Theta because an Alpha Kappa Alpha said I came from nothing and nowhere. I graduated summa cum laude because old friends said I never could.

I became a lawyer because I would earn enough money to keep up with the Joneses. I, Sharon Denise Douglas, Esquire, was a new millennium African American woman, who went to church on Sunday most times just to show off my newest tailor made suit with matching shoes and accessories. I even had a platinum Visa card with a credit limit high enough to buy an SUV. I owned my condominium in Chevy Chase, my mother's home in Baltimore, and I dibbled and dabbled in collecting fine art and rare South African wine. As a must, I only dated doctors, lawyers, and college professors. Sometimes my companion would be high profile executives, but rarely politicians, and never athletes or entertainers. My ideal mate would make over three hundred grand a year, which was twice my yearly salary. That candidate also had to have a personal and professional profile similar to my own.

Only one person truly knew everything about me, my mama, Mrs. Gloria Walker. I still knew how to shoot a nine-millimeter handgun if someone messed with us. Although I grew up in the streets, one would never know by looking at me. When my daddy needed me to, I sold crack in our old neighborhood in Baltimore. I wasn't afraid to get my hands dirty. I wore a thick mask that few people had ever seen me take off since I pledged my sorority in undergrad. But who did I need to let see the real Sharon Niecey Walker? That's why I changed my name when I graduated from law school.

About five years ago, I was in a relationship that I thought would end up in marriage with a stockbroker named Aaron Karn from New York. Our love was passionate and deliberate until one day he just stopped calling. This had me alarmed, so I waited a couple of days to see if he would call. Then a full two weeks went by without me hearing a word from him. He wasn't answering any of my calls and then just like that, his number was disconnected. Finally I decided to take an unannounced trip just outside Manhattan to find out what was going on with my man.

A brand new Mercedes sat in the driveway with a bow on it. Excited about the gift he must have bought for me to make amends for him treating me this way, my heart raced in anticipation, and I began to blush. He had said he had a surprise for me about four weeks beforehand. The house had large picture windows surrounding it with a large French door at the entrance. A beautiful lawn anchored with rose bushes captured it immaculately. One large oak tree sat on the side of the house adding to its charm.

We would have been a happy family there. I had never been to his house before. He would always come down to D.C. on the weekends. I knocked on the door and waited. To my surprise, I was greeted by a woman, with a belly as round as a balloon wearing my five thousand dollar wedding ring and band on her finger. Aaron enticed me with the wedding ring set five months prior, and I couldn't wait until he finally asked me to marry him.

"Hello, how may I help you?" the lady asked; she looked startled as her eyebrows scrunched. My eyes were bulging out of my head and I had a scowl on my face.
Standing there with my lips poked out, I put my hands on my hips and tapped my right foot.

"Oh, I'm Mr. Karn's attorney, Sharon Douglas. I am here to take care of some last minute things on his latest endeavor." I told a lie that I knew would get me in the door. The woman called for him. She held the door ajar while standing in her bare feet. Her hair was in a messy bun. It was long enough to cross her shoulders. The leggings and oversized shirt she had on didn't do her any justice but she seemed not to care. She had flour on her cheek, and the house smelled good from fried chicken. She was cute, but not beautiful.

He came to the door, took one look at me and almost dropped his phone. Beads of sweat immediately appeared on his forehead as it wrinkled. In shock he rubbed his head and let out a long sigh. I was still tapping my foot. He smiled awkwardly. She stood between us, looked at him then invited me in and excused herself. I knew he didn't expect me to just show up at his house. We stood there staring at each other.

"Who is—," He lifted his finger to my lips then led me into his study. The study had two large bookcases full of books with his many accolades shown all over the walls and his desk.
It was obvious that there was going to be an altercation because I was fuming. Annoyed, he whispered forcibly,

"What are you doing here?"

"What am I doing here? What are you doing here? And who is that fat woman, barefoot and pregnant, frying chicken in my ring you said you bought me some five months ago?" I demanded loud enough for her to hear me. I was having a conniption.

"Okay, okay. I should have been upfront with you from the beginning." He rubbed his head and let his eyes roll to the back of his head. "That is Marisa; she is my wife. I married her three weeks ago." He put some space between us then continued to say, "She got pregnant six months ago, and I just wanted everything to be okay for the baby. I never thought you would show up after I stopped calling." In disbelief, my shoulders slumped. "I just didn't know how to face you. I love you, Sharon, but you can be too much at times. I don't know if I would be enough for you. You can do better than me, so much better." He touched my arm. I guess he thought he was going to get away with it. I wasn't falling for any of his bull crap, though. I pictured him standing there with her in front of his family and friends saying marriage vows. A bolt of energy flushed over me. I was furious. Secretly, I had been planning our wedding. Just knowing he got married to another woman three weeks ago was baffling.

"Oh, you think I'm just going to fall back and believe this bull crap?" I couldn't believe him. Without thinking, I slapped him. He fell off balance, so I started whaling on him with punches. His wife came in swinging a frying pan so I pushed her over the desk. She hit the floor hard. Then she got up and crawled around the desk. He grabbed me by the arm and yanked me out of the room. His wife picked up the frying pan again then tried to hit me with it. I ducked and kicked her in her hip. Then he hit me in the eye and pushed me down. She ran into the kitchen. I got back up but Aaron grabbed me and held me down. I was in a rage. She called the police from the safety of the kitchen.

Twenty minutes later the police came in to find Aaron on top of me while I was struggling to get up. His wife told them that I attacked them. They got Aaron off of me then put me in handcuffs. The officers interrogated them while ignoring me. I kept trying to speak my piece. Both of them had bruises. Aaron told them that I was an ex-girlfriend that was obsessed with him and just showed up at his house uninvited.

I spent the weekend in jail. They decided to drop the charges once he finally told his wife the truth. Instead of firing me over the incident the senior partners at my firm put me on leave for two months without pay. I almost lost my license to practice law as well.

I lost my mind once over a man and vowed to never ever do it again. Since then I took it upon myself to always take the lead in any relationship I had with a man. If I was going to be in a relationship, I needed to be in control of how things were going to go. There would never be another chance for any man to surprise me with their issues. There was no way I could get hurt if I was in total control.

Sometimes I would let my guard down and let my heart get involved, but as soon as I saw any signs of disloyalty, I got out of the relationship and moved on to the next profile. I didn't care, though; one day soon I would find the man that was worthy enough to be my husband. It should be a she who finds a husband because these men today really didn't know what they wanted or what was good for them. I got this Lord, like you said, I can do all things through Christ who strengthens me.

Three
Wives: Destiny

One of my favorite songs of praise blasted through my speakers. I sang along to "Safe In His Arms" by Milton Brunson "Whew, glory, glory, glory. Thank you, Jesus. I bless your holy name Father. Umm, Umm, Umm." I was driving down Georgia Avenue trying to get to my hair appointment on time. The phone rang. "Shoot, restricted. Lord, please don't let this be my job calling me in," I prayed aloud. "Hello, Destiny Price." I answered the phone trying to sound chipper with a fake smile on my face.

"Karen, please. We need to talk," Stanley begged. He had been calling me for days pleading for a second chance. I didn't care. Our relationship was over. I could not marry him with the issues he was dealing with.

As calmly as I could, holding back the latest stream of tears I had been crying for over two weeks, I said, "Stanley, I don't have time for this right now. I told you it is over."

"Karen, wait. I just want—," He pleaded but I cut him off.

"My name is Destiny Karen Price, licensed clinical social worker to be exact. Or did you forget that, just like you forgot to tell me you like men." Tears streamed down my face yet again as I yelled. He was out of his complete mind if he still thought I would keep up the illusion and marry him.

"Karen, I…I mean Destiny. C'mon now. That's not even my virtuous…" I was so annoyed with him mentioning how he wanted a Proverbs 31 virtuous woman of God. It was sickening to even believe he would still try to get married knowing he was gay. He shouldn't even be thinking about marrying anyone at all knowing that he liked men.

I tried to control my temper. "Oh, don't even go there. I'm hanging up on you now, Stanley." I wiped my tears away. I was not going to listen to this fool try to explain away almost four years of deceit. He had me fooled big time. I never thought he was gay. Even though we never had sex, it never dawned on me that he could be gay. He adored me and treated me like a lady all the time. I was the envy of every woman at the church too. Even my girlfriends couldn't believe how well he treated me. Now that it was out that he was gay, all bets were off. A car beeped its horn as I almost drifted out of my lane. I quickly turned the wheel and tried to concentrate on the road and not hit anyone.

"Beloved, wait. We need to talk about this. Remember, the wedding is in five months." He tried to wiggle his way back into my heart by reminding me about the fairy tale wedding we had planned. We had spent almost eight thousand dollars already for the two hundred guests we expected. He'd been cheating on me on the down low since before we met. I let out a long sigh and started to tremble. Just days ago, we were in the perfect relationship. Now all my dreams had been shattered. I couldn't take it anymore and pulled the car over because I had been bobbing and weaving in and out of traffic speeding.

"I can't marry you. You're gay! Gay! Gay! Gay!" I screamed at the top of my lungs in disgust.

"No, no. I'm not, Karen. Baby, that was just a phase in my life. It's all over with now. I only want to be with you, all I've ever wanted was you. I need a real woman of God. I need a Proverbs 31 woman. I need a woman to have my babies and grow old with. I need a woman..."
I hollered, not holding anything back now,

"A phase? A phase? Hell, we've been together for almost four gosh darn years, and you never said 'oh, by the way beloved, I have been wrestling with the spirit of homosexuality and I need to get myself together before I mess with you.'"

"There was no need. It only happened..." he said.
I was so tired of his lies so I yelled, "Once, yeah right! Stop lying to me, you freaky bastard!" My lips poked out as my eyes rolled.

"Hey now, I'm not gonna let you keep disrespecting me, Karen," he said.

"My name is Destiny, darn it. I don't know why I let you call me Karen all this time."

Instantly I had a migraine headache. Every day now they plagued me. I was rubbing my temples when this fool said something else.

"Because you'd do anything for me," he said smugly.

Just then I rolled down my car window and threw the cell phone across the street cursing his name. "Sorry, Lord. Shoot, now I need a new cell phone. Stupid! Stupid! Stupid!" I punched the steering wheel then rolled up the window and started down the road again. I desperately needed a day of pampering and assurance from my friends. "Mama always said, fool me once, shame on you, fool me twice, shame on me. You fooled me once, Stanley Milton Reid. I'm not going to give you and the devil the pleasure of fooling me again." I reached down deep for that inner strength I always had to fall back on during hard times in my life.

While we were together our courtship had been lengthy and modest. Stanley made it a point to never touch me physically, except for the occasional hug or, when he was really feeling 'hot', a peck on the cheek or forehead. I loved that about him. He respected me, my body, and spirit enough to not spoil me before marriage. It had only been a couple dozen times that we actually French kissed.

Now, don't get it twisted. I wasn't a virgin by any means. I've had my fair share of boyfriends, some fine as May wine. But when I finally decided to really get serious about Jesus, I took a vow of celibacy and had been living my life free of fornication for over seven years.

When Stanley finally asked me to marry him, he went all out. He chose the Bahamas because I said I always wanted to walk hand in hand with my lover on white sand by the moonlight. We had dinner at the best restaurant on the island in Freeport then went to the beach. Walking hand in hand, I could hear the waves of the ocean caress the land. Our feet were wet and dirty, but we didn't care. Then he stopped in front of this big boulder, pulled me in front of him and got on one knee.

"Destiny you are the woman I've been waiting my entire life for. Would you please do me the honor of being my wife?" he held up the ring. I looked at it then at him.

"I would be honored to be your wife Stanley." We kissed and held each other as the moon shined across the sea. As soon as we returned, I told my best friends, Sharon and Tracey. They were in total disbelief because he had been dragging his feet for almost half a decade. Tracey laughed at first but when she saw my ring, I could see the jealousy in her eyes. Sharon was actually happy for me and said she couldn't wait to help me pick out my dress.

Too bad I found out six months later that my God-fearing, spirit-filled, Holy Ghost loving, man of God was a lying whoremongering bisexual. Three days before the New Year, I found a box of memories in his closet. I was innocently trying to match a pair of his designer shoes with a sweater I had just bought. Standing all of five feet five, I reached up on my tiptoes to get the shoebox on the top shelf in his closet. As I pulled it out very carefully, three other boxes fell from the shelf. One box hit me on the head, and its contents flew all over the bedroom floor.

"Ouch, shoot. Now I gotta put this crap back together, and I know how anal lovey can be." I placed the shoes back into their respective boxes then bent down to pick up the mess.

"Old hags!" There were pictures of women posing seductively. A couple of them were of naked women who would be considered brick houses. "Too late girls. I got him now, and he's all mine." I fingered through all the photos, cards, and letters. I paid no attention to what I had in front of me, until I noticed that some of the pictures were of naked men. It wasn't just naked men, but naked men in compromising positions. I gasped in utter shock.

"Calm down, lady-day." My heart raced as I started to fight for air. Then I held my chest. I picked up an envelope that was in the pile with a letter in it dated almost three months prior and read it aloud.

Dear Beloved,

I regret to hear that you have decided to turn away from your true self. Although I understand that you are saved, want a wife and a family in the near future, I cannot say that I am happy for you. Stanley, I love you, and I have never loved anybody as much as I have loved you. I don't know, maybe I should have never given you my number. Maybe I should've never let you love me for the first time back in 2004, our first time together in New York.

"Oh, my God!" I moaned in disbelief, remembering that New Year's when he said he had to go to New York on business because he was about to lose a very important client. We were supposed to go to my sorority's annual party, but he said he had to go or else. My stomach churned and I felt nauseous. I continued reading the letter as tears streamed down my face. A migraine headache formed instantly as I started to remember other times when he conveniently cancelled on our plans.

And just maybe I should've never fell in love with a man who couldn't face the reality that he enjoys being with me, loving me, adoring me. Stanley Milton Reid, I wish you all the love and happiness in the world with Ms. Price. She is truly a Proverbs 31 virtuous woman of God and will make a good wife. I just hope you can be real with her because you weren't with me and it hurts so bad.

Love Your Beloved Always,
Darryl Antonio Mason a.k.a. "DAM"

My hands trembled as I read and then re-read the Dear John letter. Crying in agony, I started reading all the cards and letters from different men and some even from women I knew at our church. I looked at some of the photos, now recognizing some of the faces. They were of men I knew from church, Stanley's basketball friends, and a few of his fraternity brothers. One face was in more pictures than all the rest, and he and Stanley were always together, sometimes kissing.

Disgusted, I threw the evidence of his iniquities all over the room. The mess fell on the bed and floor making piles everywhere. In a rage, I tore up photo after photo, cards, and letters, screaming uncontrollably. I grabbed a pair of scissors that were sitting on the nightstand and was about to slit my wrist, but I stopped abruptly. I then remembered something my mother used to tell me when I was just a little girl. "One day, when it's all said and done, you will be able to look that devil right in his face and tell him boldly, you ain't got no power in hell to destroy my faith in God."

I picked up the last of the things I had left untouched by my fury. I put them and the Dear John letter in a bag with the sweater. I cleaned up my mess. "Bishop said sometimes you have to eat your dung right in the midst of your enemies and let not the taste spoil you because you are always at battle with the enemy and every last one of his imps and demons. I see you now, devil. I am declaring war right now. You will not destroy my faith in God. This ain't over. You have messed with the wrong one for the last time. I could sure use one of your songs right now, Sister Shank."

I fell on the bed and wept in anguish and pain over a marriage that would never work, waiting in the dark to confront my fiancé.

Four
Destiny

I jumped out of the car and trotted across the street as fast as I could. My big butt shook all over the place as I tried to get out of the way of a car that was zooming past.

"Ooo-wee, it must be jelly 'cause jam don't shake like that," one of the old guys standing in front of the fish joint yelled at me from across the street.

"Get ready for the drama," I said as I entered my best friend's shop, Ooo-La-La Inc. Nelly rapped his latest hit over the radio. Two little girls danced along to the beat, kicking their feet in the air in the play area. Their mothers cheered them on clapping with black caps on their heads. The smell of burnt hair and chemicals permeated throughout. I didn't care, though. I needed to be here and relax my mind.

"Alright now, there goes my idol. How are you doing today, Ms. Destiny Price?" Tony asked. He was one of Tracey's youngest stylists. He always picked on me about being fat and fabulous. When he finally saw a picture of Stanley, he made a big deal about it by asking how in the world did I catch a fine man. Now every time I walked into the shop he had something crazy to say but today was not the day.

"I'm fine, Tony. How are you?" I said, trying to avoid talking to him. Since I found out about Stan's down low lifestyle, I had less and less patience for people like him.

"Fabulous, let me see that rock again, baby," he said.

"Tony, leave that girl alone." Ms. Diane braided a little girl's hair.

"Stay out of my business, Ms. Diane. Let me see that stone, Ms. Thang." He continued to pester me. A little disgusted, I reluctantly showed off the engagement ring. I had lost it while tearing up Stan's room but pulled myself together. Once found, I got it appraised and insured. I still hadn't told everyone about our breakup because it was too shameful. Tony and the new girl gawked at the beautiful three karat pear shaped ring.

"Um, um, um. Girl, you must be working some serious voodoo on that man because I know that's a couple grand." He stood up and slapped ten with Lamar, the other male stylist who was also gay.

"You deserve it, girl." Lamar reached out to hug me. I faked a cough and told him I had a cold to get out of touching him. Lamar was a nice guy and all, but I was so hurt by Stanley. Now every gay man I came in contact with made me sick to my stomach.

"Oh, you need some cough drops, boo?" he gave me a tissue and looked for a cough drop in his satchel.

"No, no. I don't need anything fro—," I got cut off by Tracey who asked Lamar to turn up the radio because Missy Elliot was on. She could tell I was about to be disrespectful by the way I rolled my eyes and smacked my lips. She didn't want any mess to get started in her shop. What I didn't know about until later was the powwow Sharon and Tracey had in the stockroom.

"He's gay," Sharon told Tracey in disbelief. They both stood there just staring at each other when Tracey finally broke the deafening silence.

"No, he is not," Tracey said. Perplexed Sharon said,

"Yes, that bastard is so gay," she put her hands on her hips and stared at Tracey confused.

"He might be bi, but he ain't gay," Tracey sighed.

"What is the difference? Bi just means you're gay and greedy. And why are you so nonchalant about this, Tracey?" Sharon asked, trying to get Tracey to cut the crap.

"I had a feeling," Tracey told a lie omitting the full truth that she had known for at least three months he was on the down low. Sharon tapped her foot. Her face flushed and her heart raced.

"Uh-uh, heffa. You knew, or you know somebody who

knew."she showed her frustration with Tracey.

"It's not like that, Niecey," Tracey said.

She tapped her foot faster. Sharon begged, even more frustrated and angry now. "Not like what? She's our friend. How could you let her go through this all this time, Tracey?"

"Shoot, she's a grown woman. Plus, she got 'vision.' Why couldn't she see it for herself?" Tracey said putting up quotation marks trying to act as if it was no big deal. She was tired of everyone always tiptoeing around me and my issues. Totally disappointed, Sharon said,

"Because sometimes the devil can be staring you right in the face, and you don't even know it because you're too blind to see. You are so wrong for this, Tracey." Tracey kept it real, reminding Sharon about her own fling with Stanley.

"Oh, look who's talking, Ms. Oh my God, I slept with him in undergrad."

"This is different. That bastard asked her to marry him," Sharon replied. Coyly, Tracey said,

"Well at least now I know I don't gotta waste no money on no ugly dress." The two left the conversation closed for now, but it would reopen soon, because Sharon had finally had enough of Tracey's two-faced ways. Tracey was notorious for saying one thing in your face while saying something contrary to the fact behind your back. Sharon had witnessed her do it to a few of our sorority sisters and didn't want to believe she would really do it to either one of us.

Lamar looked at Tracey as she came back to her work station. Tracey turned her face to the ground as she walked out of the stockroom. About eight months ago, she and Lamar went clubbing in Dupont Circle. Lamar told her it was about time she found out how to really party like a true diva. While they were at Club Red, Stanley walked into the club looking very GQ smooth. Stan was a regular at the club which was one of D.C.'s hot spots.

"Hey, isn't that Stan?" she asked Lamar. He shouted, dancing to the music,

"What? I can't hear you girl,"

"Ain't that Stan over there?" Tracey pointed across the club to the bar. Lamar turned and looked, and sure enough Stan stood all six foot two and as fine as he wanted to be. He nodded his head in agreement and yelled, still dancing, feeling no pain.

"Um-um. Yup that's him, and I know a sistah who loves to sink her teeth into that milk dud daily,"

"Yeah, Destiny knows she pulled a fine one," Tracey said. Lamar dropped his drink all over Tracey's shoes.

"Watch it boy!" she shouted, not paying attention to the total change in Lamar's demeanor. Lamar had stopped dancing and stood there as other party goers bumped into them. He put his hand over his mouth and shook his head in disbelief. He couldn't believe what he just heard her say.

"C'mon. We gotta go," he said, grabbing her by the elbow and ushering her towards the door. She wiggled out of his clutches.

"Go? Boy, it's rocking in here. What you talking about?" Tracey was having a good time and was totally blind to what she had just told Lamar. She stood there looking at him in protest with her hands on her hips annoyed.

"Yeah, but I know another place that you'll like even better than this," he said trying to avoid Stanley and Darryl.

"Well, lead on my sistah. But let me finish this apple martini first." Just as she took a sip, Darryl began to dance seductively with Stan. Lamar grabbed Tracey by the arm again and pulled her out of the club. She followed him as he pulled her quickly to his Yukon truck.

"Lamar, now I got this mess all in my dress. What in the world freaked you out?" she asked trying to wipe herself down.

"C'mon. Let's get in the truck." As they drove to Obsession nightclub, Lamar told Tracey about Stan's down low lifestyle. At first, Tracey wanted him to turn around and go back to Club Red so she could drop kick him in the forehead. But then she remembered he ain't her man and that's my cross to bear.

Since we all attended the same church, we each knew Stanley Reid some kind of way. He was the catch at First Metropolitan Baptist Church. Everybody wanted him, and it was pitiful how women in the church threw themselves at him. He and Tracey went out once while they were in high school, but he said she was too street for him. In a nutshell, Tracey knew he meant too ghetto. He waited months before he stepped to Sharon at Howard. Neither of them would ever admit that they dated, let alone had sex their freshman year.

Then one Sunday morning, I was singing a solo with the choir. He got up and started clapping and shouting. Now this wasn't unusual because I could really sing. Nevertheless, that Sunday my voice seemed to put a spell on him. He chased me for months, buying me this and that, before I finally agreed to go out with him. Even then, I said it had to be a group outing because I was trying to stay chaste. We often double dated with another young couple at the church. We rarely showed any signs of affection towards each other in public. Oftentimes, Tracey wondered if it was the Holy Spirit that brought us together or me holding out on the panties. Either way, Tracey couldn't understand how the fat girl got the best man.

Δ

I tried really hard not to show my emotions after the argument with Stanley, but just listening to Tony got under my skin. Even though I was not homophobic, I did not agree with homosexuality. It was against the word of God. It was good to see my girls finally. We had not seen each other since our sorority's New Year's Eve party.

"Hey, sweetie." Sharon opened her arms.
I responded dryly hugging her. "Hello."
"How have you been?" Sharon asked as chipper as she could without being too insensitive.
With a sheepish smile on my face I said, "I've been well and you?"
"Okay," Sharon responded, a little confused because if she were in my shoes she would definitely be more upset and showing it.

"Hey, Tracey," I said.

"What's up, girl? What are we doing for you today?" Tracey said trying to ignore the subject more for herself than for me. I replied,

"The full service, girl," Dramatically Tony said, "Alright now, getting ready for him tonight." Ms. Diane voiced,

"Stay outta grown folks business." And continued braiding hair.

"Or just shut up," I blurted, vividly annoyed by his antics.

"Oh no she didn't. Just because that rock is almost as big as your fat behind doesn't mean you gotta change attitudes on people," Tony said nastily putting his curling iron in its cradle. Trina the nail tech put her two cents in, "Oops! Watch out now. This is gonna be good." Shaking my head in disgust, I shouted,

"And just because I don't feel like hearing the wiles of a devil don't mean I gotta be all sweet and nice!"

"Oh, uh-uh." Tony picked up the hot curling iron like he was about to karate chop me. Sharon got between us to stop the impending massacre.

"Oh, no. Uh-uh, not up in my shop. Tony put that rod down," Tracey demanded as she tried to continue tending to her own client's hair.

"Well, you better get her," Tony yelled, putting down the curling iron, snapping his finger at me and rolling his eyes. He tossed his hair my way and tried his best to show his disdain.

"You can be so emotional," Lamar said laughing at Tony.

"Shut up, trollop," Tony spat.

"Growl," Lamar teased. Everybody laughed. I stood there remembering that this was one of my hiding places from the world. I didn't have to go off and be so demeaning with a chip on my shoulder. I would not let this trial in my life change the person that I was. God would provide and heal my broken heart. I remembered a sermon Bishop Franklin once gave, talking about Delilah and Samson. Yeah, the story may have to be flipped around a little for my situation, but I truly got away from a trap set by the devil himself. I still had my strength, and I wasn't gonna settle for form and fashion. I smiled and said,

"Sorry, Tony. I've just been having a messed up New Year."

"Well, diva, my divine, don't let sour grapes ruin your nurtured vine! If that nigga is actin up, put him back in check." Tony snapped his fingers and cursed.

"Two dollars, please." Ms. Diane shoved the no cursing jar in Tony's face.

"Hey, that's the song!" Trina started dancing to Prince's "When Doves Cry" on the old school radio remix and just like that all was well again at the salon. I got the full service and even let Tony wrap my hair. Sharon, of course, had her regular: a wash, set, dry, nails and brows. She never let anyone touch her feet. She said it's because it's too unsanitary. But if you let us tell it, it was because she had monkey feet.

Five
Tracey

    I walked through my walk-in closet full of the trendiest clothes out today trying to figure out what I was going to wear. Most of the clothes were gifts from my many boyfriends and admirers over the years. I decided on a nice pair of Tommy jeans with matching sweatshirt. I put on some blue Timberlands and slapped on a ponytail for my date with Rob Thrasher. He was also a native Washingtonian in the pharmaceuticals industry. Although he held no academic degree, he attended Howard long enough to learn advanced chemistry and take intro to accounting. He owned a house in Fort Washington and had an apartment in Southeast D.C. where he grew up.

    We met one day when he dropped off his then girlfriend Angel to the shop. When he came back to pick her up he dropped one of his cards on the floor next to my chair "accidentally." Knowing the game, I picked up the card, waited about 15 minutes and called him on his cell phone.

    "Did you forget something?" I asked.

    "Just You," he said.

    "Oh really," I smiled into the phone. Even though I knew he was probably a bad boy he was charming.

    "Yes really,"

    "So, what do you do and what do you want from me?" I asked.

    "To make you my lady," He answered my second question ignoring the first.

    "Why?" I asked even more flattered now.

    "Because you da fattest dime piece I've seen in a long time," he said as he ignored his girlfriend.

    "And what about her?" I asked nonchalantly.

"What about her?" He answered affirming that his girlfriend did not mean anything to him.

"So, when are you taking me out?" I wondered aloud.

"Tonight, when you close up," he said.

"Where?" I demanded.

"You like the water?" He asked.

"I like anything that moves smoothly." I flirted.

"Well, I guess that means we'll be cruising tonight,"

"Oh, a waterbed," I asked ready for whatever snide remark he was about to say.

"Naw boo, we just met. Spirit of Washington," he said to my surprise.

"Oh, sounds nice, but can you afford me." I asked.

"Baby, if I wanted to I'd buy that shop from the owner and sell it to you for $50," he said.

"Well, I'm not selling it." I hung up on him. That night Rob and I went out and had a good time. He said Angel was one of his baby's mamas but he was looking for someone to settle down with. He told me he owned two barbershops and a club in Baltimore, but he left out the fact that he was a major player in the drug game and managed a prostitution ring. Rob and I had been dating for almost nine months and I might stay with him longer. He treated me right, bought me anything I wanted and I ain't had no problems with his baby's Mamas. The phone rang and so I answered "Hello?"

"Hi baby." Charles responded to my bubbly voice.

"Chucky...how are you." I responded truly surprised to hear from him so soon. He had been on vacation for the holidays all by himself in Mexico. He was upset because I decided not to go with him and went to Barbados by myself instead. His calling now totally took me off guard because I thought he wouldn't be back until next week.

"I'm back in town," he said smiling in the phone.

"Since when?" I asked not ready to see him yet. I wanted to still have my cake and eat it too with Rob.

"I left a message yesterday, talked to mother too," he

sounded happy to hear my voice.

"Oh really." I rolled my eyes because mother was always meddling in my personal life. If it was up to her, we would be married already. I didn't care if we had been dating for almost three years. I wasn't ready to get married even though I would wear his ring proud because I know he was gonna spend a lot of cash for it.

"So, where do you want to go for supper this evening?" Charles asked waiting in vain.

"Supper, hum oh." I stammered while putting on my boots.

"Oh, c'mon Trace, we haven't spent much time together this past holiday season and you said after you returned from Barbados it would be just me and you. And that's been almost a month." Charles whined.

"Chucky, darling mami got a lot of stuff to do, it's the New Year and business has been booming. I've even had to come in for full days to handle the demands of the new semester," I said lying and smirking at myself in the mirror while I fixed my hair and makeup. Rob would be here any minute now and I needed to get Chucky off my phone.

"Mami, I know, but papi needs to see his Bodiqua," he said in his baby voice.

Disgusted with the baby talk, I responded sternly. "Now, come come now Charles Alexander Pryor Jr. We will see each other tomorrow."

"What time mami?" He kept up the baby act probably turned on because he loved it when I got forceful with him. He was a big mama's boy really into the baby talk and submissive male thing. I hated that stuff, but I'd do anything to please my main squeeze.

"Brunch." I told him.

"I'll cook for you," He suggested.

"Of course you will." I said under my breath but too loud.

"Huh? I can't hear you mami." He said.

"Uh, How nice of you papi." I cleaned it up laughing at

myself while posing in my full length mirror. I was a dime piece which was why I always had to beat all the men off with a stick.

"Tomorrow then." He asked again.

"Yes." I responded affectionately.

"I love you Tracey,"

"I love you too Chucky." I said sweetly. He hung up the phone. Whew, that was close. One of these days I would be busted for sure. I kept putting on my makeup thinking about Chucky, the love of my life.

Charles Alexander Pryor Jr. was the son of Charles Alexander Pryor "CAP" Sr. CEO/President of Pryor Associates. Their firm was the most renowned African American owned accounting firm on the East Coast. Chucky was a junior partner at the firm and pulled in about seventy five thousand a year. He was a good, God fearing, strong man but very sensitive. If you asked me, he was entirely too sensitive.

Mother got the bright idea of getting the two of us together after a Christmas party about three years ago. I made the mistake of walking up under the mistletoe where Charles stood less than two feet away.

"Aww, now you know the rules." Mother said brightly.

"Hey, Chucky come on over here and give my daughter Miss Tracey Simmons a kiss." She called out to him. Charles turned around and stared at me. He told me later he thought I was probably the most beautiful girl in the world, at least to him. He put on his biggest 'I am the man' grin and walked right up to me.

"So where should I kiss the most beautiful flower in the garden?" He looked me up and down searching to find the perfect spot to plant his lips. I cocked my head to the side and rolled my eyes to the sky. Mom pinched me and whispered for me to fix my face. He grabbed my hand as if he was going to kiss it, like a gentleman, but kissed me on the forehead instead. I thought that was cute. I loved it when men kissed me on the forehead. It was so endearing.

"Oh, how sweet." Mother said holding both of our hands

together and winking at me.

"Mother!" I whined annoyed trying to wiggle out of her grasp. She was smiling from ear to ear trying to get my dad's attention. Daddy took one look at us and toasted us with the drink he had been nursing all night long.

"What? Girl, you know you liked it. This is Charles Alexander Pryor Jr. His father is CAP Sr. you know, he plays golf with your father." Mother attempted to familiarize me with the assumed catch of a lifetime. She did it as if I needed to know the boy's past, present and future.

"Okay." I responded and said under my breath "and you're telling me this because."

"Oh, you two would be just wonderful together. Jim," She motioned to the hired photographer. "Jim come over here and take a picture of these two. Don't they look wonderful together?" Mother said admiring her work of art. Although we did look like the perfect couple in that picture which I kept on my nightstand, I still had one big problem with Charles Alexander Pryor Jr., he was a mama's boy.

Δ

The doorbell rang and I went downstairs to get the door of my row house in Northwest D.C. I kept my place tight. My art deco theme made the house look modern. It was built back in the fifties. I made the necessary upgrades every chance I had and even though I had money, because my parents were doctors and gave me a nice trust fund, I never really touch it. I made it a point to earn my keep which is why I owned Ooo-La-La, Inc. No one was ever going to say Tracey Ann Simmons had everything given to her. I worked for everything I had. I opened the door and saw my other suitor standing firm and dark as night with a red Roca Wear scully cap on with matching bomber jacket.

"Ready Boo?" Rob asked bending down to kiss me. His

Burberry cologne intoxicated me. He was at least six feet inches tall to my five feet six.

"Yeah." I replied kissing him passionately. My knees almost buckled. I could taste the beer on his tongue and smell the weed in his coat. I didn't care though he was my thug passion and I was his thug misses.

"Grab your good coat, its cold; plus, I want you to be seen at the game," he said. I grabbed my three-quarter inch white fur coat, put on the security alarm and walked out the house.

"Can I drive babe?" I asked.

"Yeah, do you," We switched seats and headed out of D.C. to FedEx Field. Along the way Rob talked on his blackberry to his different partners while I styled and profiled in his new two thousand and six onyx colored Cadillac Escalade. Weed smoke was filling the air and I was trying to control my cough. After a while I tried to open a conversation with him and asked where our seats were avoiding the real reason why I wanted to talk.

"At the twenty, with some of the player's families." He answered.

"Must be nice to rub noses with the stars all the time," I said.

"Yeah, that's why I need someone like you on my team at all times. But don't front. You know a few yourself." He pinched my thigh.

"A few is right." I cussed in disgust. Cars were piled up at the exit ramp off the four ninety-five. The car in front of me stopped short and I almost hit him.

"Watch that mouth." He pinched me again.

"I mean darn, traffic." I corrected myself.

"It's cool relax. Game don't start for another two hours anyway, and I got a good parking space,"

"Robert?" I asked now with a little more vigor.

"Girl, why you calling me by my government name, what you want Tracey Ann?" He asked laughing at me and twisting the end of my pony tail.

"Do you know somebody named Gary Turner?" I asked

shyly. I had heard so many rumors about what Rob was really into and I was getting concerned.

"Why do you ask?" He asked and sat up in his seat.

"I just want to know." I admitted.

"Well, in that case. No, I don't." He said but I knew he was lying. Too many people had told me they'd seen him with Gary walking through the hood or sitting in his truck.

"You sure?" I asked again, pressing the issue. I was trying to pay attention to the road while still getting a read on Rob's mannerisms.

He uttered vulgarities and asked. "Why you always asking me about my business? Just drive the darn truck." He yelled angry and annoyed putting his blunt in the ashtray.

"Why you yelling at me?" I whined. Robert then turned up the radio and blocked out my voice with music.

I had heard many rumors about Robert's so-called business. I recently overheard a conversation one of my customers was having about him and the infamous Gary Turner, a big time cocaine dealer. He also ran a prostitution ring. It took me only a couple of weeks to figure out Robert was lying about what he did for a living. But see no evil; hear no evil as mother always said. Plus, I loved all the attention I got from him and he checked me when I needed to be checked which was something Chucky never did.

"Robert?" I tried to gain his attention again while 50-Cent blasted through his new speakers. "Robert!" I shouted.

"What Tracey!" He shouted frustrated and annoyed.

"We need to talk, this ain't over." I said.

"What girl? What in the hell do you want?" He yelled again.

"This conversation, it ain't over." I said cowering from the forcefulness in his voice.

"Look trick, just drive this darn truck and keep your nose out of my business alright." He pointed at me trying to end the conversation.

"Trick?" I said. I couldn't believe he just disrespected me

like that.

"Yeah, trick. You acting like a little trick right now messing up my buzz this whole night," He said now putting out his blunt he was smoking. He had had enough of my inquisition, but I wasn't done with him yet.

"How is that? I just asked you a simple question and you got all defensive like you got something to hide," I said.

"Why you acting like this now? You know so much about me already why you asking all these questions now." He asked me, sounding concerned. "Yeah you've heard things at your little shop where those trollops run their mouths all day. You do know they're just jealous of what we got boo," He said putting his fingers in my bangs trying to smooth things over a little.

"Robby it's not like that, I'm just," I said trying to cover it up.

"You're just what? You ain't got nothing to be worried about, I don't mix business with pleasure," He said now angry again. I couldn't get a read on his behavior.

"Oh, just forget it," I said, dropping the issue because I didn't want to make matters worse. Plus, he was getting too upset about it and he looked like he was about to hit me for a second there.

"Now you want to just forget it. Man, you always know how to screw something up." He started yelling at me defensively and I yelled back. We bickered for about ten minutes then I finally said "Whatever." and sat there pouting. I could see him smiling out the corner of my eye. Then he started pinching me on my thighs again. I got the wool pulled back over my eyes long enough for him to get whatever he wanted from me that night. By the time we got back to his house in Fort Washington, I was laying on my back enjoying the perils of lust in his bed.

The next morning, I got up to find I was alone. I was about to get up and start preparing for church and then the phone rang. I had never answered his phone and figured it wouldn't make a big difference. We'd been together for months now so what could it hurt. I answered the phone.

"Hello?" I asked looking around for Rob.

"Why are you answering my phone?" Rob asked.

"Rob? Uh, um. It just." I said flustered and surprised

"It's just what?" he said, trying to start something.

"It kept ringing and, wait—why are you calling your own house? Where are you at?" I asked not falling for it.

"I'm in Miami," he said.

"Miami? When did you leave for—," I was cut off.

"Look, don't start again Tracey. I need you to do me a favor." he said.

"What Robert?" I asked annoyed now. He was getting on my nerves even though he made me shiver in delight less than six hours ago.

"I need you to put some money away for me for about a month or so,"

"For what, don't you have accounts?" I asked now going through his dresser drawers.

"Yeah but I don't want my baby's moms to know about it. It's only for a couple of weeks babe c'mon." He begged trying not to give out too much information.

"How much is it?" I asked not really wanting to agree to what he wanted. I didn't mix business with pleasure either.

"A couple thousand," I could hear a police siren in the phone driving by.

"A couple thousand? Rob, why do you have or how did you?" I asked concerned and not wanting to give in to his demands.

"Don't worry about that. Look we'll talk about this more later, I've already said too much on here anyway," He said about to hang up before I could ask more questions.

"What does that mean?" I asked.

"Nothing. Look, get off my phone. I left the keys to the truck on the kitchen table. Keep it for a week. I'll see you then," he said.

"But wait. What about?" he cut me off again.

"No. I'll call you later."

"Okay." Rob hung up on me before I could say goodbye. I didn't give it a second thought as to why he needed me to keep some money for him. Even though he never said it, I knew he loved me and that I could help him change. Besides, sooner or later we were gonna get joint accounts anyway, so it really wouldn't matter.

Six
Destiny

"Good morning Saints" Bishop Franklin said to his congregation of about fourteen hundred mostly African American Christians.

"Good morning Pastor" The members of First Metropolitan Baptist Church greeted their Pastor, Bishop James E. Franklin, on a beautiful winter Sunday morning.

"I want to give a special good morning to one of my dear brothers in Christ, Pastor Mobley from Bibleway Missionary Baptist Church out of Greensboro, N.C. Let's give him and his lovely family an old fashion Metro welcome." Bishop Franklin motioned to his wife who then got up to hug Pastor Mobley as the choir sang.

"Aww, yes praise Him choir." He said.
Why does he keep staring at me? What did he think that because he just broke my heart I would not come to church? I was raised better than that you stupid fool. I'm not letting the devil within you stop me from praising God. I thought to myself all the while singing and gesturing in my favorite choir robe as if nothing at all was wrong. The pianist began to play one of my songs and motioned for me to step to the microphone. Just then Stanley yelled "Sang Karen!" And I cut my eyes at him so fiercely that everybody who was watching me looked back at Stan as if to say "boy, you in trouble."

Nobody in the church really knew what was going on between us. Yeah, we'd been seen together and Bishop had even suggested we make an appointment with him and his wife to discuss the relationship. Nobody knew except three people: Eugene Carson, a deacon, who had a relationship with Stanley six years ago. Monica Perch, one of the most popular women in the church, who contracted herpes and passed it on to her husband after sleeping with Stan for three months back in 2001. Then there was twenty-one year old new member, Jamal Hunter, who met him at another church's singles function.

Almost like clockwork every month, Stan would search the DC/MD/VA area for different single events or events for young adults and entrepreneurs. At these functions Stan stalked new prey for his slaughter and exchanged phone numbers and later other pleasantries with both men and women. Unlike me though, Jamal would not take things lying down without a fight. He found out on New Year's that he was engaged to the church's gospel star and was furious to say the least.

I sang my heart out to Reverend Milton Brunson's "For the Good of Them". The choir director, Sister Shank, ushered us to sway along to the music. I hit a high note then the choir exploded with the next phrase in the song.

Saints in the congregation started to stand and clap. Some were crying and shouting as their hearts were touched. Mothers in Zion who had been through some things in their lives began to praise and worship the Lord the best way they knew how.

"Oh, don't y'all just sit there. God is in the house." Bishop's voice echoed over the people. Like a school of fish, the congregation went to collectively worship God. Men lifted Holy hands in worship, some crying, others just yelling "Jesus". There was even some bending down on their knees like some of the women in the presence of God. Little girls and boys watched intently as their parents shouted out to Jesus Christ the Savior.

The choir continued to sing the song with passion. I crooned the lyrics to the song until the words just stuck to my ribs and filled my whole heart. Not singing anymore, I stood there and just cried. I cried like a baby who had lost its mother as another choir member took the microphone and a nurse's aide rubbed my back and helped me to my seat. All one could hear was weeping and wailing throughout the church. The choir began to lower their voices to a permeating hum as the pianist and other musicians played softly. Just then our Pastor stepped to the podium.

"Ah just play that a little more, real softly." He said to the musicians. "My brothers and sisters today God is working it out." He encouraged his flock and began to move into his sermon for the morning. By then the ushers opened the doors so that the late comers, including Tracey, could quickly find their seats and hear the word proclaimed.

"I would like for those of you who have their Bibles to turn with me to Luke, chapter ten versus nineteen and twenty. When you get it please stand and read along with me. Behold, I give unto you power to tread on serpents and scorpions. All"

"Hallelujah!" I yelled.

"Yes, yes. Read." Bishop said.

"And over all the power of the enemy: and nothing shall by any means hurt you." The congregation read the verse.

"Thank you, thank you." I yelled over and over as others join me saying "glory be to God" and the like.

"Continue." He said to the church folk.

"Notwithstanding in this rejoice not, that the spirits are subject unto you; but rather rejoice because your names are written in heaven." Everyone read together but I was still caught in the Spirit and started to shout glory to God rocking myself back and forth engulfed in a stare down with Stanley.

"Today Saints I'm gonna remind you of the power God has given you to destroy, dismantle and to defeat the devil just because your name is written in the book of life as one of the saved. Folks we're gonna talk this morning about our God given rights to defeat the devil. Amen." He said.

"Amen." The congregation responded to the Under-shepherd of the house. Just then Stanley grabbed his stuff and walked out of the church as Bishop began preaching. I watched his every move from the choir stand but remained in my seat listening intently to the sermon.

Δ

"Girl didn't Pastor preach this morning?" Tracey said hugging Sharon.

"Girl yeah. How are you doing Sister Louisa?" Sharon responded and started to ask about the health of Sister Louisa Fuller who was recently diagnosed with breast cancer.

"Oh, I'm wonderfully blessed girl. How's your mother." Sister Louisa asked Sharon.

"Oh, she's doing fine." Sharon answered.

"Well tell her we miss her visits over here." She replied.

"Okay." Sharon answered sort of fake. "I don't know why every Sunday she wears that ole' tired wrap. We all know her husband got it for her three Christmas' ago." Sharon said to Tracey.

"Girl, You a mess. Where is Dee Dee?" Tracey asked.

"I dunno, probably changing. Did you hear Sis bring the house down this morning?" Sharon asked.

"Girl yeah, and I heard that fool so called cheering her on calling her Karen." Tracey said.

"You wasn't even here yet." Sharon wondered aloud.

"I was in the overflow then came back around when I saw the early birds leaving on cue." Tracey responded.

"Oh yeah, he got issues. He better leave her alone though. I know that much." Sharon said.

"Yeah. Hey Brother Smalls." Tracey said to one of our deacons who walked past us.

"Oh, Sister Sharon you look lovely this morning, are you losing weight?" Brother Smalls asked her.

"Aww, I don't know," Sharon responded.

"Well you're looking good." He said moving in to hug her.

"Well thank you. Have a good week," Sharon hugged him back and winced.

"Oh, you too." He winked at Tracey and smiled.

"Gay," Tracey whispered in Sharon's ear as he walked away.

"And fabulous," Sharon said. We giggled at the sight of him sashaying past us.

"Oh no," Tracey muttered almost yelling.

"What?" Sharon asked her.

"It's Stan," She said pointing.

"I thought he left," Sharon turned and looked now alarmed.

"I guess not, c'mon let's go find Dee Dee and leave out the other way." The girls went off to find me but I was in the basement talking to Pastor's wife.

"Oh, good morning ladies," Sister Franklin said to my best friends.

"Good morning mother," They each hugged and kissed her on the cheek.

"And Ms. Tracey, why were you prancing in here late this morning?" She asked her.

"Oh, umm, I was out in Fort Washington ma'am," Tracey replied.

"Un-huh. Well are you girls registered for the Women's Retreat on Valentine's Day Weekend?" She asked.

"Oh, umm, no I dunno," Sharon replied.

"Well you all need to register, especially you Ms. Tracey. I will be teaching a workshop on how to go from single to married, the Godly way. And Elder Jackson will have her series on the Proverbs thirty-one women of the new millennium," She said.

"Oh, that sounds wonderful Sister Franklin," I assured her.

"Yes, seeing as I believe Sister Price will soon be making that jump over the broom it's about time you two girls join her," She said smiling and rubbing Destiny's back.

"Well that's still to be seen," Tracey said.

"Excuse me?" Sister Franklin asked concerned and looking at me.

"Oh nothing, could you guys excuse us for a moment please?" I asked my friends.

"Sure," Sharon and Tracey answered and stepped away so I could talk to Sister Franklin in private.

"She hasn't told her beloved mentor Sister Mother Pastor Patricia Franklin," Tracey asked Sharon teasingly.

"She's just waiting for the right time," Sharon pronounced.

"I bet she ain't even told Ms. Juanita or Granny Mae either." She continued asking about Destiny's aunt and grandmother.

"Hunny, I bet Granny Mae already knew Stan had an issue," Sharon said.

"Or two," Tracey added and the slapped five giggling.

"Or two what?" I interjected after finishing with my conversation with Mother Franklin.

"Nothing boo. How are you doing this morning?" Sharon asked me.

"Oh, I'm just too blessed to be stressed," I lied still torn about the break up.

"You haven't told Pastor yet?" Tracey asked.

"Drop it Tracey," Sharon butted in and shook her head no.

"No, no I haven't Tracey. Stanley and I will tell them together," I said lying because I had just scheduled an appointment with them to tell them myself because he was refusing to tell them anything.

"Oh really," Tracey said not convinced.

"Yes really," I said a little indifferent at how she was acting.

"Since when?" Tracey continued to press the issue.

"Hey, come on you guys. Let's go I'm hungry," Sharon intervened pulling us in the opposite direction of where they saw Stan last.

"I'm parked this way," I said.

"Well, I'm driving," Tracey said.

"Oh really," Sharon taunted her.

DIMES, PROFILES AND WIVES

"Yeah, Rob let me get the keys to the Escalade." Tracey threw the words in Sharon's face trying to make her jealous because Sharon didn't even have a man yet, that we knew of.

"That's fine but you know that means you have to drop me back here by 5:30," I said.

"Oh, you have to sing tonight too," Tracey questioned.

"Don't I always," I responded smiling. I loved to praise the Lord every chance that I got.

"I don't know why you just don't go get a record deal. You can sing just as good as that Cookie Smith, Karen Clark Sheard and Kim Burrell. Shoot girl you even better than that new girl, what's her name?" Sharon asked.

"Delores Catherine Cox," I answered.

"Yeah, I mean she can blow, but Destiny heffa you can sho nuff sang girlfriend, and you know you can so don't try to even act shy," Sharon continued.

"Huh?" I tried to act shyer.

"Oh, heffa don't even act like you don't know what—" Tracey was cut off as Stan appeared in front of the side entrance to the church.

"Good afternoon ladies." Stanley said. Irritated Tracey and Sharon answered him with much attitude.

"Hey,"

"Hello Stanley." I said.

"Hello Ka, I mean Destiny. Do you have a moment?" He asked trying to sound as sincere and sweet as possible, the way any man would after being caught with his hands in the wrong cookie jar. Stan had been planning this short meeting for weeks now. He knew that if he used the church as the meeting place I would be less inclined to make a scene and more open to listen to him. I was such a conscientious person and loved the church too much to desecrate it even over him.

"We're about to go out to eat so she can't talk—" I had to cut Tracey off abruptly.

"Girls can you go bring the car around?" I asked.

"I can stay here, that's if you need me to," Sharon said.

"No, here take my things. I'll be right out when you pull up," I said sure of myself.

"Oh, by the way, Stanley. Go straight to hell!" Tracey said as politely as she could then walked out the door. Sharon looked the man up and down, sizing him up ready for him to say one word so that her alter-ego, Niecey, could come out and drop him in church.

"Five minutes Dee," Sharon said now making eye contact with me.

"Thanks girls," I said and smiled handing her my purse, Bible bag and choir robe.

There was a long awkward silence between us. He was standing there trying to find the words that he thought would get me to change my mind. Of course, he said the wrong thing.

"So, I guess this is the only place that I can talk to you," He asked.

"Stanley cut to the crap. What do you want?" I demanded.

"Baby it's time for us to work this out. I mean it's been weeks already and you won't return my calls," He said smoothly.

"I told you it's over," I affirmed.

"But Beloved, all of that is in the past," He tried to sound even smoother.

"It doesn't matter, it's over Stan," I affirmed and put my weight on my right leg.

"So that's it. You don't believe me," He threw up his hands frustrated.

"Why should I?" I put my hands on my hips and huffed.

"Because you know I love you and would do anything for you," He said as a matter-of-fact.

"No, no I don't," I assured him not at all impressed in his antics.

"Oh, so you've told your grandmother or how about Ms. Juanita?" He hit a nerve.

"Don't go there Stanley Milton," I told him pointing at him.

"That's what I thought. You haven't said anything to anybody yet because in your heart of hearts you still love me and want to be my wife," He said like he'd won the argument.

"Stanley, believe what you must, but I gotta go," I conceded because I didn't want to make a scene and really tell him where he could go today.

"But I got reservations for us at Phillips and I wanted to continue discussing our plans." He said like he knew he had me in the palm of his hands still.

"You just don't get it do you," I said, taken aback.

"I get that we both need to go through with this. I mean, when was the last time you had a man in your life before me that treats you the way I do. All that I have I still want to share with you Karen," He said sounding like the Stanley of old.

"Oops, there are my friends I gotta go," I was happy the Lord brought them out just in time because I was seconds away from letting him have it right there at church.

"Wait!" He grabbed my arm. Tracey blew the horn because she saw us.

"Let go of me. Don't you touch me, don't you ever touch me again!" I shouted angrily pulling away from his grasp.

"We'll talk about this later," He let me go because one of the deacons heard me and started walking towards us.

"No, no we won't. There is nothing else left for us to talk about," I told him sternly.

"Destiny please, this can still work out for both of us." He said trying to ignore the deacon who was steps away from me.

"Bye Stanley." I pushed past him through the door and walked briskly to the truck and the safety of my friends. We rode in silence listening to a CD of the sermon we just heard being reminded yet again that we each had charge over our enemies no matter what the situation.

Seven
Sharon

"Mama, I am on my way right now," I spoke into my I-Phone.
"Well what do you have on?" Mama asked.
"One of my suits, why?" I replied.
"No reason. Okay so I'll see you at the church." She said.
"Yes mother." I drove my Lexus down to Baltimore from Chevy Chase. A few weeks ago, my Mama invited me to her church's annual Love Revival. She had been begging me to make sure I would come all week. My mother figured since her daughter was still single, it was Valentine's Day and a Friday night what better way to spend the night than with the Lord. Therefore, Sharon Denise had better have her butt in a pew. I just hoped she wasn't trying to hook me up again with yet another saved (wife abusing), sanctified (adulterous) and set-free (bastard hiding) God fearing Christian man. I have had my fill of fake and trifling "Christian" men who dare to blasphemy the name of God just to get my phone number.

Greater Mount Sinai A.M.E. was packed for a Friday night. Okay, am I pulling up to Club Love or a church? I realized that the subtle bass I was hearing was not coming from my speakers but from the church. People were still walking in and it was almost 8:00 p.m. Services started at 7:00 but hey, better late than never Mama always said, especially when trying to get to church. Just then I saw a limousine pull up in front of the church. Oh Lord, see as soon as a small church gets some money they go spending it on frivolous stuff! I wonder just how much this super preacher cost them tonight. Now appalled, I began to reminisce on the days I was a trustee in training and realized that some preachers actually expected you to pay them a flat fee before they preached the word of God to the congregation. Or at least the word they felt the money was worth for preaching at that particular church.

To my surprise, out jumped seven adorable teenage girls dressed in cotillion like gowns in some heels and flawless make-up and carrying oil lamps.

"Excuse me Ma'am. Would you please step aside and let these precious young ladies in waiting come through? The bridegroom is coming; and they have oil prepared." A tall lanky young man said to me as he opened the door to the church for the girls. Each young lady stepped into Greater Mount Sinai with virtue written all over her faces. They looked straight ahead, not speaking to anyone. For a second there I thought I had new pledges standing in front of me. After they passed I was let in with the other late comers. The youth were in charge of service and the first three rows of the church were full of debutantes and escorts. Just then I heard.

"Oh, my sweet Jesus. Niecey, baby-girl is that you?" Mother Abigail Howard proclaimed. I turned to find old Mother Howard standing in front of me. "Well Lord, the prodigal daughter has returned," She said hugging me and fussing at my clothes and hair.

"Ooo, you don growed up so healthy. I see that ring finger still bare," She said.

"Yes, Mother Howard, how are you?" I asked her.

"Well the Lord has been good to me. You see that last batch of virgins, the tall gal is my last grandbaby and she ain't got no kids, ain't on no drugs and she graduate this year. Now I don't really know if she really is a virgin, she looks too healthy to me, but as long as she don't fall into one of those three lists she fine by me," She explained.

"Yes ma'am. Have you seen my mother?" I asked.

"Oh yeah, she's up there with the rest of the nurses. Come here young man," She told one of the youth.

"Yes mother Howard?" He responded.

"Go up there and fetch Sister Walker. Thank you," She instructed him.

"You're welcome ma'am." He responded to the Mother.

"Just wait here in the vestibule. She probably got a seat for you already," She confessed. Mama always saved me a seat next to her near the front whenever I came to visit here.

"Oh, thanks Mother Howard, you are always so sweet to me," I said.

"Baby you're welcome. You know we are still your home no matter where you go for services on Sunday." She said and went inside the sanctuary leaving me to wait for mama.

"Yes ma'am." Just then the youth choir, a good thirty or so, started to sing a beautiful rendition of "Jesus loves me" as one of the ladies in waiting sang the lead.

"May I take your coat?" Asked a handsome stranger. I turned bracing myself to see yet another fake Black Christian man.

"No, no thank you. I have everything under control," I answered the stranger. Although I was usually very cautious about men who tried to start up any kind of conversation with me in church, I got a good vibe off this tall dark and handsome man. With a quick once over I saw he had no wedding band, or no impressions of one on his ring finger indicating he just took it off. He was carrying a Bible and notebook that both look worn, but he could've just picked that up somewhere. He even had some nice non-flashy Kenneth Coles on his feet, which screamed he had style and at least one hundred dollars in my wallet.

"Well I just thought it would be easier to find a seat without one," He said then smiled. His smile could break the law with his chiseled chin and thick juicy lips covering pearly white teeth.

"Oh no. My mother is saving me a seat," I explained to the inquisitive man.

"I thought you looked a little familiar," He crossed his arms and proceeded to look me up and down like he was making a mental note of who he had in front of him.

"Oh, really and how is that?" And the game began, men are so typical. I thought to myself but was nervous all a sudden.

"Niecey, boo. Niecey come here girl, oh hey there Brother Marcus." My mother said.

"Hello Sister Walker," The man said and hugged her.

"I'm glad you two have met." Mama said standing between us.

"Oh no Ma'am not really. I was just telling this beautiful young lady that she looked familiar," He said grinning from ear to ear. I tried not to let a slight smile creep on my face.

"Well that would be correct. This is my daughter Niecey Walker," She declared calling me by my birth name.

"Sharon Denise Douglas, Esquire actually," I corrected her.

"She go by my maiden name and she a lawyer too," Mama said.

"That's great Sister Douglas," He reached out to shake my hand. I shook his. "Well I see there's a seat opening up and the choir is just about done. We'll talk again soon," He said.

"Okay Brother Marcus." Mama said.

"Is that okay with you Sister Douglas?" He asked me and cocked his head to the side.

"Oh, call her Niecey." My mama said.

"Sister Douglas is fine, and yes speaking again would be fine," I surprised myself answering him.

"Enjoy the service." He touched my arm and walked into the sanctuary. My heart fluttered.

"You too," I said grinning like a goofball.

"Umm, umm, umm. God is working in here tonight," Mama said vividly happy.

"Mama please. Why you still got everybody up in here calling me Niecey?" I asked.

"Chile hush and c'mon so we can go sit down. You late but the girls haven't danced yet so you're just in time." About fifteen minutes and a dozen announcements later about twelve ladies in waiting appeared in front of the congregation. There were about four from every age group up to around twenty-one. They did a wonderful liturgical dance to "Mary's Alabaster Box."

Listening to the song and just watching the girls made me realize just what the Love Revival was truly about.

It was about getting the virgins ready to meet the bridegroom and His love for the church. There were ten virgins preparing to meet one bridegroom and only five were ready to travel with him to the wedding chamber. Five virgins that were ready: untouched, undefiled, and pure ready to meet Him and receive all the love He had for them. Finally, the Pastor stepped to the podium with the scripture. Not to my surprise he went to the parable of the ten virgins, but he didn't concentrate on their oil, those that had it ready and those who did not. He did not talk about Christ coming back for the church either. Pastor James concentrated on one word and one word only: tarry.

Now usually I could figure out what the preacher was going to say just by the scripture they choose, but tonight I was stumped. Pastor James began his sermon and then came to the subject. "Tarry, hmm, tarry, tarry?"

"Yes pastor," Terry Knowles answered him.

"Oh, I'm not calling you out son. Church let's close the book for a moment and take a quick survey. When was the last time you tarried over a thing? Now think before you answer Saints. Tarry. What does that word mean, what does it entail people? Another word for it is sojourn, is that right Sister Niecey?" Pastor asked. Almost half of the congregation turned to look at me.

Embarrassed and shocked I answered, "Uh, yeah, I mean yes pastor."

"Good to see you this evening daughter." He smiled at me and moved on with the sermon. As he continued I felt as if he was talking directly to me, that I was the only one at church that night and he was all in my business. Whenever I heard the word church, my name was there instead. I felt like I was finally getting that spoon fed tapioca pudding that me and Daddy used to eat every Sunday afternoon after church when I was a little girl.

"Niecey to tarry means to wait." Pastor continued. "Waiting involves patience but patience is not just a noun it is an action word. Now listen, because I'm about to drop a seed in your womb that within the next nine months your husbandman will come unto you." Just then I got all excited because I just knew I was ready for everything he was about to say. "Church, God don't need another list from you to tell him how to create you a husband or a wife. He doesn't need your help finding your mate doing background checks and all that. All He desires of you is for you to wait, be patient, and prepare. How do you wait? You go to work every day the same way you would when you finally do get married. Marriage doesn't mean you stop working and they take care of you. Oh no, if you got that in your heads ladies and gentlemen y'all need to quit playing. Ladies you do know there are some men out there who think if they find just that right woman she'll take care of him, don't fall for that old scalawag. Be patient brothers and sisters. Don't stop all your hobbies and things because you think it's time to get married and God got one ready for you tomorrow, " he preached.

"Remember that our timing is usually never in line with His. And prepare. Can I talk about preparation for just a moment folks? It's not about who, what, when, how, or why just do it. Prepare for the person who ain't gonna ever leave your house, even though it's in your name. Prepare for the friend who will run up the phone bill calling their mama for hours at a time. Prepare for the baby who gets sick in the middle of the night and whines, cries and moans every time you move to make yourself more comfortable in that big king sized bed you always wanted. Tarry church tarry," He took a sip of his water and wiped the sweat from his brow.

"You see it's not all about the bomb career position, good credit, money in the bank, a nice car etc. No, it's about the fruits, those same fruits of the spirit I've been teaching on that you need to become a wife or husband to your mate. Anyone can be a bride, here just put on a nice frilly dress and it don't have to be white. Oh, but you need a ring, here you go, a nice three karat diamond solitaire for you, yes little ole you. And let's not forget the oh so necessary wedding party with all the trimmings yup, there you go," He said.

As he was preaching about tarrying the young ladies moved in line collecting a little keepsake from a young man with a basket who got it from the first lady. One by one they filled the rest of the choir stand until the end of the sermon. That's when I realized I had been doing a lot of stuff, just not tarrying like Pastor James was talking about.

I mean I had a slew of applicants who would make a good husband for me, especially Cornelius, who I'd been dating sparingly behind the girls' backs. I thought I had it all down, but I guess not. As I listened to him finish his sermon I made a promise to myself and to God to be patient and haste not for anything because He was going to supply all my needs, especially my need for the husband of my dreams. After the service mama and I went out to dinner.

"So, baby, what did you think of the service?" she asked.

"It was lovely, and Pastor really preached that sermon," I responded.

"Yeah, so are you tarrying?"

"I haven't, but I will start," I said trying to finish the last of my fried chicken.

"Good, because I think Brother Marcus would be good for you," she said not to my surprise.

"Mama, see there you go again," I started to chuckle starting on my apple pie. We were eating at one of her favorite restaurants, the Bistro.

"Oh, hush now. Brother Marcus is perfect for you. Works for the city, no kids and is God fearing," she reiterated.

"Here we go again," I said exhausted already.

"What?" Mama's voice went up an octave and she took a sip of her lemonade.

"Mama every year you do this and to appease you, I date these God fearers only to find out they either whores, violent, crazy or gay," I told her the truth as I saw it.

"Who's gay?" Mama asked, concerned putting her hand on her chest.

"That's not the point, we date a couple of times and then I have to dump the idiots. They never live up to my standards and you think they are the best thing since Big George," I continued to try to make her understand where I was coming from.

"Okay now you stop it. Your Daddy ain't no where near the caliber of men I've introduced you to. According to them you're too uppity and expect too much too soon. You are from right here in south Baltimore Niecey Walker. You ain't this Sharon Denise Douglas you made up. I gave birth to you, I know better," She said sternly.

"Mama please," I responded.

"No, now you listen to me. So, you want a rich fine husband that you can serve tea to and know all those famous important people. Well let me tell you something girl, it's easier for a camel to fit through a needle than a rich man to enter heaven. You better stop chasing after that fairy tale and get with someone real," she said then tried to get a piece of my pie. I gave her some on her plate.

"Like who, Brother Marcus?" I threw his name in her face.

"No, like a man that actually works for his money," she said as a matter-of-fact.

"What is that supposed to mean Mama?" I asked annoyed.

"I see you still playing church and don't know the real word of God," she said.

"Get to the point, mother," I said even more annoyed now.

"You watch your tongue Niecey; I still know how to swing a belt," she said as I kept eating my pie and rolled my eyes.

"Okay, okay I'm sorry," Mama pulled out her Bible and turned to Proverbs 12:11.

"Niecey, a man that has wealth gotten by vanity shall be diminished, but he that gather it by labor shall increase," she said.

"Ma, what are you getting at?" I pouted crossing my arms in defiance.

"Oh, Ms. I gotta law degree can't figure this out," She said pushing my buttons even more.

"Mother," I clanged my fork against the plate.

"All I'm saying is this, money ain't gon get you what you need, a man that really loves and respects you. Why do you think I broke up with your Daddy?" she asked.

"Cause he went to jail," I said which was an afterthought for me.

"No, because he loved money more than he loved me and his family. So much more that he destroyed your brother's life and got him killed. Shawn had no business being there that night. No business, George got my baby killed over a thousand dollars," She started sobbing.

"Ma, don't cry. Big George didn't know they were gonna get robbed," I said and rubbed her hands across the table.

"Yeah, but he was too young to be there period," she said. It's a wonder she still gets so choked up about Rayshawn and it's been almost eighteen years since his murder.

"Let's change the subject," I said.

"Yes let's. Now, back to Brother Marcus," she said.

"Aww Mama." I whined as Mama listed all the attributes that her latest prospect had available.

Eight
Tracey

Rob and I had been on a roller coaster ride for the past two months and as spring came around he was clearly pushing me over farther and farther. For Valentine's he gave me a tennis bracelet to match the new Coach leather upgrade for my Lexus SUV. In return he asked me to make him a nasty video of myself with another man for him to keep. I didn't want to do it at first, but when I saw the bracelet and the sexy dark skinned adonis he had picked out for me, I decided it was well worth it especially if the video was for his own personal collection.

In the middle of March, we took a trip to Walt Disney World. However, he sent me back in tears early because he needed to go to Miami to take care of some business and wouldn't let me come. While he was away he gave me the keys to the house and full run of his rides. So, while he was away, I played house with a couple other men I liked to keep on the side. I even drove Chucky around in Rob's Benz the week before he came home telling him I was test driving it. We made crazy love in the car and I made sure to leave evidence there for Rob to find later.

The day he returned from Miami I pulled up to the terminal at BWI and saw Rob coming out of the airport followed by a very beautiful Latina woman. They both walked to the truck. I popped the trunk and the woman put her overnight bag in after Rob's luggage. She then went to open the back door as Rob closed the trunk and walked to the front door.

"Who are you?" I hollered to the woman envious of her physical attributes. She had to be at least five foot ten with green eyes that sparkled in the sunlight.

"Hola, como estas?" The woman said to me looking

dumbfounded. She had the nerve to flip her long brown hair at me.

"Aww hell no!" I yelled as Robert got in the front seat. I crossed my arms. He reached over to kiss me on the cheek,

"Hey babe." I moved out of the way and stared at him like he had lost his mind. "Rosa this is Tracey, Baby say hello," Rob said very nonchalant starting to roll a blunt.

"Who is she?" I demanded now popping my gum and putting my foot on the gas while still in park.

"She's one of my good friends from Miami. She just got here from Nicaragua and wants to move to DC," He said clearly unfazed by my irritation.

"And, so where is she gonna stay?" I asked.

"At the apartment for a while,"

"The apartment only has one room," I reminded him.

"Yeah, and," He threw a piece of the narcotic in the ashtray.

"Robby I aint that stupid,"

"Oh, no," he chuckled smugly. "no, she will be working for me at the club, she dances," He continued to chuckle now amused by my antics.

"You a trip, why didn't you tell me this before?" I said understanding everything now but still concerned because stuff wasn't sitting right in my gut.

"Because it was none of your business. I'm only telling you now, so you won't trip if you come to the apartment and see her there," He said getting serious now sounding a little upset.

"But she don't even speak English," I told him with a slight attitude.

"She speaks enough to make me some money," He said coyly.

"So she don't understand nothing we say," I asked rhetorically.

"Nope," He shrugged and lit a match.

"Rosa," I called to her.

"Si." Rosa answered.

"Stay away from my man or I will hurt you," I told her using my hardest gangster girl attitude trying to impress Rob.

"You think you so hard little girl, but it's all good. She ain't thinking about me boo. How is my money doing?" He asked.

"It's fine, still there if that's what you mean," I replied.

"Good, cause I gotta make another deposit," He declared.

"But I just put the $6,5000.00 in yesterday," I said concerned about all the deposits he's been making into my business account.

"That's cool. I just need you to hold on to it a little while longer, maybe for a month or so," He said not fazed by the obvious concern in my voice.

"Why can't you deposit it into your accounts? I mean darn, this is starting to be a lot of money Rob and this is my business account," I asked to make my concerns heard clearly.

"I already told you why," He responded still trying not to get into an argument in front of Rosa.

"It just seems like there is more to this story than what you're telling me," I said finally.

"Stay out of my damn business Tracey," He lost his temper then cursed.

"I'm just saying, in the last couple of months you've deposited almost $100,000 in cash into that account. And you say it's only so your baby's Mamas don't find out," I said trying to get him to understand my concerns.

"Yeah, so what's your point?" He said motioning for me to drive the car. I put the car in drive and started out towards DC on the parkway.

"It's just," I tried to form the words for how I really felt. I ain't that stupid, like he thought. I would have to account for all that money some kind of way, especially if we stayed together for the rest of the year. I didn't play with Uncle Sam nor my business. He just flipped his wrist at me dismissing my concern.

"It's just nothing Tracey. It'll be gone before you know it and you can have a good five grand for doing me this favor. I just need it to stay there for a while. You love me right baby," He rubbed his hand up my thigh while I drove. As if he just lit a match to my fire, I began to melt at the steering wheel because I finally got to say I love you too. Umm, now I can get rid of that fool Chucky, well maybe not, he's really the better catch and I need somebody who can play clean up whenever this fool messes up again.

"Yeah, I love you boo." I admitted smiling from ear to ear.

"Then don't even worry about it. We gonna take over the DMV. Stick with me kid. I got plans for us." He pinched my thigh and relit his blunt.

For the second time I had fallen for the deception of yet another charlatan full of lies and deceit who manipulates my body and mind. Rob was nothing but a sniveling weasel of a man that would use any woman to his advantage even prostituting his own "woman" for profit. He loved nobody but himself and used his charisma and good looks as a noose to hang women with every chance he got. However, this fleecing was not all his fault. I was just as much to blame as Rob was for falling again for the bull crap. Too bad I didn't see the trouble that was on the horizon.

Nine
Destiny

I was sitting in choir rehearsal on another Friday night after a crazy week at work. Singing always made me feel better no matter what happened during the day, so I was glad to be here.

"I don't need anybody else" The choir sang.

"No, no, no. Altos let me hear that again," Sister Shank stopped the choir from singing. I was sitting in my seat trying to ignore the stares and snickering of some of the choir members.

"I heard he's been like that all along and she knew it but couldn't take it anymore when her parents found out," Sister Jackie Smalls whispered loud enough so I could hear her. They were so catty.

"Girl no, they don't even know the wedding is off," Sister Geraldine Gephart said and had to be shushed by Elder Coffey.

"Umm, excuse me Geraldine, but we are trying to prepare for this concert and you are still flat," Sister Shank told her, making me laugh out loud.

"Humph, I wouldn't be laughing too much if I were you," Geraldine said smugly.

"The joy of the Lord is my help," I retorted just as smug, and then whispered, "at least I did have a man."

"She so fake," Geraldine tried to continue the dialect.

"Uh, uh. It's getting too street in here. This is still the Lord's house and I will not have this mess going on while I am in charge," Sister Shank declared. "Sister Smalls and Geraldine y'all go take a break and work on those notes for about ten minutes. Dee Dee start teaching the sopranos the next verse of the song. Altos one more time, let's go. And one, two, three sing," We continued the rehearsal for another forty five minutes. After choir rehearsal Sister Shank stopped me in the vestibule.

"Dee Dee, sweetie is something wrong?" she asked.

"No Ma'am. Everything is alright with me, how about you. You seemed a little worked up today," I answered trying to sound more concerned for her than depressed.

"Well, I've been hearing a lot of stuff around here about you and Brother Stanley. You know you can talk to me about it, about anything for that matter. I know your mother would have wanted you to talk to someone about all of this," she said.

"No, no really I'm alright. I just had to stop something from going terribly wrong in my life that's all. Brother Stanley has been good to me and we have been talking to Pastor," I lied.

"Well, okay. You two are in my prayers." We both walked out the church to our cars. I didn't have to lie. Why am I lying to people? It's obvious that nosey Mable Thomison told one too many people that our wedding was cancelled after I had to tell the Pastor alone that me and Stan were not getting married. Not only that but I had to tell him the boy was gay or bisexual which was something I should not have had to tell our Pastor by myself. He should have been man enough to at least show up for the meeting and tell it himself. I just wished we hadn't already had the date posted on the church calendar because then I wouldn't feel so ashamed for having to cancel my own scheduled wedding. Just then someone walked up to the car and tapped me on the shoulder.

"You have such a beautiful voice," The stranger admitted smiling ear to ear. He was a small little man but had beautiful hazel eyes.

"Thank you," Recognizing the man from the choir.

"My name is Jamal," He said, reaching to shake my hand.

"Oh yeah, welcome to the Metro," I told him and shook his hand.

"Thanks, hey you wanna go out for some coffee?" He asked a little too forward for me.

"Umm, actually I'm on my way to meet someone," I told him truthfully.

"Oh, I'm sorry. Yeah, a woman as pretty as you would have someone waiting for you," He said trying to insinuate something I couldn't understand at that moment.

"Oh, it's not like that at all," I responded.

"Don't apologize my sister. It's good when a man finds a good woman to spend some time with," He said smiling like a goof ball again. I later found out Jamal just wanted to find out where Stanley was and bust him out or find out when the wedding was going to be and make sure he made a mockery of the whole affair. He was a man scorned by another man, and men like him didn't play. So, whether I liked it or not, I was about to be a friend to him and lead him to the promised land of sweet revenge. Too bad he hadn't been to church in a couple of weeks because the word was out the wedding was cancelled.

"Yeah?" I questioned his response and myself. "Well I gotta go,"

"Well see you Sunday." He said and tapped me on my shoulder.

"You too, God bless." I got in my car. Now he's a nice young man, wonder if he's gay too. Probably, I seem to be a magnet for them types lately.

Δ

The girls and I were having dinner at one of Sharon's favorite restaurants, the Hamilton in DC. She always liked to hobnob with all the movers and shakers in the DMV area who would come here to have their business meetings or impress their next client.

"Douglas party of three please," Sharon told the maitre d.

"Ah, Ms. Douglas your table is right this way." He led us to our table. It was one of DC's premiere restaurants. The seafood was just delectable. She always talked about it and I was happy when she finally decided to invite us here. I definitely could not afford it on my salary.

"Um, it's so nice in here Niecey," I said to Sharon.

"I thought I'd take you two heffas downtown somewhere nice for a change. Especially you Dee Dee. You deserve to be pampered after all you do for the world and us." Sharon said.

"Especially us and after finally canceling that wedding," Tracey added her two cents.

"Well I had to, there was no way in the world I was going to do that to my family and friends," I admitted.

"More importantly to yourself girl, to yourself. Boo, you're a strong woman but all of us have our limits. And Stanley Milton Reid was yours," Sharon added.

"Where are all the brothers at up in here?" Tracey asked Sharon.

"There are plenty of men in her Tracey, don't start acting up. Be on your best behavior in front of these people some of them are future clients or people I will be rubbing elbows with," Sharon touted proudly.

"I don't care, is the food good?" I asked.

"Oh no, just because you had to let that Negro go don't mean you are going to pig out and gain all that weight again Karen," Sharon called me by my middle name to annoy me and make a point.

"Whatever Niecey, I'm gonna eat to my heart's desire," I tried to get her back for picking with me. She really hated when we used her birth name.

"Go on ahead and let the heffa eat, she gotta get her kicks somewhere because Lord knows she won't be getting them any other way now," Tracey started giggling picking with me.

"Forget you Tracey," I laughed a little uncomfortable but happy she got me to laugh.

"Don't start y'all," Sharon intervened. We sat there for less than three minutes before the waiter came to the table. Their service was so on point already. I knew we would have to leave a hefty tip.

"Hello ladies, I'm Justin. What will you be having to drink

this evening?" The waiter asked.

"I would like a glass of the Chardonnay please," Sharon said.

"Anything else, hors d' oeuvres maybe," The waiter asked.

"Y'all got any cheese fries," I asked trying hard to get on Sharon's nerves acting really ghetto.

"No, Dee Dee," Sharon snapped embarrassed pinching me in my arm.

"Fine, I'll have the calamari then and some Pepsi," I said.

"And you ma'am?" He asked Tracey.

"I'll have some Mad Dog 20-20," Tracey said trying not to laugh.

"Excuse me?" The waiter asked confused. We all giggled and he stood there looking at us like we were crazy.

"Oops, I forgot," she winked at Sharon. "I'll have a glass of Dom," she said trying to mock Sharon the best way she could.

"I hope you're paying for that," Sharon said.

"But of course, mademoiselle," Tracey said in her best French accent.

"You are so stupid," Sharon couldn't help but laugh at her friend acting like she didn't have no home training. Now understanding they were no longer paying him any attention the waiter excused himself and went to get our drinks and food.

"So, Dee Dee how was choir rehearsal?" Sharon asked.

"It was fine, but that darn Geraldine keeps running her mouth," I responded.

"Well you know after you told Pastor and he told that flighty Sister Johnson all bets were off," Sharon stated.

"I don't think he told her all the details though," I told her not wanting to believe our Pastor would be so haphazard with that kind of information.

"No, but you know how people like to make up their own stories," Sharon said continuing to make her point known because she knew how our church secretary sometimes runs her mouth too much.

"Yeah," I sighed. "well Sister Shank asked me if everything

was okay, I just said yeah. I didn't want to tell her the full truth," I explained.

"You have nothing to be ashamed of Dee. He lied to you, not the other way around," Sharon tried to uplift my spirits and reached to rub my arm.

"I know it's just so hard. All this time and I never had a clue," I admitted.

"Never?" Tracey asked.

"No, never. I thought he was a Godly saved man. We met at church, never once got fresh with me, even when I begged him to," I said.

"Begged, girl please, he ain't that fine and ain't no sex worth begging or paying for," Tracey crossed her arms and tsked.

"Shut up Tracey," Sharon said shaking her head.

"Yeah Tracey, but for real I thought he was just being respectful. He even said he wanted to wait until our wedding night, so we'd at least be virgins to one another," I said.

"And all the while that nigga was a meat packer," Tracey sipped her drink and started laughing.

"Tracey!" Sharon almost yelled because she was really getting on her last nerve now. The waiter sat a bottle of Cristal in ice next to their table. "From the gentlemen in the corner Miss Douglas." He said and motioned with his hand to a corner table full of fine looking men.

"Uh, who is that?" I asked Sharon. We all turned to look at four gentlemen sitting at a table near the back. One handsome man nodded and tipped his finger at us.

"Um, um, um, he is too fine," Tracey added.

"Ladies that would be Mr. Wynd," Sharon said putting a seductive smile on her face.

"No way," I said.

"Here we go again. I don't know why you even bother. He's a Wynd, and they all blow away sooner or later," Tracey told Sharon annoyed. She downed her drink then reached for the new bottle on the table.

"Don't hate," Sharon told Tracey and grabbed the bottle before she could reach it.

"Congratulate," I finished the clause.

"He probably ain't no good just like his brother," Tracey continued to push the envelope.

"We'll just have to see about that, now won't we? What didn't happen for you could still happen for me, don't be jealous soror be happy for me. Anyway, I haven't made my final decision about him yet though. He may be just too good to be true," Sharon said.

"You can't be serious," Tracey was even more annoyed and poured some Cristal in her empty glass.

"And why not," Sharon retorted.

"Niecey, his little brother broke Tracey's heart," I added.

"That was years ago, and he's not Eric," Sharon continued to back up her choice for a suitor.

"No, no it's cool. Go right ahead Ms. Opportunity," Tracey conceded and sipped her drink rolling her eyes to the sky and smacking her lips "it's your funeral."

"Like you wouldn't do the same thing?" Sharon asked a little taken aback by her attitude and not wanting to understand why she even cared that she dated him.

"I already did," We all laughed as Cornelius made his way to our table.

"Miss Douglas, how nice to see you this evening," Cornelius said kissing Sharon's hand.

"Mr. Wynd, thanks for the Cristal," Sharon said smiling from ear to ear.

"I thought you lovely ladies wouldn't mind if I shared it with you," He said.

"It was a new bottle," I tried to correct him.

"But of course it was," He looked at me quizzically.

"Oh, how rude of me. Cornelius these are my best friends, Tracey Simmons and Destiny Price," Sharon introduced us.

"Hello, hello." He shook our hands. "You wouldn't happen to be related to Dr. Jeremiah Simmons II?" He asked.

"Why yes, he is my father," Tracey answered him.

"I often play golf with him at the club. CAP's son sure did find him a diamond in the rough," Cornelius said, obviously not impressed with all of the jewelry she had on. Tracey sometimes wore too much especially when she was trying to prove she had money even though she didn't have to.

"Excuse me," Tracey said letting the street come out now. I decided it was time to cut in before my friend went all the way in on Mr. Wynd.

"So, you're a lawyer as well," I asked.

"Why yes, I dibble in the law, and what do you do?" He asked me.

"I'm a social worker, I work in foster care," I said.

"Ah, you'll never go hungry," He said trying to get away with poking fun at my weight.

"What?" I said now feeling the punchline like Tracey.

"Uh, Cornelius, um who are you here with?" Sharon cut in before we both did the go off.

"Just the guys. I was wondering though Miss Douglas when were you going to take me up on that offer I made weeks ago?" He asked.

"I told you, this is a busy season for me," She tried to get off the subject in front of us.

"For me as well, however all work and no play, well you know what they say," He told her. He was so pompous. But I could see why Sharon was attracted to him. The man wore a suit like he was a god.

"We will see," Sharon ended the conversation.

"Yes, we surely will see. It was nice meeting you all," Cornelius said taking her hint to leave us to our dinner.

"Yeah" I said annoyed followed by Tracey's "Un huh". Once he was out of ear-shot Tracey begun "I know you really can't be serious,"

"He didn't mean anything you guys," Sharon tried to make excuses for his rudeness.

"Oh please, he practically called Dee Ms. Piggy," Tracey

said frustrated.

"He was talking about how social workers are always in need," Sharon still tried to back him up as if she was already his wife and defending him for the millionth time to friends who tried to tell her from the beginning he was a jackass.

"He better had, and where is our waiter," I said irritated.

"And when or how long have y'all been talking?" Tracey asked her.

"We met officially in the lobby of the court house in January. I accidentally dropped my briefcase," Sharon confessed.

"Yeah right," I looked at her like she had a beehive on her head.

"He doesn't even remember me," Tracey said.

"Well he was in Europe when you were dating Eric remember," Sharon reminded Tracey.

"Yeah, but we met a couple of times," Tracey said a bit ticked at how he acted towards her.

"It's better this way anyway," Sharon admitted aloud.

"How so?" Tracey asked.

"Because he doesn't know me through you and his crazy brother. It's all about the image," Sharon admitted.

"But sooner or later he'll find out," I pointed out.

"And I'll act surprised," Sharon confessed her web of lies and deceit already spun for her latest conquest.

"You got this all figured out don't you," Tracey added.

"Well you have to, to attract the right element," Sharon sipped her drink.

"Ladies, what are we having this evening?" Said the waiter finally.

Ten

Sharon

I was sitting in my office trying to find a file that I had told my assistant I needed to go through. He was getting on my last nerve and if he couldn't find it I was writing his butt up.
"Alex, I need that file on Mr. Weathers," I told him again. This corporate takeover was worrying me too. If they couldn't figure out their actual earnings for the last twelve quarters they could forget about it.

"Yes Miss Douglas," he said as the phone rang.

"It's Mrs. Walker on line two."

"Put her through," I told him. A second later he walked in with the file in hand. He waited for me to say something but I just flipped my wrist at him to leave my office and motioned for him to close the door.

"Niecey," Mama said, sounding like I was still ten years old.

"Yes mother," I answered, readying myself for another candid disagreement with Mrs. Gloria Walker.

"Did you get my message?" She asked a bit rushed.

"Yes mother, but I'm really busy right now," I explained to her trying to get her off the phone.

"Okay, so you will be in attendance," She pushed.

"Mama, I might be busy Saturday too," I whined trying to get out of another set up for sure.

"Oh no, Sharon Niecey Walker, I told you about this dinner weeks ago," Mama said.

"But Mama," I continued to try to get out of it.

"No butts. Bring that lovely girl Dee Dee and her fiancé too," She sounded like she was cooking because I heard her clanking pots together.

"They broke up mama" I told her reading through the ex parte on my desk.

"Broke up, when? Why?" she asked, sounding concerned.

"He's gay mama," I told her a bit testy.

"Gay, um, um, um, and he was such a fine boy too," she said.

"Yeah, and God-fearing," I said to her chuckling under my breath.

"You watch your tongue chile," Mama scolded me.

"Well who all is gonna be there?" I asked, remembering how she liked to pop surprise guests on me usually cloaked in sheep's clothing only to be wolves ready to pounce.

"Otis, Sister Charles and her husband, and your auntie and Uncle Byron, and a special guest," She said proudly.

"Let me guess, Brother Marcus," I said.

"Well, you said it not me," Mama said chuckling.

"Mama, I told you I wasn't going there this time," I told her firmly.

"Oh, just come out and have a nice time with your family. Mr. Otis ain't seen you in so long he done forgot what you look like," she said trying to smooth over her date party.

"Okay Mama, what do you want me to bring?" Because I knew she wanted me to cook something to try to impress the precious Brother Marcus.

"Make that pound cake you bake so good. It'll make a nice impression on Brother Marcus and dress nice, bring a change of clothes so we can go to church together in the morning," She responded.

"We'll see," I said knowing full well if I don't bake the cake she would talk about it all night and that meant we would have to have another date party where I would not only have to bake the pound cake but cook as well.

"For real Niecey, I'm getting old in age and you still got time to give me at least one grandbaby," Mama said.

"Why, you already got eight." I said.

"Speaking of which, your niece Nikisha turns sixteen this

month and she don't even know you. Now baby, family should be the most important thing in your life besides the church. It is a shame before God that you don't get along with your sisters and brothers cause you all were born of my blood, grew up in the same house with the same parents and y'all act like you don't know each other from a stranger on the street. That breaks my heart baby, it just breaks my heart. Especially since you are doing so well, you should be an example for your nieces and nephews along the way," She gave me the woe is me speech again.

"Mama I don't have time for this. You know that Lakeya, Jasmine, Hollis, and Stevie all have their own lives to lead. That's just how it goes; it's not my fault that they don't like my success," I told her really trying to mask the fact that I didn't like communicating with them because they could be so ignorant and crass. They always had something to say about me going away to school and moving to DC instead of holding down the block when daddy got in trouble.

"Oh, chile please. You spend more time in that fancy office and with your friends than you do with your own family. You don't even visit your brothers and sisters because you're so busy or you think you're too good," Mama told me the truth.

"Ma, I have to go, my two o'clock is here," I lied to get off the subject and the phone.

"There you go, I swear if I wasn't for the fact you call me a few times a month I wouldn't even know I had a middle child named Niecey," She said sounding hurt now.

"Mama, I love you, but I have to go." I still tried to get off the phone not fazed by her attempt to make me feel bad for having the life of my dreams and being important in the world.

"Okay, go on and do what you gotta do." Mama finally said and hung up the phone. I knew she really wanted me to be at her little dinner date but sometimes I just wished she would leave well enough alone. I already had the man of my dreams on the hook, I didn't need a new one who couldn't compete if he tried.

Δ

Two days later I pulled up in the driveway of Mama's house. I had long since stopped begging her to move to a better neighborhood. When I made junior partner, I paid off the house and got it landscaped. It was the best looking house on the block and one of the few that was actually owned by the owner.

"Hey Mama," I kissed her on the cheek. I put down the cake box then took off my jacket.

"Hey baby. You remember Mr. Otis?" She asked, pulling something out of the oven.

"How can I forget," We hugged each other. Mr. Otis was Mama's special friend, which was old people's talk for a boyfriend. He liked to fix stuff around the house and would take Mama to the IHOP for pancakes every Saturday morning.

"Hey there gal, you show nuff is pretty. Look like yo Mama from back in the day," He smiled trying to hug me again.

"Thank you, Mr. Otis," I chuckled at his old nasty behind.

"Your auntie and Uncle Byron in the family room eating cheese and soda crackers," Mama said.

"Okay, here's the cake," I handed it to her as the doorbell rang.

"Cookie can you get that," Mama asked her sister while walking past her. Aunt Cookie opened the door and let Sister Charles and her husband in.

"Hey everybody," Hellos went around the room as I took their coats and put them in the closet.

"We got cheese and crackers, oh and coffee if you want it. One more person is going to come so we'll wait till they show so we can eat," Mama said.

"I'll take a cup," Mr. Charles said.

"Me too," His wife added as the doorbell rang again.

"I got it," Aunt Cookie said. I walked into the kitchen, but

Mama stopped me at the entrance and turned me around, so I could be seen. "Where are you going? That's him. Hold on, let me fix your hair." She said putting her fingers through my bangs.

"Mama, stop," I whined as Marcus Anthony Washington walked through the door in a nice Harvey Bernard coat, a couple seasons old, with a pot and flowers in his hands.

"Good evening everyone," He said standing there just as smooth as he wanted to be. He could dress a little bit, if I did want him I'd only have to upgrade his wardrobe a little because it looks like he had the kind of style I liked in a man. Umm, he got the nerve to be a little sexy too. I was expecting him to give me the flowers in his hand.

"Hello," Everyone responded almost in unison.

"Hello Sister Douglas," He acknowledged, separating me from the group.

"Oh, call her Niecey," Mama said grinning from ear to ear.

"Hello Brother Marcus," I responded.

"Marcus let me get that pot. Oh, what lovely flowers," Mama reached for the pot.

"Oh, they are for you, but I didn't realize Niecey would be here too," He took one of the flowers from the bouquet and gave it to me.

"You don't have to," I said.

"Thank you, Marcus, that was so sweet of you. Sit. Sit. You want some cheese and crackers?" Mama asked, cutting her eyes at me behind him.

"Oh no, that'll spoil my appetite," He said.

"Well the food will be done in a sec," Mama told him.

"Hey there brother Charles," Marcus said.

"Hey Marcus, You still with the Metro," Mr. Charles asked.

"Yes sir, going on fifteen years now," Marcus said.

The Metro, "oh no" I said under my breath. He was a bus driver, now Mama knew better. He didn't even make sixty thousand a year. How would it look, me marrying a bus driver as successful as I am? He would not blend in well with the kind of lifestyle I wanted to have, how could I introduce him to Mr. Brooks and the other partners. Image was everything; good looks and the Lord could not compare to image and the law. See this was exactly why I said this whole relationship would not work, he's not good enough for me. But I could spin it for my plans to build my own firm and become a judge later in life.

"Yeah, well they still got them good benefits, right?" Brother Charles asked.

"Yeah, they come in handy too," Marcus answered.

"So, Marcus, uh what's your last name?" I asked as if mother hadn't already told me every detail she could find about him twice.

"Oh, it's Washington," He said.

"Where did you grow up?" I asked.

"Born and raised right here in Baltimore. I went to Height High School and Morgan State," He answered.

"Oh really, what kind of degree did you obtain at Morgan?" I asked more interested now.

"Oh, I didn't graduate, I dropped out to work and help take care of my family," He answered, shifting his weight almost seeming uncomfortable which was good because it was time for my full court press.

"Family, you have children?" I said now a little flabbergasted.

"Oh no, my dad got sick with cancer and passed away while I was at Morgan, so I stopped going and helped out Ma with my younger siblings. She never forgave me, but she realized that was the only way the family would survive at the time," He explained.

"That's too bad." I said. There was no way in the world this man would ever live up to my standards.

"Oh, not really, I put my brother and sister through school and got Mom the care she needed as she got older and sick with Alzheimer's," He continued to explain his life to me looking like he enjoyed telling it to somebody.

"That's right, how is she sweetie," Sister Charles asked him.

"Oh, she's doing well," He responded.

"She still remembers you?" She asked.

"Yeah sometimes she'll call me Ant and then I know she was feeling alright," He said.

"Ant?" We all questioned mocking him giggling.

"Short for Anthony, my middle name. Mama used to call me that because I would save and hide candy in my room all the time to eat later," He said.

"Storing it away like a little ant," Mr. Otis said.

"Yeah. So what kind of law do you practice?" He returned the questioning to me.

"Cooperate mostly." I explained. I crossed my arms readying myself to be interrogated.

"You went to Howard right," He asked.

"Yeah, the only one in the family, that's my Niecey," Mama confirmed then put on a big smile.

"Yup, nobody thought she could do it but look at her now, driving a Benz and everything," Aunt Cookie added.

"Oh, that's yours huh," Marcus stretched his neck to look outside the window then smiled.

"Yes, I own a Lexus coupe also," I added uncrossing my arms while crossing my legs.

"Oh, that's great, you live in DC?" He continued the dialogue as everyone watched and listened intently. We both realized now that this was really a set up for the two of us and they were just the buffing zone.

"I own a condo in Chevy Chase," I replied.

"Oh, I own a house in PG County," He said.

"Oh Really" I said intrigued once more. I wondered how he pulled that off, it's probably his mother's old house or something like that.

"Well I have a part time job working second shift to help out with the bills since I'm not married and don't have any kids. I have the time and energy," Marcus answered.

"Oh, Marcus you've never been married?" Sister Charles asked him.

"No ma'am," He said.

"And why not," Aunt Cookie asked him, winking at me.

"I haven't found the right lady to meet me at my needs right now. I've been looking for the right one prayerfully though," He said.

"Well take your time son," Uncle Byron put his two cents in.

"Yeah, but I am looking," He said now looking at me. I smiled sheepishly. He might be okay.

"Dinner is ready," Mama said, walking back from the kitchen. Everyone went into the dining room to eat dinner. Mama asked Marcus to bless the food. Afterwards we all sat and enjoyed a nice meal together making some conversation as we ate.

"The food is delicious Sister Walker," Marcus said.

"Thank you, Marcus, but wait for dessert," She said.

"Oh, what did you make?" He asked.

"Oh, not me, Niecey," She boasted putting on another broad smile.

"You're a cook too," He looked at me across the table.

"I dibble and dabble a little," I tried to play down my true skills. Even though I don't like to cook I could burn when I needed to impress a man.

"Well what did you make?" He asked.

"A pound cake," I said proudly flirting now, just a little bit because I didn't want him to get the wrong impression. He still got too much work to do to be able to compete for my affection.

"Umm, my favorite," He said rubbing his stomach and smacking his lips. My stomach flipped because he looked really good doing that. Now I realized I had truly been set up for sure. More polite conversation went around the table as Marcus and I took quick glances at each other over our plates. Some kind of way the conversation got back around to marriage except they put me in the hot seat as Marcus sat and listened.

"So Niecey, when are you gonna take that long walk down the aisle?" Aunt Cookie asked.

"As soon as the right man who is worthy enough to be

with finds me," I replied.

"And how do they have to be worthy?" Mama asked a little concerned because I sounded real uppity suddenly.

"Oh, I have a list of demands they need to cover and meet," I said without apology.

"A list," Marcus asked, taking a bite of his chicken.

"Yes, a list," I affirmed.

"Well, what's on this list may I ask?" He said putting down his fork and paying more attention to me.

"Oh nothing, just your garden everyday things, this and that, six figure income, home owner, no kids, no drama, nice car, good family background, college degree etc," I said as a matter-of-fact.

"Now that's a list," He said and sipped some of his lemonade.

"That's just the major stuff, most men won't meet it," I told him, wiping the corner of my mouth with a napkin.

"What about being saved and living a Christian lifestyle?" He asked crossing his arms

"Well yeah, that too," I added as an afterthought.

"So, you got it all figured out." He wiped his mouth with his napkin.

"Pretty much," I told him, noticing that he had stopped eating and looked a little upset. I didn't know why, but it was all good because he was not the one for me anyway. Friends were all we could be.

"Let's cut the cake," Mama interjected trying to save me from myself.

"Oh, I'm full, but I'll take a piece home," Marcus told her then looked me directly in the eye. I felt like I had been scolded like a child the way his eyes focused on me. I found out later that he got tired of all the crap he'd been taking off me the entire night. He knew I was gorgeous, but he also thought I was too full of myself to deal with. I would make a good trophy wife, but he was looking for something more than that, maybe we really could be friends. He didn't know, so he decided to just chill and maybe get to know me better.

Plus, I hadn't said two words about God and how good He had been to me in my life. It wouldn't surprise him if I wasn't saved, just one of them people who had been going to church all their life and thought they were going to make it into the gates of Heaven by association. Christ was important in his life and he needed a woman who loved Christ just as much if not more than they did him in order for their relationship to work. I just needed to work on my faith walk, but it was too bad I already thought I had it all figured out.

Everyone else took a piece of cake as Marcus prepared to leave for the night. I got his coat and we shook hands before he left. He gave Mama a hug and told her he would see her tomorrow then headed home. The Charles' then left, and nobody was left at the house but family. Just then Mama confronted me.

"Why do you always have to act so asinine and stuck up around my friends? Look what you did. You practically shoved the man right out the door and your life," She snapped.

"Mama he's a bus driver for God's sake," I said unimpressed.

"So, and," She retorted, not understanding.

"And, I'm going to end up making almost three times as much as he does in a couple of years," I explained the facts because clearly, she was mistaken if she believed he had a prayer of living up to my standards.

"But he's a good man Niecey," She tried again to change my mind.

"Good and broke, Two jobs and no college degree," I started putting away the pots and pans in the kitchen to speed up this conversation and get her to concede.

"He had to help out his family," She tried to defend his lifestyle to me to no avail.

"Yeah right," I said, keeping up appearances because even though he was merely a bus driver he was fine and my type. Old enough not to be into a bunch of games and no rug rats to worry about. The fact that he sacrificed his education to keep his family alive was admirable too. I wondered if there was something else though because he was pushing forty hard.

"Girl I swear, you wouldn't know a sure blessing from God almighty if it slapped you in the face," She said and started helping me put up the food. My black berry started to ring.

"Hello," I answered.

"I hate them things, get off that phone and clear off the table," Mama said.

"Hold on, mother I'll be right there," I said.

"So, you're answering your phone now, and on a Saturday night," Cornelius said.

"I was having dinner at my mother's," I told him.

"Have brunch with me tomorrow?" He asked.

"I'm in Baltimore," I responded to his offer.

"So, I'll come there," He said, trying to encroach on my life too soon.

"I don't think so," I retorted swiftly. He didn't need to know what neighborhood I grew up in.

"What about dinner then?" He tried another way to get to see me before the end of the weekend.

"I dunno," I said flirting.

"C'mon, please, I promise I'll be nice," He begged a little, which is what I liked coming from him. It meant he really wanted to be in my presence and spend some quality time with a good woman.

"Let me call you back." I said, still trying to be elusive.

"Dinner then," he asked one more time.

"Okay, Okay," I finally gave in knowing it was going to be a wonderful evening.

"Great, I'll send my driver for you at six o'clock," he said.

"But you don't know where I live," I said.

"You'd be surprised what I know about you Miss Douglas." He said connivingly.

"Niecey!" Mama yelled.

"I gotta go," I said smiling on the phone.

"See you tomorrow then," he said, sounding excited.

"Bye." I said.

"Okay, bye." Cornelius hung up. The next morning church service was very exciting. People were shouting and praising God so much the Pastor didn't even preach. At two fifteen it was over, so I gave Mama a hug and kiss and started walking out of the sanctuary to get my coat. Just as I reached for my Prada coat Marcus stopped me.

"Oh, let me get that for you," He said, smelling good from Burberry classic cologne.

"Well, thank you Brother Washington," I said. He was looking too good in his suit this morning, it was probably from Burlington though.

"No problem, it's pretty icy out there still, I'll walk you to your car," He offered.

"Okay," He got his coat and belongings and we headed outside to my car.

"Your cake was good," He said, helping me into my coat.

"Oh, thanks, I'm glad you liked it," I said letting him be a gentleman.

"I'm going to have to return the favor one day," He said and stepped to the side of me.

"Oh, that's alright," I said, trying to stop him from embarrassing himself. I hadn't changed my mind about him and I was meeting a real profiled candidate tonight.

"Now c'mon now. Let me be a gentleman," He demanded.

"Okay," I gave in too quickly.

"So, Sister Douglas, may I call you Niecey?" He asked, trying to flirt now.

"No, you may not." I shut him down before he got too ahead of himself.

"Ouch," he said mocking me then chuckled

"But you can call me Sharon," I said to soften the blow. I could still flirt with the man. He was fine.

"Fair enough," he smiled. "so, Sharon, how about lunch sometime?" He asked.

"Don't you have to work?" I asked, sounding concerned.

"I can take some time off for you," he said to my surprise.

"Oh, no, I can't let you do that," I told him even though I was flattered.

"Why not, I can use a day off in the company of a lovely lady such as yourself," he said.

"I dunno," I said trying to figure out a way to get out of going on a date with him.

"You dunno what. Just because I work hard for a living doesn't mean I can't take time off now and then to treat myself. I got enough time stored up to take off a few days and well, I'd like to spend at least one with you is all. No big deal, if it's too much that's fine, it's not a date. It's just two friends eating and talking over some drinks maybe, harmless fun." He explained grabbing my hand.

"Well I just thought you needed all the hours you could get to keep up with—" He cut me off before I could I put my big foot in my mouth.

"See now you trying to offend me. Hey, I heard you and your list. I know I have a fat chance of living up to any of those expectations and who says I even want to, I just think it would be cool if we could be friends. Plus, it takes more than an application to get the job," He was sure of himself which was something that turned me on big time.

"Fair enough, you've made some good points counselor," I said now realizing that we were holding hands and walking to my car as if it was the natural thing to do.

"Well you know how I do. So how about it, believe me I won't miss a few pennies either way it goes," He said as we stood by my Mercedes.

"Alright. Here's my card. Call me and we'll get together this week sometime," I said.

"Good. You have a blessed week Niecey," He said trying to get away with it.

"Uh." I said reminding him he wasn't allowed to call me Niecey just yet.

"I mean Sharon." He corrected himself. I watched him

walk away before getting in my car. He had potential but that wasn't enough to get my love. Who knows, maybe I can introduce him to one of my sorority sisters or something.

∆

At six o' clock sharp the doorbell rang at eighty-two fifteen Crosswinds Place in Chevy Chase, MD. I took one last look at myself in my long length mirror. Dangling just enough, my D & G was fitting just right tonight. I headed for the door as the driver rang the bell again.

"Hello, I'm here for a Miss Douglas, courtesy of Mr. Wynd," The driver said.

"Yes, I am she," I said excited because the car behind him looked like the new Maybach.

"Please, let me help you to the car." The driver took me by the arm and led me to the car.

A new Maybach fifty-seven was parked in my driveway. "Um, I knew he was flossing but this is just too much." The driver opened the door for me and ushered me in. As he sat in the driver's seat I asked where Mr. Wynd was? The driver said he was just supposed to take me to the restaurant where Cornelius would meet me. Just then my black berry rang.

"Niecey, you got a minute?" Tracey asked.

"Yeah girl, I got plenty of time. I'm just relaxing in a Maybach fifty-seven fully loaded reclined in the back seat." I bragged then giggled in delight.

"Lemme guess, you're with Corny Wynd," she said.

"Shut up heffa," I said trying to be oblivious to her jealousy.

"Anyway. I may need some legal advice," she stated.

"Yeah, what's up?" I asked her because she was not sounding like her usual self. She sounded scared for some reason, her voice was shaking a bit.

"First can you do a background check on somebody for me?" she asked.

"Yeah who?" I replied.

"Robert Thrasher." she said.

"You know his social?" I asked getting out my organizer.

"Nope," she said with a short response.

"Birthday?" I asked.

"I think it's November 29, 1965," she said.

"You think, but you've been sleeping with this man for months Tracey," I said scolding her now.

"Hey, I ain't Inspector Gadget like you. So, are you gonna do it or what?" she asked, sounding desperate.

"Why all of a sudden you suspicious of him?" I asked knowing full well that the man she was so smitten with was a dog of the worst kind.

"Let's just say I think I might be in over my head," she sighed.

"Isn't that the truth?" I said trying to get her to realize the truth of the matter.

"Look, if you ain't gonna do it I'll get somebody else," She huffed impatiently.

"I'm gonna need a little bit more to go on, like what am I looking for in particular?" I asked trying to get the truth out of her because I knew there was more going on than what she was telling me. I already knew the man was a drug dealer and a pimp, even killed someone, in self-defense people said. But Tracey wasn't as stupid as she tried to play like she was, and I don't like being taken for no fool, so she needed to come forward with the info.

"Never mind, forget it," She snapped.

"No, no wait. I'll do it," I said more so for my own knowledge than hers.

"Good, when do you think you'll have something?" She asked, sounding rushed.

"By the end of the week," I told her as the driver weaved in and out of traffic effortlessly. Dang, this car was so plush, I could not wait until it was all mine just like his house in Montgomery county sitting on twelve acres.

"Friday, can't you get me something sooner?" She asked, sounding even more desperate as her voice cracked.

"A full make-up is gonna take at least that much. I do have a career you know," I said.

"Fine, thanks girl," She said and sighed, sounding like a bunch of weight had been lifted from her shoulders.

"Tracey," I said.

"Yeah?" she asked.

"Be careful alright," I said.

"Ain't I always." she said. We hung up on each other. I was starting to really worry about my friend. Even though she could be ghetto, she really deserved better from these men she often had flings with behind Chucky's back. Chucky was a good man, all she had to do was concentrate more of her efforts and affections towards him and there was probably nothing he wouldn't do for her.

Eleven
Tracey
Spring

I was over here at Rob's apartment in southeast DC waiting to go to dinner. He was supposed to be here almost an hour ago. This heffa Rosa was getting on my nerves speaking Spanish like I had any clue what she was fussing about.

"De donde es Roberto?" Rosa yelled.

"Speak English!" I yelled back.

"Donde es, donde es? Roberto!" she yelled following me throughout the apartment.

"Robert, why?" I asked.

"Necesito más dinero, no tengolo." She said in more Spanish.

"Dinero, you mean money. He ain't paid you." I asked her, totally confused.

"Mas dinero, mi abuela necesita, droga como dice metformin," She said looking really concerned.

"You need drogas. Oh, hell no, that sounds like drugs. Where is this boy at?" I speed dialed Robert's club. "Isis, let me speak to Robby."

"Who is this?" Isis asked. She was a short little tart with a boob job gone wrong.

"His woman!" I yelled ticked off.

"Shoot, which one." she retorted coyly.

"Look, get him on the phone or else," I said firmly.

"Or else what?" Isis yelled on the phone. I heard somebody ask her who she was talking to. "Somebody looking for Mink." Isis answered.

"Put 'em through and quit playing." I heard the voice of

Black Sam yelling at her.

"Ugh, hold on," She told me.

"Yeah what up." Black Sam asked, sounding all smooth.

"Who is this?" I asked.

"Who is this?" He demanded.

"This is Tracey, Robert's girlfriend," I told him.

"Oh yeah, which one are you," He said then busted out laughing. He was head of security at Rob's best dance club Delicious.

"Don't play with me Black Sam, it's me T-baby," I re-assured him of who I was.

"Oh, what's up girl why didn't you tell me it was you?" He said, sounding more relaxed.

"Where is he at?" I was still pumped up.

"He should be in the south east by now. What's up?" he asked, now sounding a little concerned.

"This Mexican heffa is over here trippin' talking about money and some drugs," I told him about Rosa's craziness. She had been going off since I got there.

"Ah naw, she bet not be smokin'," He started laughing again.

"I dunno, most of the stuff she's been saying is in Spanish," I admitted to him.

"No habla espanol?" He laughed some more.

"Ha, ha very funny Sam. When did he leave?" I asked.

"About an hour ago. Call his cell," Black Sam said blowing air into the phone no doubt now smoking a cigarette.

"He ain't picking up," I told him ticked off at his demeanor.

"Well, I don't know what to tell you baby girl. I stay out of the boss's business. One." He ended the conversation.

"One." I hung up thoroughly pissed off now. Rosa picked up the phone and started going off in Spanish again. "English! Speak English!" I yelled as my cell phone rang. "Hello?"

"Hey get Rosa and y'all come outside," Rob said.

"Where have you been, we were supposed—" he cut me

off.

"Look Tracey. Just do what I said. I'm pulling up now," he demanded.

"Rosa, c'mon," I said.

"Que? We go now?" she asked.

"Si, yes Roberto we go now," I told her, she was so stupid.

"Aya ya!" She yelled what I was sure were some obscenities in Spanish.

"English, speak English," I said, wanting to knock her upside the head.

"Okay, okay." She said looking in the mirror again and fixing her top.

Robert's truck was parked outside the apartment building with the music up. We got in.

"Hey baby. Que pasa Rosaria?" He said like nothing was wrong with him being late and ignoring my repeated phone calls.

"Callate Roberto, necesito mi dinero!" Rosa yelled. She was pissed but I had no idea what she was talking about even though I was pretty sure she just told him to shut up.

"You'll get paid when I pay you," he told her as she started cursing him again in Spanish.

"Shut up hoe!" Out of nowhere he turned and slapped her across the cheek. She flew across the back seat.

"Robby, what is up with you? What is really going on with you and this girl? You act like you pimpin' her or something?" I shouted at him scared.

"So, what if I am." He responded oblivious to what he just did. He put the truck in drive and took off down Brandywine.

"What is that supposed to mean Robert? This girl has been here for almost a month living in your apartment and I know she ain't been dancing in no darn club," I said trying not to look at Rosa in the back seat fixing herself up.

"Look, you don't have to worry your pretty little head about my business. She's waiting on her papers. Until then she just does private parties, like bachelor gigs and stuff," He tried to clean up his improprieties.

"And that's it," I asked again, not impressed with his obvious lie.

"Darn Tracey, why are you so worried about this piece? It ain't like she is a sista or something. She is just some tramp from Mexico or Cuba looking to keep her grandmother healthy. Let her do her hustle and you do yours," he retorted.

"What I do ain't no hustle. It's a legitimate business that makes money without using and abusing people," I was ticked off now. He kept trying to belittle my career.

"Just stay out of my business," he stated firmly.

"Look, we've been together for a few months now I think I deserve the truth," I said.

"You got all the truth you're gonna get, hell, you can't even handle the truth. I can't tell you everything I do Tracey," he said.

"Why not, you know everything I do," I replied.

"And that's the difference between me and you. I'm a man, I got a lot of stuff going on that will keep you in Gucci and gold so don't worry yourself none about what it is that I do. Just know this, I'm a true entrepreneur with my hands in a few thangs," He said, trying to end the conversation.

"What about drugs?" I slipped that in just to see what he was going to say.

"What, where the hell did that come from?" he asked knowing I was trying to be slick.

"She was asking about drugs," I blamed it on Rosa to save face because he wasn't buying my innocent act.

"For her grandmother. See; stay out of my business Tracey. I make sure her abuela gets her medicine and pays her under the table from the club," Robert said, trying to still end the conversation. He sounded like he was getting tired of explaining himself to me. He knew he was doing dirt and didn't feel like he needed to explain anything to anybody, especially not me. I was just another dime piece he had been doing until the next best thing came around and little did I know I was already being replaced.

"But she hasn't even been at the club, you just said that yourself," I said, still not fazed.

"I'm opening a new one, nothing but dancers at this one," He stated.

"Is that what all that money is for?" I asked trying to get to the bottom of some things.

"Darn, what's up with the fifty million questions? Yes, yes. That's what the money's for," He said, still trying to end the inquisition.

"Well is it or isn't?" I wouldn't let it drop.

"Why does it matter?" He said.

"Because it's in my business accounts!" I finally yelled.

"Oh, you won't have to worry about that too much longer," he said smugly.

Now a little hurt because I didn't want to push him away, I said. "Hey, there's no real rush. I just want to make sure everything is on the up and up, since this affects me too." I tried to clean it up.

"Of course, it is. I'd never do anything to hurt my boo. I need you at my side girl, you the only thing that's real out here even with my baby mama's." he replied reassuring me. He stopped in front of a spacious two-story home near the Hill. "Hang tight. Rosa c'mon." he said getting out of the truck. A man opened the door, looked at Rosa, gave Rob a package and shook his hand. Rob ran back to the truck and we went on with the rest of our date.

Twelve
Destiny

There was a knock at the door as I sat down to watch my favorite shows on BET. "Aww man. Who is at my door this hour of the night?" I looked through the peephole. I was really looking forward to just sitting down and watching some TV. I didn't want any company or drama.

"I heard that," Stanley said, hearing me fuss.

"Go away Stanley," I said.

"No, we have to talk," He demanded.

"About what?" I asked unmoved by his prowess.

"About whatever it is you told Pastor Franklin," He sounded ticked.

"I told him the truth," I said matter-of-factly.

"That's not the whole truth Karen," He said.

"Look just leave Stan. There is nothing else to be said between us, it's been months already why do you keep doing this. I said it was over," I started putting my hands on my hips getting upset now.

"No, you owe me an explanation," He yelled at me. I yanked open the door because I was beyond pissed.

"I owe you an explanation, you an explanation. Negro please, you've been sleeping with men for years behind my back and I owe you an explanation!" I yelled.

"Lower your voice," he said, noticing one of my neighbors opening their door to see what all the shouting is about.

"No! Let me tell you something you low down dirty bastard. You've had your chance, all the chances I'm gonna give you. I don't want to see you anymore. Don't call me, quit emailing and sending me cards and flowers, don't even speak to me at church," I said shaking my head and putting my hands on my hips in my angry Black woman stance.

"You don't mean that," He tried to smooth the situation over.

"Oh, I don't. Why not Stanley? Because I'm a virtuous woman of God," I asked.

"No. No, I mean—" I cut him off.

"Oh, come off it Stan. You are about as saved as a penny in a homeless person's pocket. Do I look stupid to you, that naïve, that needy?" I questioned.

"You're still wearing my ring," He made a very valid point.

"This piece of crap. Here take it. And go straight to hell Stanley Milton Reid!" I threw the ring at him and slammed the door in his face. Stanley stood there speechless. He finally realized that he had lost the best part of him. The only woman who had ever loved him and treated him like a man. That's why he was so attracted to me in the first place. Yeah, I could sing, and was truly a Proverbs thirty-one woman, but I always carried myself as a lady. Not too prissy and never butch. He loved that about me, I reminded him of his mother.

Shoot, I forgot rule number one, never return the jewelry. To my surprise I heard something fall to the floor and footsteps walking away from the door. I waited a couple of minutes then opened the door. The three-karat diamond engagement ring sat there shining in the moonlight. I hesitated then picked it up. Maybe it's a sign. Who am I kidding. I placed the ring in the mail basket by the door. I'll pawn it, or at least get it reset. Now back to the Black entertainment network.

Δ

Three days later at the office I got served at my office. I opened it and started to read it. It looked real serious. As I read the papers I realized that Stan was suing me for the money for the wedding stating that he couldn't get the deposits back from anyone. He also had the nerve to put something in there about personal pain and strife over me ending the engagement. Of course, this called for a call to my favorite lawyer. I don't know why he's pulling this crap, he knows I'm best friends with one of the best lawyers in the area. I dialed Sharon's work number.

"Ms. Douglas' office," Her assistant Alex answered.

"May I speak with her please?" I asked.

"May I ask who is calling?" he asked.

"Yes, this is Ms. Price, from Lutheran Social Services." I answered.

"Oh, how are you doing today Ms. Price." he said.

"I'm fine and you," I asked him.

"Doing well. It'll be just one moment," he said and put me on hold. I listened to the jazz and kept reading through the paperwork.

"Hello, this is Ms. Douglas," Sharon answered the call.

"Hey," I tried not to sound too upset.

"Hey, what's wrong?" she asked, realizing it was me.

"I think that fool is trying to sue me for palimony," I explained.

"What, you're kidding right?" she asked.

"Nope, I just got served with some papers at my job. He is saying I've caused him to go to a shrink to remedy his sexual issues because I outed him or something crazy like that. The man is crazy. What am I gonna do Niecey?" I whined.

"Bring me the papers so I can see if there is really any damage he can do. This just might be a tactic he's using to get back at you for outing him at the church. You know how they like to keep a lot of stupid crap going for no reason. Don't worry about it boo," she affirmed.

"I'm just mad because he could've said something about it when he came to the house the other night. He's just a sorry bastard I swear. And you know I'm mad because he got me about to start cussing," I said. In my head he was every son of a so and so in the book.

"Like I said, don't worry yourself about it, okay. Don't call him or anything. I will handle this for you as your lawyer. He hasn't seen a palimony suit yet if he wants to act all ugly. What have you been up to though by the way?" she asked.

"Nothing, working and going to choir rehearsal. I met this guy named Deitrick James, he wants to do a recording with me leading a song," I said now sounding more upbeat.

"Girl that's great. You should do it, it'll keep you busy and get your name out there for when you record your own record," she said.

"I don't know. I know I can sing but I don't know if I'll sound good recorded," I said, "there is a difference you know,"

"Girl you will sound wonderful. I don't know why you're acting shy. You know you want it, just go after it," She encouraged.

"What I want to do is kick a faggot's behind is what I want to do," I said now reading my casework for the Jenkins.

"Don't even sweat it. Remember God never puts us through something we can't handle and you've handled way worse than this," Sharon reassured me.

"Still though, I got words for him. How dare he," I was so ticked off.

"Dang, I ain't never heard you this mad before, do I need to come see about you?" she asked.

"No, my pressure is just up though. Where is Tracey, I can get her to beat him up," I said and chuckled.

"Uh, no you don't. Then I would have to get her out of jail for assault," Sharon laughed.

"Well let me go, I got a couple home visits to do in the southeast. Don't want to wait until late in the day to do them," I said getting off the phone.

"Take your mace girl." She advised.

"Mace ain't nothing in the hood, I need a nine-millimeter to carry with me for this," I busted out laughing.

"You so stupid, but you right," Sharon laughed too.

"I know why you think I got one for real," I told her the truth.

"Stop it Dee Dee, you are making me laugh too hard girl," We shared a good laugh for a moment.

"Gotta make sure I make it back out alive," I said as tears of joy fell from my face.

"I'm about to hang up," Sharon said.

"Thanks for everything, I'll fax this stuff to you okay," I said calming down.

"Or you could just take half a day and come up here to my office, you haven't seen it since I got the new desk," she said.

"Okay, that'll give me an excuse to come to Georgetown and shop,"

"So, when are you coming?" she asked.

"I'll do these visits and call you from the car,"

"Okay,"

"Okay, bye." I said.

"Bye." She said. I sat there and read through the whole document and said a short prayer. Father, let your will be done in this thing because right about now I want to really do the go off.

Thirteen

Sharon

It was another day in the office for me and I was trying to get through it without any big hang ups. Cornelius had been pressing me to see him almost every other day now. He had been sending little presents to the office and sometimes at my home address just to sweeten his offers. Last week I learned I got at least four bouquets of red and pink roses from FTD. He knew he could be a romantic sometimes.

"Alex can you bring me the Younger case file." I asked my assistant.

"Yes ma'am. Oh, you've got a delivery," He said.

"More flowers," I asked.

"Yes ma'am." he said. "Dang whoever this is must be sprung. Oops I;m sorry Ms. Douglas, I didn't mean to overstep my boundaries," he said.

"It's okay. Ah, the spoils of war. I'll call Mr. Wynd tomorrow. By then he'll be a bit irritated but not so much to not want to see me," I said.

"You have mail." my computer uttered.

"And who is this?" I opened my email to find a new message from Cornelius.

I know you got my messages and the flowers. You like having the dog chase the cat. I love a good challenge. – CW

"Hmm, no response to your emails either CW." I loved the way I was being chased by him. For a few weeks we had been playing tag through phone and email. I had him right where I wanted him, so I thought. Little did I know he thought the same thing, so we just played the dating game like two college students in love for the first time. We were getting to the point where we could get physical without being strangers. It all added up to one goal, landing the husband I had been wanting for the past two years.

"A Mr. Washington on line two," Alex interrupted my daydream.

"Where's that case file?" I demanded.

"Coming right up," he said then left my office. Sometimes he really acted like such a peon.

"Hello," I said.

"Hello Ms. Douglas," Marcus said.

"Mr. Washington, if I didn't know any better I would think you had forgotten all about me," I flirted then sat back in my chair flipping my hair.

"Oh no, never that. How has your day been?" He asked.

"Full,"

"Okay. You have plans for lunch tomorrow?"

"Oh, now you know the rules."

"Don't tell me you actually follow those," he stated.

"Of course I do. I'm a lady, aren't I?" I told him trying to be cute.

"Well you will be breaking them tomorrow," he said showing his confidence.

"Oh really, how so?" I was taken aback but impressed by his assertiveness.

"Because I have reservations at Morton's,"

"You don't say," I responded. He can't afford that. "You know I kinda have a taste for some Mexican food," I said after pausing to try to sway him toward something a little more affordable for him. He didn't have to try to impress me; he didn't really have a chance at being my man. I mean I liked him, but I don't like him.

"We'll do that some other time, but tomorrow it is Morton's," He affirmed.

"I dunno, let me check my schedule and get back to you," I told him trying to get out of it. It sounded so tempting but I didn't know if I wanted to date Marcus or not right now. I had my hands full with Cornelius already, but if I juggled I could be closer to my goal in no time.

"Well okay. Call me by 7:00 this evening and let me know what's going on," he said.

"Oh, I have a deadline," I asked.

"Yes, my time is precious as well," He said like I'm two short of being a ten.

"Okay, I'm scared of you," I said, really liking his take charge attitude. If he didn't stop showing me he knew how to be self-confident he might have a chance.

"Don't be. I'm as tender as a lamb," He said now pouring on the charm.

"Then I must be a wolf," I stated.

"In sheep's clothing." He chuckled.

"You are so silly." I blushed.

"Well, I gotta go. My break is about over," he said.

"Okay," I said.

"Talk to you later?" he asked.

"Okay," I stated.

"Bye Sharon." He stated almost sounding like he was singing my name.

"Bye Marcus." I said cheesing. If I didn't know any better, I would think this man was really trying to put in his own bid at being my number one man. Still though, I couldn't let that happen.

The next day I met Marcus for lunch at Morton's and had a nice time. He knew he was old school, very chivalrous and everything. I mean opening doors, pulling out seats and even bringing me some beautiful red roses. Doing everything I wanted, even had the nerve to know something about what I did for a living which was something I loved in a man. There was nothing better than having a conversation with someone who at least took the time out to learn something about you, even if it was trivial. At least Marcus thought about me on a level deep enough to do some kind of research. He had me laughing and just feeling like myself. I never had to put on airs or anything, shoot I even got a drink which was something I never did when I knew I had to go back to the office. We made a date to go to Applebee's the next weekend. I think we're going to be good friends.

I just didn't see myself dating him seriously though. Plus, it wouldn't matter, he didn't believe single people should really date anyway, something crazy about no such thing as having a boyfriend or girlfriend. He said he got the concept from some evangelist he met at the church and it's something his pastor has been teaching the singles of the congregation for a couple of years now. He said if I wanted to know more about the concept to pick up the book I Kissed Dating Goodbye.

Marcus said he used to be the type of guy who would get into these long monogamous relationships with beautiful women only for it to blow up in his face some years into it. He believed according to scripture men and women are not supposed to date anyway. We were supposed to keep to our families until a man finds a wife who is comparable to him and then marry. He even had the nerve to say he didn't believe in premarital sex and had been celibate for nine years. I had to commend him for that because a heffa like me knew she had needs and would be letting Cornelius give me crazy orgasms in about two weeks.

But I don't know though, Lord. Marcus is a real nice guy. He was really into God and the church. He was even committed to doing community service with at risk teenagers at the YMCA to pass the time. I didn't know where he got all the time and energy to do everything he does but he says it keeps him from getting into trouble with the ladies because he gets lonely at times. Still though, he just didn't measure up to Mr. Wynd.

I mean let's do the list. Cornelius was a premiere lawyer, well worth his salt and a partner at one of the largest law firms on the East Coast. They had clients like Proctor & Gamble, Wal-Mart and people like Gerard Cummings and Michael Portis on their team. They've had some of the most notorious cases in the District. I sometimes wished I could trade places with him for just one day to be on the payroll.

Marcus was a bus driver. He drove the bus. What kind of career was that? Driving the bus. Shoot I hadn't been on the bus since I was in high school and I didn't know anybody who still rides it. I mean he was cute and all but, a bus driver, come on. I could do better.

Cornelius collected African art. Marcus collected medicine bottles from his mama. Cornelius raced horses in the Kentucky Derby. Marcus went to the horse races and bet a hundred dollars for fun. Cornelius drove a Maybach, c'mon. Marcus drove a late model used Nissan Maxima. Cornelius got his education at Yale and Marcus dropped out of Morgan State. They both didn't have any kids, thank you Jesus. And they were both sexy. One was a saint, the other a low down dirty freak. Basically, it was a no brainer. I would date and marry Cornelius and be a good friend to Marcus. Maybe try and get him to drop the celibacy act.

Fourteen
Tracey

It was my turn next in line at Chase Bank. I had at least two thousand dollars in cash to deposit plus the booth rentals for the month. Coming here on the first of the month had always been a hassle, but I loved making deposits anytime. The teller was a short blonde girl who clearly hadn't been working there too long because she didn't recognize me. My family had been banking here all my life starting when it was just Bank One, NA. I gave her my transactions and she started typing in the system.

"I'm sorry ma'am but it looks like this account is frozen," She placed my deposit back on the ledge of the counter.

"What do you mean the account is frozen?" I demanded pissed off because this stupid teller wouldn't complete my transaction.

"Ms. Simmons if you would just calm down," The teller responded, trying to make the situation calmer.

"Calm down, calm down. I've been banking here for years and all of a sudden my accounts are frozen. Get me the manager!" Now livid I shouted.

"Yes, yes ma'am. If you would please just calm down and take a seat." She went to get the manager.

"You just go get your darn manager," I fumed as she stood at the bank counter.

"Ah yes. Ms. Simmons, if we could just go into my office," Mr. Tnosky said, smiling as if nothing had happened. He better quit smiling before I went Postal up in here for real.

"Yes, let's," I responded as we walked to his office. By now everyone was looking at us. "Uh, can I help you?" I asked this nosey white woman talking on her cell phone, laughing and staring at me. She rolled her eyes then quickly turned her back on me. I started to turn her butt around and slap the taste out of her mouth but she was not the problem. We got into his office and he started to explain himself.

"Ms. Simmons, we ha—" I cut him off.

"First of all, I want all my darn money out of this racist bank," I said.

"Ma'am if you would just let me explain," he said motioning for me to take a seat.

"Explain what, your racist policies," I told him sitting down.

"Oh, come on now Ms. Simmons. Your family has been customers here for many years and I can remember when you yourself first opened this business account. I personally signed off on your first business loan and everything. We would never do anything to lose a customer of your caliber," he stated trying to smooth things over.

"Yeah, well I'm quite sure they all will close their accounts after I tell them about this," I told him, not fazed by his sucking up.

"Now wait, let's not get hasty. It is federal law that we report large cash deposits from any of our customers regardless of race," he stated firmly.

"But this is my business account. I have deposited large amounts of cash before in fact, at the end of the month it's almost guaranteed that I deposit about $12,000,"

"Yes, we know but within the past three weeks over $90,000 in cash has been deposited into your account,"

"And?" I asked not wanting to give up my stance.

"Well, that is a large amount of cash, especially since that is close to your yearly average. I mean if you have funds elsewhere, at another banking institution, it would be much easier to wire the funds here. We can always do that," he stated.

"And how long will it take for my funds to be available?" I asked now realizing this is all Rob's fault. I should have never ever let him use me like this. Sometimes I could be so stupid when it comes to men. All in the name of love, I swear.

"Oh yes. You have to fill out these forms explaining to the IRS where the funds are coming from, especially if they are from closing retirement accounts or CDs. Your other bank should have sent you similar forms." He gave me the forms.

"How long will that take?" I asked.

"Oh, about two weeks to thirty days. Your personal savings account has available funds if you need cash today. I'll even verify funds if you need to write checks or pay bills out the business account until we get this all squared away. So, if you would please just fill out these forms." He laid out the forms before me on his desk. I shifted through them not understanding some of the jargon written on them.

"Can I take them home?" I asked looking them over some more and noticing how much info they were asking for that I could not provide right then and there.

"Of course, Ms. Simmons, and again I do apologize for the inconvenience," He said standing to shake my hand.

"So, you're saying that I have over $250,000 in the account now," I asked.

"Yes, actually about $292,545.15 to be exact. Yesterday's deposit of $21,000 is what flagged the account," He said.

"Yesterday?" I questioned.

"Yes, one cash deposit was made right before closing. My lead teller was surprised. We didn't know you were engaged," He revealed.

Astonished my mouth dropped. "Engaged. Oh, um, yeah. I'll just take these forms with me and fill them out at home. The money is from his accounts anyway." I rose from my seat to leave.

"Oh. Well if you have any questions here is my card, just call me." He gave me his card and walked me to the door.

"Thanks Mr. Tnosky." I said.

"You're welcome Ms. Simmons, and congratulations." He said and we shook hands.

Yeah right, wait till I talk to this fool. Robert is gonna get his money out of my account as soon as possible. What has he gotten me into? Niecey work!" I yelled into my cell phone. "Put me through to your boss," I said to her fine assistant as soon as he answered.

"She's in counsel at the moment," he said.

"Okay, this is one of her clients, Ms. Simmons. Tell her it is imperative that she calls me ASAP on my cell," I told him, running to my car from the bank.

"Is this an emergency?" He asked, sounding concerned.

"Yes, it is, as a matter of fact, I'm on my way to her office," I said as I got in the car throwing my purse and Coach briefcase across the passenger seat.

"Okay I'll tell her, but what is this in reference to?" he asked being nosey.

"It's about my sole proprietorship,"

"Okay. I'll pass this along to her,"

"Thanks."

"You're welcome Ms. Simmons." He responded then we hung up the phone. A migraine was coming on swiftly so I rubbed my right temple while steering with my left hand. Zooming thru traffic I yelled in my cell phone again.

"Robert!" it dialed his number and he picked up right before it went to voicemail.

"Yeah, what up?" His voice irritated me.

"Robert, why didn't you tell me you were going to deposit over $20,000 into my account?" I demanded.

"Oh yeah. I needed to stash it for a sec. I'm gonna need it right back out by this weekend." He said not fazed by the tone of my voice.

"There's a hold on the account Robert," Cynically I responded.

"What do you mean a hold, it's a business account ain't it," he sounded pissed off now.

"Yeah, didn't the girl say something to you about it when you went last night?" I asked.

"Yeah, she asked me all these questions, but I figured it was procedure or something. But merchants get special privileges for cash deposit limits, right?" Now he sounded a little panicky.

"Yeah, but I have a maximum deposit limit on this account and they flagged it because the amount was so high, and you've deposited over $100,000 in less than six weeks fool. You should've said something, so I could've warned the bank," I tried to smooth it over, but I was equally as pissed.

"That sounds like some straight BS to me," Trying to defend himself. He always had some excuse for his crap.

"We'll see, I'm going to see my lawyer about it now. And for further references just do a wire transfer for large amounts of cash like that," I retorted.

"Yeah, I'll work on that," He said sarcastically knowing full well that the money is from his drug trafficking and that if he didn't have her to wash it for him this time he'd be in a mess.

"I'm serious. This could mess up my business funds," I said with tension creeping up the back of my neck just thinking about losing my shop over him.

"Tracey, I dun already told you what you could do with that shop. It's chicken bones compared to what I got," he said boldly.

"Well I like my chicken bones. And what's this about us being engaged. Where is my ring at then?" I was still trying to figure out where this relationship was headed.

"I had to tell them something to get her off my back. You know I got love for you boo, thanks for holding it down again, much props. Let's go to the Four Seasons for dinner," he suggested trying to weasel out his crap.

"Maybe after I take care of this mess," Now a couple of streets away from Sharon's office, I found a parking space.

"Alright, one." he said.

"One." I hung up the phone and parallel parked the car. Trotting across the street to her office I thought about all the possibilities and worse case scenarios. I didn't realize at first that I could end up in jail messing with this fool Robert Thrasher.

Δ

"So, what you're saying is if they can't put a paper trail together for this money, the accounts, all of them, can be seized and I could get audited," I asked Sharon as the excruciating migraine headache made me feel like I was going blind. We sat in her office with the door closed and she was trying to explain the in and outs of a possible audit.

"In not so many words, yeah. Why would you let him put all this money in your accounts in the first place? You really don't know nothing about this fool do you. I finally got all the information you needed on him," she stated and pulled out this big file from her bottom desk drawer.

"I could even lose the shop," I whined aloud.

"Did you hear what I said Tracey?" she asked me.

"I can't lose my shop Sharon, you got to do something. Tell them something, fill it out and tell them anything so I won't get audited." I almost started to cry realizing how stupid I had been over this man.

"I'm not compromising my license to bail you out because you in love, or lust which is more like it," she said, flipping through the file she pulled out.

"That's not fair. He loves me," I announced, still trying to prove to her I had a good man.

"No he doesn't. He's a drug trafficking pimp from Florida. Here; take a look." She tossed the file across her desk at me. I went through it looking at a record from when he was nineteen.

"Attempted murder," I exclaimed as I re-read the charges staring up at me.

"Yes. And he got more than one child Tracey. What in the hell have you got yourself messed up in? You just got to go after these thugged out fools. Well you really got you one this time. And he likes to put his hands on women; especially those who tend to get pregnant by him. You need to end this relationship before he takes you down with him," Sharon said.

"Girl, all this can't be true. Look this attempted murder charge was tossed out of court and he was only twenty. So was all these domestic violence charges," I said, trying to make it sound better more so for myself than her.

"Just because the girls get scared and decide not to go ahead with the charges don't mean a thing Tracey," She told me, crossing her arms and shaking her head.

"Is this all you got on him?" I asked.

"Shoot that should be enough fool." She retorted.

"Don't call me a fool Niecey, that crap ain't cool. I can handle this myself. He's gonna tell me what's going on as soon as the time is right. I just wanted to know some stuff up front first. Plus, I need to know what's going on in Miami that keeps him up there every other week or so." I said, still trying to save face, why I'll never know.

"Ain't it obvious. Why are you acting so stupid over this man? Is he that good between the sheets? I always knew you were a sucker for some good sex, but this is extreme even for you. You know you could do better, look at Chucky." She tried to put some sense in my head. "You won't even give him the time of day because of this loser. Look, I'm going to fill out this paper work and get you out of this crap this one time, but no more. I've warned you once and I swear to God if you come to me with anymore BS about him, I don't want to hear it." She took the paperwork from out of my hands and started to tidy up her desk. "You're too old for this Tracey. And too good of a person for him and I know you know it. Don't put yourself in harm's way just to spite your father girl. Life is too short." She finished her spill.

"Who died and made you Freud?" I asked trying to lighten the air in here.

"See, you think everything is a joke. This man is a criminal of mass proportions. He could hurt you for real about this money. There is no telling what he'll do if you don't get this taken care of," She said and walked to her bar stand.

Laughing uncomfortably because she was making a lot of sense. "I'm gonna break it off after I get my accounts together. I promise. He's having a party in about three weeks; I'll do it after that. You wanna come?" I asked and wanted to take it back as soon as the words left my mouth. She turned around with a scowl on her face.

"I wouldn't be caught dead there." she said pouring some tea in her Georgetown coffee mug.

"You know what, forget you Sharon Denise Douglas, Esquire. You ain't all that," I said pouting, crossing my arms and legs.

"Forget you too. Now get the heck out of my office. I got more things to do as Sharon Denise Douglas, Esquire and that'll be an extra $150 for your psych counseling as well," she said trying to be funny.

"You'll be dead before you get any money out of me for psych counseling. You suck at it." I told her and laughed. I walked out of her office a bit relieved but still concerned that I could lose it all dealing with this man.

Fifteen
Destiny

After I counter-sued Stan for mental strife, stress, and cheating he dropped the lawsuit and sent me a long ten-page letter begging me to give him another chance, lying about his sexual preferences. I'm still not over the whole thing but it's been almost six months and summer was coming up. Today I was at the church in counseling with Mother Franklin who has been a Godsend since this whole thing has happened. She and Pastor have had my back and continue to pray for me. They said I should pray for Stan, but I just haven't gotten that far healed yet.

"Mother I just don't know what to do now. How can I trust another man again?" I asked in dyer straights.

"Baby, you have to put all your trust in God, and you must find it in your heart to forgive him," She assured me.

"I can't, I just can't. I am so angry. I'm angry with him for lying to me and leading me on, myself for trusting him and falling in love. And I hate to admit it, but I'm angry with God," I admitted almost crying.

"Why?" she asked.

"Because God should've given me some kind of sign before I fell in love with him like I did," I responded.

"But you needed that love at that time," she replied.

"But at what cost," I asked contrived.

"None," She said easily as if I should know this already. Not liking her attitude, I asked.

"What do you mean none, look at me," I said.

"Look at you. You have walked away from the deadliest trap the devil had set for you in that marriage unscathed. And God revealed the truth to you right in the nick of time," she said just as condescending as before.

"But why let me go through loving him like I did?" I asked still wanting her to explain this to me, break it down in layman's terms.

"Because you needed him during a painful time in your life. Yes, it turned out to be not what you intended but God always had everything in control. Stanley was there for you when you lost your mother, he helped you go back home and deal with all of that," she reminded me.

"My girlfriends were there too," I added sitting up straight.

"Yeah, but there was a difference between them and Stanley. He loved you as only a man could love a woman," she said and settled back into her chair.

"How could he love me and have sex with men too?" I asked rhetorically.

"The same way a married man can truly love his wife and cheat on her with a woman. Sex is sex, fornication is fornication. The Bible says if you live in sin you will die in sin and I have yet to find one sin that is higher on the totem pole than the other. It does tell us about the ones that lead to the fiery sea, such as homosexuality, fornication and idolatry. But baby you have to forgive this man regardless of what you think God owes you because honestly, He owes you nothing but His love and protection that He gives you freely," she explained then took a sip of her tea.

"You always make it sound so easy. So, what should I do now, just forgive and forget?" I asked, trying to make sense of it all.

"Well yeah," she said.

"It's not that easy mother. Don't you know he had the nerve to come over and ask me what I told Pastor?" I told her about that awful night.

"Yeah, I bet he did. My husband had a few choice words for Stanley Reid," She giggled.

"I hope so." I giggled too, finally feeling better about the situation.

"Yeah, Stanley is wrong. No doubt about it, and maybe at one time he was very earnest about wanting to be your husband. But there is no way Pastor would let him marry you or any other woman knowing his issue. Not at Metropolitan." she said and sipped her tea.

"That's good." I said wringing my hands.

"So, changing the subject. Did you hear?" she asked.

"What?" I was a little taken aback because I really didn't want to drop the subject.

"We've chosen the new youth pastor," she said excitedly, smiling from ear to ear.

"Oh, that's great," I was not amused. "I hope he can put some holiness in our youth." I said slouching in my seat. She was starting to get on my nerves.

"Well, that's God's job." she reminded me. "But he sure enough can preach."

"Who is he?" I asked, trying to sound interested.

"He's Elder Michael Daniels from Grace Temple in Hampton, Virginia. I think he's originally from North Carolina. I'm gonna need you on the welcoming committee with Sister Hamilton. You know how she gets around single men." she asked me and started shaking her head.

"Oh, mother, you know I can't get in her way when she gets her eye on somebody." I said mocking Sister Hamilton's wide-eyed stare.

"Yeah, well I'm still gonna need you to run some kind of interference so she doesn't run the poor man back to Virginia." She said and we started talking about the event. I was curious about who this new youth pastor was. I didn't want to be on the committee but I knew if we really wanted to make an impression I should help get it together and be there for Elder Daniels.

Δ

About three weeks later we had the welcoming service for Elder Daniels at the church. Even though I didn't feel like being there, I put on a pretty peach dress with white flowers in it to look half way decent. If I didn't know any better though you would think I was trying to catch a man because the dress was a little form fitting and hitting in all the right places.

"Hello, hello, hello and welcome to First Metropolitan Baptist Church of Washington, D.C. Elder Daniels. I'm Sister Renee Hamilton and this is Sister Destiny." She walked up and hugged him in her too tight cocktail dress.

"Hello Elder Daniels, I'm Sister Destiny Price, are you hungry?" I shook his hand which was way more appropriate than this hag throwing herself all over him.

"Hello my sisters. And yes, I am famished." he answered me looking kinda cute.

"Our youth have put together something very special for you Elder. Please follow me to the Curtis L. Smith auditorium." she said as she sashayed in front of him in her new black cocktail dress that was two sizes too small and short enough just to show off her thick legs. She had the nerve to wear some fishnet stockings with a black line up the middle, just too darn much.

"So how long have you ladies been members here at First Metropolitan?" He asked as we walked through the church. He seemed very personable.

"Oh well I have been a member here since I was a little girl. I used to come here with my mom and grandmother," Sister Hamilton answered first.

"And you Sister Price?" he asked me with a smile that would break the law.

"Oh, I've only been here for about thirteen years. I started coming here while I was at Howard," I answered him, trying hard not to look at him too hard because he was so handsome.

"Oh really, where are you from?" He asked, sounding very interested.

"I was born and raised in Columbus, Ohio and moved here to fulfill my dreams of becoming a dedicated social worker for our young Black youth. I've been singing in the choir since I could talk, and I love to praise the Lord," I stated proud of my singing abilities.

"Well, well. I love to hear good ole fashioned traditional gospel music," he said looking me dead in the eye. We had stopped walking and let some of the mothers pass by. All of sudden I started to blush. If I did say so myself I thought this man was flirting with me. Am I tripping Lord, I think he is flirting with me.

"Well there will be plenty of that here at the Metro Elder." Sister Hamilton interjected trying to gain his attention again.

"You sing as well, Sister Hamilton?" he asked.

"Oh yes. I sing, usher, the chairperson for the hospitality committee, teach Sunday school and I'm the best cook in the church, just ask Pastor," She listed all her attributes and auxiliaries at the church.

"Oh, an all-around dedicated Sister of God," He smiled at her just as easily as he did me. This man was very charming. The sisters of the church were all going to bat their eyes and swing their hips at him in no time.

"Saved, sanctified and washed in His blood," she said proudly.

"All right. Oh, my word. This is too much ladies," He exclaimed as we entered the auditorium full of about one hundred and twenty five youth, members, and ministerial staff. Sister Hamilton motioned to the youth and they all said welcome to Metro Elder Daniels then began to sing "Welcome Into This Place" by John P. Kee.

"This is really not necessary, but I love the warmth of my new church home," he said as he held his hand to his chest. He looked a little taken by the gesture of the youth.

"Oh, expect nothing but warmth and uplifting the Lord here at the Metro Elder," she said to him as she moved into his space. I noticed he was uncomfortable by the way he scooted away from her as Sister Hamilton reached to hold his hand.

"This tramp knows she ought to stop." I said under my breath and looked at Pastor and Mother Franklin who looked at me like please save him from the leach. Thinking quickly

"This way Elder, Pastor and First Lady are seated at the front table. The youth have prepared a down home country dinner with fried chicken, collard greens, macaroni and cheese, potato salad and cornbread," I said ushering him to his seat.

"Hot water cornbread," he asked in excitement.

"Uh, sorry no they only know how to make Jiffy. But I made some peach cobbler and we have vanilla ice cream to go with it," I added then he pulled out my seat.

"Umm, umm, umm my favorite," He said rubbing his belly. He had to be a good five foot ten with short hair and beautiful hazel eyes. Sometimes they looked like they turned a darker brown depending on how he was standing in the light. I don't know why I am paying so much attention to him. I needed to get over that fool Stanley before I could even think about another man.

"Oh, well I supervised all the food preparation and seasoned the greens to perfection," Sister Hamilton said proudly trying again to out shine her competition.

"Well I'm sure everything will be just delicious," Elder Daniels said to her sitting down next Pastor and First Lady who both looked at me as if to say thank you for getting him here unhitched.

"Okay settle down everyone, settle down. Elder Daniels, would you bless this food prepared by our wonderful youth," Pastor Franklin asked his new protégé.

"Ah yes, yes sir. Everyone let's bow our heads. Oh, merciful and all wise Father God. We come to you in the matchless name of our Lord and Savior Jesus Christ. We thank you for this food, for the nourishment of our bodies and our souls. Let us enjoy this fellowship together on this evening and continue to be doers of the word and not hearers only. Father, I thank you for bringing me to First Metropolitan Baptist Church to pastor a young generation who needs you Lord. They need you so desperately in these here last days," he prayed.

"Yes, Father yes!" Sister Hamilton shouted holding up her hands. Pastor, Mother Franklin and I looked at each other and tried not to laugh.

"Let not my heart be troubled as I lead and teach these youths how to love and adore you Lord," he continued. Some of the mothers praised the Lord. But then Sister Hamilton took it to a whole other level trying to praise dance to no music.

"Praise Him, praise Him," Sister Hamilton gestured again and Mother Franklin nudges her husband who is shaking his head at her. She looked across at me and whispered: "She knows she needs to stop." Reading her lips, assistant pastor Henderson burst out laughing.

"We give you all the honor and the praise. In your Holy name we pray. And let us all say, Amen." Elder Daniels finished his prayer then everyone sat to be served by the youth department.

"He is kind of cute." Sister Marisa Capers whispered in my ear as she sat next to me.

"Yeah, well he has a job to do here at Metro. Our youth needs someone with compassion but demands respect and believes in Holiness." I responded knowing full well that I agreed. He was fine, and just my type, I thought to myself. "But you're right, he is cute." I told her and wondered why a man like him was still single.

Sixteen
Sharon

For about three months now Marcus and I have been hanging out going to gospel plays, concerts and listening to jazz at Utopia. Although I had no intentions of making this a serious relationship, I really enjoyed his company. I could be myself around this man. And it doesn't help that he's fine. I hated to admit it but he's a very nice guy and was probably the first man I've met who truly loves the Lord and diligently attempts to live by the word of God.

He was not a "holy-roller" playing church, he truly believed that walking upright to glorify Jesus could be done by anyone who just stepped out on faith and dared to be different. I respected him, even if he only earned $55,000 a year. Plus, he loved to debate, which was my second nature. The thing was, I liked him enough to go out with him, but I wouldn't dare fall in love with him, or fathom the idea of being married to an everyday hard working bus driver. So, of course I wasn't expecting anything different from him when I met him at Applebee's this weekend.

The place was packed as usual for a weekend. I walked in forgetting where I was and asked for the Washington party. The waiter looked at me smirked and said, "If you see them I'll walk you over there to their table." I had to laugh at myself because I knew better. I finally saw him and the waiter ushered me through the crowd of people at the bar to his table.

"Hello," He stood up and greeted me with a hug, then pulled out my chair.

"Hi," I responded sniffing his cologne, no doubt some Burberry, my favorite.

"Would you like something to drink or one of our appetizers this evening?" The waiter asked, pulling out his pen and paper.

"Yes, the lady will have a Sprite and I'll have the same," Marcus said and looked me over. I smiled at him warmly and wondered where he got the shirt he had on because it was actually nice and in season.

"Anything else sir?" The waiter asked, trying to work on his tip.

"Yeah. You want some nachos?" Marcus asked, making eye contact.

"Uh, yeah that's cool," I said relaxing and just enjoying his chivalry. Marcus treated me like a lady all the time, pulling out chairs, opening doors and stuff like that. My other dates did that too, I just didn't expect Marcus to be, well to be so debonair. Unlike the men I profiled before I dated, I felt like I had to put on airs with them all the time. I would dress to the nines; get my hair laid out and used words an everyday lay person would swear were not in the English dictionary.

When I wanted to really impress a man I'd use some of my Latin and massage their egos. Shoot, I had a full court press that I created to entice and satisfy the right candidate seldom if ever letting myself go and just be plain ole Niecey. Yet with Marcus I found that I didn't have to fake it. I always felt relieved when I knew I was going to be out with him because I could sit back, sip my drink, eat whatever I wanted, listen and be heard.

"So, how was your day Ms. Thing." he asked, squeezing a lemon into his drink.

"Oh, don't even get me started. My administrative assistant lost one of my files, or claims he gave it to the courier who of course says he never got it. My boss has been haggling me about the Clarion case even though I told him everything was under control and of course like clock-work Tracey calls me with her drama," I poured out the day's events unloosing my top button and unbuttoning my sleeves so I could roll them up. It was so nice being able to let off steam.

"What's up with Tracey?" he asked, sounding so sincere

with a hint of worry.

"I love my girl and everything, but sometimes she can be just plain naïve. About two months ago she let her boyfriend deposit over $100,000 into her business account," I started to explain the story of Tracey Ann for the one-millionth time.

"Okay, well that sounds cool," he said.

"Well it is, but the fool decided to put in over half of it in cash all at one time into a small business account with deposit limits on it," I attempted to explain.

"I'm still not understanding," he stated quizzically.

"Well most banks adhere to the federal mandate that they report any cash deposits over ten thousand to the IRS immediately. He had been depositing maybe eight or nine for weeks then made the bigger one fifteen minutes before the bank was supposed to close. Of course, he lied to the bank about who he was and where and what the money was for, so they flagged her accounts and froze them." He looked at me even more confused and asks another question.

"But it's a business account," he wondered aloud.

"Yeah but she has a maximum cash deposit limit of fifteen thousand at one time. I told her then she needed to leave that fool alone especially after I got the full background done on him," I drank some more of my Sprite as the waiter sat down some nachos in front of us.

"You don't say," he said trying to act like he already knew all this information. "You did
a background check on him hey. Have you done one on me yet?" he asked, picking up a cheesy nacho to shove in his mouth. His lips were so full and juicy.

Lying I answered him. "Aww, now you know I wouldn't do that to my new best friend." Not only did I know his grades in high school; I also knew how much he had in his savings account. He popped another cheesy nacho in his mouth. The said,

"Best friends. Oh, so now we're best friends." The waiter interrupted him and asked us for our order, he told him to come back in a minute. "So, uh are you going to answer me or what,"

He lightweight demanded firmly.

I hesitated then answered. "Well, yeah. We have to be friends first before anything else can articulate,"

"Articulate? Wow, I'm scared of you," He mocked me laughing.

"You know, grow," I gestured by spreading my hands out.

"I know girl. I ain't stupid, I did go to MSU," He smiled.

"Nothing compares to the Howard University," I replied proudly.

"Except our Bears," he teased, "but on the real, you do know I'm looking for more than just another friendship or girlfriend," He ate another nacho. I picked one up too, so he wouldn't eat them all before I got to taste them.

"What do you mean?" Trying to act like I didn't know exactly what he meant.

"Well you know I don't believe in the girlfriend/boyfriend thing. I also don't date effortlessly trying to weigh my options with different women all the time," he said.

"Okay now you've really piqued my curiosity," Because according to mama you want nothing more than to find a good woman and get married I think to myself. Correction, a Proverbs 31 woman, which mama made me read and began preaching to me about. Gloria Walker loved her daughter and knew she attended church regularly. Her concern though was I really getting fulfilled by the word of God or still just playing church waiting hastily for it to be over, so I could go home and spend time eating pudding with my father like I did when I was little. Marcus ate a couple more nachos and then responded.

"It says in His word: A man that findeth a wife findeth a good thing. It don't say anything about a girlfriend. And it sho' nuff don't say nothing about the woman finding a husband," He pushed the rest of the nachos toward me and I took one.

"True, but you have to be friends first before anything romantic occurs," I justified my point.

"Right, but God never said go play house and see if this woman is the one for you. He says 'find' 'look for' not 'borrow' and 'rent'." He said coyly, putting up quotation marks for each word to prove his point.

"Oh, so being in a relationship is renting a person. You can't be serious." I cocked my head then flipped my hair.

"Alright, let me break it down for you Ms. Esquire. What happens when you put the cart before the horse?" he asked and smiled.

"Nothing," I responded.

"Exactly. Nothing, nothing can come out of a relationship between a man and a woman if it's out of the will of God. He created Eve for the sole purpose of satisfying Adam. Not Steve, Kenny then Adam," He ended his rant.

"Oh, so it's the entire woman's fault," I protested.

"No, I'm not saying that. As men we have the innate desire to find a woman to define our manhood. God made it so. We find favor if we find a wife. But women also have the innate desire to define herself as a woman therefore bearing a child. She needs a man to do this and has to wait until the right man finds her and they satisfy their innate desires together in the will of God," he grabbed another nacho and chewed for a second before continuing. "Basically, we have to keep searching for the right mate in order to satisfy our flesh, but the Lord will only reveal or give a man that woman when he knows they are both ready. Not before, during or after. Just at the right time to glorify Him," He closed his case so effortlessly. I loved it when he got all Christian on me, but a heffa was hungry.

"Can we order now?" I interrupted and asked another question to continue the conversation. "So, what you're saying is don't have a relationship before marriage,"

"In a sense, yeah. You have your single years to glorify God and do his will in your life. When it's time for marriage you'll know it and seek the right person easily,"

"But how are you going to know if you and this person are right for each other. You have to know if you love someone in order to be with him," I plead my case again.

"Okay, let me put it to you this way. Do you think I'm

sexy?" he asked then put on this devilish grin. Off guard I pondered my answer because I knew there was a hitch to this question. "No, don't think about it. If we were alone right now, would you have sex with me?" he asked again.

"Okay, I'll bite. Yes, I would." I gave in then grinned like a goofball.

"Why?" He asked and started chewing his food.

"Because I do think you're sexy," Sipping on my drink trying to play it cool.

"Do you love me?" He stopped chewing then looked me right in the eye.

"I barely know you, how could I love you," I uttered swiftly.

"But you would have sex with me simply because you find me attractive," He smirked.

"Yeah, so," I stated.

"That's the problem with this whole boyfriend/girlfriend thing. You don't even know me, but you will have sex with me because you think I'm sexy today. Love has nothing to do with it. That's why it says in I Corinthians 7:9 "if they cannot contain, let them marry, for it is better to marry than to burn because of fornication". Don't you know in your heart you've already fornicated because you desire me," He motioned for the waiter.

"Boy, I'm not married," I told him knowing full well there had been plenty of times that I fornicated and enjoyed every second of my sin.

"And that's the point. Whatever a man truly believes in his heart so is he. You're not married yet in your heart you have already sinned which is why it is more important for single Christians to care more about how they can please God and what belongs to God then worry about getting to know or falling in love with a boyfriend/girlfriend," he said with a stern face.

"You're pretty knowledgeable about this whole marriage thing," I said coyly.

"I have to be. I've been doing it wrong for so long that I could never find peace in my heart with or without a girlfriend.

It wasn't until I truly understood what the sole purpose of marriage is for in the first place." he said.

"Don't say having babies," I clarified.

"Yeah, duh,"

"Oh no you didn't." He laughed at me and pushed a piece of hair out of my face.

"No, it's about the love of God. His exaltation and your fleshly desires being met which stops you from committing a whole bunch of sins,"

"So, I guess what you're saying is don't worry about pleasing your boyfriend/girlfriend. Just please God," I asked.

"And all these things shall be added unto you," he said then sat back in his chair crossing his arms.

"So why aren't you married then Mr. Know it all," I asked, trying to break the Christianity mumbo jumbo and get to the real.

"Because I haven't asked her yet," He said then smiled and winked at me.

"So, you're not looking." I tried to ignore what he just said because if he was serious he would stop me in his next sentence.

"Yes, I'm looking. I'm getting pretty close too. Can't you tell," he said.

"But you just said—," I was cut off by the wave of his hand.

"Girl, quit trying to over qualify everything and let's eat. I swear you probably really do give people a run for their money in court," He ordered our food. The waiter had been standing there for at least five minutes listening to us go back and forth.

"Desert?" The waiter asked.

"None for me, I have to watch my figure," I said.

"Oh, quit actin'. We'll have the apple pie a la mode after dinner. Thank you." I adored his take charge attitude. If only he made more money. At least then I wouldn't feel like I was settling. The ringtone for my text messages went off in my purse. It was Cornelius wanting to meet me later at the house. I answered it and told him I'll call him back and finish dinner. So far, Marcus has piqued my interest and if anything had made me horny because all I could think about for the rest of our time together was what he looked like naked.

Seventeen
Tracey

Running around like a chicken with my head cut off, I pulled my outfit for the night out of the closet. Trina was sitting on my bed reading the latest Essence magazine and listening to some Maxwell as I got ready for Rob's party. He had asked that I come dressed to impress, because he wanted to show me off. I invited Trina because there was no way I was gonna get Dee Dee to come with me and Niecey thought she was too good for my crowd.

This party was just what I needed because the IRS had still not responded to my explanation as to where I got that money. It was freaking me out and I needed to be cute and sip on some champagne just for the heck of it. Plus, these kinds of nights wouldn't be around for too long because I was breaking up with Rob as soon as I got his money out of my account. Maybe Niecey was right, maybe it was time for me to settle down with Chucky and have a baby or something. I was getting too old for this. Plus, it would make my parents happy and then maybe Daddy would speak to me about more than just business.

We hopped in the car and took the 495 to Fort Washington to get to Rob's house. Once we got on his street it was clear that the true ballers were out in full force. Trina fixed her breasts to pop out of her dress a little more. "Looks like I might meet a man tonight." She winked at one of the football players walking up to the house.

"Girl, you'll meet more than that with them things," I told her as I parked. We walked up the walkway to the house and rang the doorbell. Black Sam from the club opened the door and let us in. He pulled at Trina's dress and she slapped his hand away as we went inside. It was so crowded that you bumped into people as you walked through the place. The music was on point, too. DJ Premiere was spinning some of the latest tunes and there were people dancing on all sides of the front room. We headed for the bar as I looked for Rob.

"Wait a minute. Ain't that Senator Keeley over there?" Trina asked as we walked past a small group of white men surrounded by women in high-priced designer clothes. Some of the girls had on red bottoms and wore expensive jewelry. This one girl I knew had on a five thousand dollar choker. I looked and to my surprise it was the Senator and probably some of his friends.

"Oh my God. It is. I swear, Robby knows everybody," I said, proud to admit my man got it going on the social scene. Trina shimmied a bit and sipped her drink.

"Well, you know people in his industry gotta know how to get the product to the highest paying customers." I tried to act like I didn't know what she was talking about. Rob was into to some messy stuff, but I couldn't knock his hustle. As long as I could get this money situation together there was no reason to judge the man. Plus, he had been in the game since he was fourteen, you couldn't teach an old dog new tricks.

"Girl, what are you talking about?" I asked her while looking at some heffa walking around half-naked in a BCBG dress and some Jimmy Choos.

"Don't even play that dumb role with me, heffa. I've known you from the womb. You know that man ain't nothing but a big ol' pimp." Trina swayed her body to the beat of the music.

"Girl, please," I said. "He just has dancers." Still not ready to admit anything to anyone but myself I kept up the appearances. If anyone could understand that I knew, Trina could. We had been friends since we were seven and she moved to D.C. from Brooklyn.

"Who sometimes trick. I mean look at this room. All these model type chicken heads and what maybe twenty or so men, all ballers and a senator. C'mon Tracey open your eyes." She stopped dancing and looked at me with her hand on her hip.

"He owns a popular club and some of these guys have been there on nights when these girls strip. That's all. Stop hating," I said mostly to myself because Trina had turned a deaf ear to my childishness.

"Ain't no need to hate on the truth. He's been moving women here from all over the country. Yeah, they might dance for a month or so, but then he puts them on the market for real," she said, winking at one of the Raven's players.

"You don't know what you're talking about." His friends started looking at us. I waved at them.

"Okay, let's see. What about that girl from Miami? She came here with nothing and look at that heffa now. Shoot, she got on Christian Louboutin and you know she ain't make that kind of money on no pole." I started to remember when Rosa first came to the Chocolate City and now she was wearing shoes and clothes I had only seen Niecey wear sometimes.

"I'll be back," I told Trina and strutted off looking for Rob. I couldn't stand for people to tell me the truth when I didn't want to accept it, especially when I was trying to get my groove on. I walked into the kitchen and there he was standing at the counter with some girl in his face. He saw me and walked over.

"Hey, babe. I need you to do something for me," he said seductively while playing with my hair. I tried to ignore his flirting.

"We need to talk first."

"Aww, boo. C'mon just do this one favor for me, please." He pulled me close and started nibbling on my neck knowing it would make me do just about anything he wanted me to do. I felt myself relax because he had me in the palm of his hands. "I need you to help the Senator with a little problem," he said seductively and started to pour me a drink.

"Yeah, like what?" I smiled devilishly.

"Just go on upstairs and we'll meet you there. It's something real simple. Here, take this champagne." He handed me a glass of the expensive stuff and led me to the bottom of the stairs. "Just wait in the sitting room," he told me then kissed me passionately, groping me and rubbing his hard member against my thigh.

"Okay," I said, gulping down the drink. I turned and started to walk up the stairs when Trina yanked my arm.

"Don't go up there," she insisted and pleaded with me. Now she was starting to piss me off.

"Girl, you tripping. Let go of my arm, my boo wants to spend some sweet time with me." I twisted out of her reach and stumbled a bit, feeling woozy suddenly.

"Tracey, I'm begging you. Don't go." She stared into my eyes. "You don't know what he's up to, girl. Haven't you noticed only couples going up and down them stairs all night," She pointed out the facts.

"None of them hoes have been with my man. He's been waiting for me all night and I'm here to please," I said, now dizzy but still ready to get my freak on.

"Fine, go on up there but don't say I didn't warn you." She turned to walk away. I stumbled up the stairs not sure why I was out of sorts and horny.

Δ

Upstairs, I took a seat on the brush gold finished Victorian fainting couch with my blouse opened to expose my ample breast. I felt so free and sexy that my hot box was literally throbbing. In a few minutes Rob would come upstairs and I was ready to please him. The room was spinning all of sudden, but it didn't really matter to me. I heard the door open and close. In walked a white man who looked like Senator Keeley carrying a champagne flute.

"Ah, you're a sight for sore eyes," he said, sipping the champagne. Trying to stay focused, I asked him stuttering,

"Do I know you? Where's Rob?" He came over to the couch and stood over me. I was starting to feel uneasy with him being in the room but for the life of me I couldn't voice my fears at that moment.

"Oh, he'll be up in a sec. He said I can take my time, you won't let me down, you black whore!" He slapped me and threw champagne in my face. He pounced on me and started pulling my clothes off then began to force himself on me. I tried feverishly to push him off even though my body was disobeying my will. He yanked my panties off and was trying to push himself inside me.

"No," I said weakly even though I was screaming it in my head. He whispered obscenely in my ear while trying to kiss me. I moved my head away. He then grabbed my face and spat on me.

"Don't you dare deny me!" he yelled, smothering me. Just then, I kicked him violently in the groin. He yelled and rolled off me crouching and holding himself in pain. He screamed at the top of his lungs words that only a drunken sailor would shout. I heard someone burst into the master bedroom.

"Tracey, Tracey. Oh my God. Tracey," Trina yelled in a panic. She ran into the sitting room to find me disheveled and inebriated. I could hardly hold myself up. "Tracey, oh my God. Get up, get up, girl. C'mon." She tried to help me up. The Senator yelled at us.

"Oh no. I paid my money one of you is going to serve me tonight." Trina pulled a blade out of her purse. She waved the knife in his face in a defensive stance, egging him on. She blurted out her own devilish words putting her New York stamp on it while putting room between us and him with her blade.

"We'll see about this." He got up and zipped his pants while cautiously moving around us. "I didn't pay for you people to ruin me." Trina uttered some more obscenities as he turned and darted down the stairs.

"C'mon girl. We gotta get you outta here," Trina said.

"I'm so sorry, Trina," I mumbled, about to cry. "I don't know what happened, it wasn't supposed to be this way. I feel so woozy and high." I leaned on her as she led me down the stairs. Robert saw us and walked past the Senator who was demanding his money back still holding his privates.

"Where in the hell do you think you're going?" he asked.

"She's leaving with me," Trina told him and continued walking towards the door.

He looked at me in disgust. "You must be crazy, she got a job to do. Tracey, go back upstairs and make me my money." He flicked his wrist at me like I was nothing. I was starting to realize he was a demon. There was no way in the world I was going back upstairs no matter what he said. He would have to force me if Trina had anything to do with it.

"She's not going anywhere," Trina objected firmly, holding onto her knife. Everyone was standing around watching the drama unfold. Trina walked me closer to the door. When Robert grabbed me by the arm Trina turned with her knife and slashed his Versace shirt. He called her a female dog and raised his hand to slap her. Senator Keeley interjected, holding Robert's arm back from hitting Trina.

"No. No, wait a minute, Rob. I can't be in the middle of a scandal. Let them go. We'll settle this another way. There is plenty of loose fish in here to satisfy me." Robert retracted his hand and let us pass. He motioned to Black Sam to open the door as I turned to face him.

"Why Robby, why?" I asked in desperation. He looked at me with another one of his devilish grins.

"Just business baby, never personal." I looked at him and realized just how much of a hellhound he really was. I remembered every man who had ever let me down, including my father, and I got enraged. With all my might, I slapped him.

"That was personal!" I yelled then spat in his face. I mustered up the rest of my pride and walked out the door with my head held high and Trina right beside me. We got in my Mustang and rode silently back to D.C. I started thinking over the events of the night and things that had been happening since I started dating Rob. There was no way in the world I should have ever been in any type of relationship with him. He was beneath me and I knew it. It was his street sense that turned me on. Finally, I interrupted the eerie silence feeling a little more sober.

"A senator attempted to rape me tonight," I realized aloud.

"But God moved in the nick of time," she replied.

"Yes. Yes, he did. Plus, your crazy self was there to help."

"By His divine intervention," Trina said.

"Turn around," I told her.

"What?" she asked, confused.

"Take me home to my parent's house. It's time for me to get real," I said, finally realizing my responsibility in this whole mess. Trina didn't say another word and exited the freeway to go back to PG County. She knew I had old demons to exorcise and wasn't going to stand in the Lord's way. We got to my parent's house and I told her to take my car with her, I would call her in a couple of days to pick me up and take me home. She asked if I was alright. I told her everything was fine knowing full well that I was about to face a past that I had tried to forget.

I entered the house from the maid's entrance and headed straight towards his library. The light was still, so I knew he was in there; probably watching one of his movies and doing what he does to stop from giving my mother the love she needed at night. I swung open the door catching him in the act.

"Daddy, your daughter is a tigress, just like that girl on the screen," I said.

"How dare you waltz your butt into my private study," he demanded, covering himself up and turning off the T.V.

"No, no. Turn it back on. I need to know why you and Senator Keeley think I'm such a vixen. So much so that you would do me any old kinda way to get what you want, when and where you want it," I told him in defiance. I was finally going to face the music and deal with the spirit of lust that had been consuming my life since I was a teenager. He was the reason why I knew at an early age how to be the temptress that I was.

As he stood to pull up his pants he said, "Don't you provoke me to hit you, Tracey Ann Simmons. I never did anything to you and you full well know it."

"Oh, you didn't? Daddy, you had me sit there and watch these tapes with you and told me that's how real women are supposed to please their man. You may not have touched me, but you brought the spirit of lust into my life early, which is why it surrounds me daily now. It was always in your eyes. I knew what to do with my private parts before I had hair on them," I admitted.

"Okay, Tracey, something is wrong. I am sorry for doing that to you, but you must remember a lot of those times I was drinking and not myself. I would never do that on purpose, baby. You have got to believe me," he said, sounding sincere.

"Daddy, it's too late for that, the damage is already done," I protested.

"What happened tonight?" he asked and pulled himself together to come towards me. I put up my arms. "Stay where you are, don't touch me. I'm so tired of men thinking they can touch me and do whatever their lust thinks they can get away with. I was almost raped tonight by Senator Herbert Keeley at a party tonight. My ex Robert Thrasher thought it would be cool to get me drunk and sell me to the highest bidder." Daddy was livid and threw the remote to the TV against the wall.

"I'll kill them!" he stormed through the house to his gun display. He took out his rifle and some ammunition then started to load the gun with it. "Where was this party?" He demanded then cocked the rifle.

"Daddy, put the gun down. I can't allow you to go to jail over my irresponsibility." I had to talk him out of going back to the scene of the crime. Once we were both calm he talked me into going to Howard University Hospital to have a rape kit done and get my blood checked to find out what had me so high. When we got back to the house we sat up and he listened to me pour out my broken heart to him.

I told him how much of a vixen I really was and how I enjoyed it. He thought it was time for me to get married and stop flirting with death in the sheets. Mother must have heard some of it because she came in his library crying and hugged me. I told her not to worry, I knew what I was gonna do; press charges and get Senator Keeley thrown out of office.

I told her it wasn't her fault, neither was it daddy's because the truth was it's my body which was a living sacrifice that should be holy and acceptable unto Christ, not used to please nasty men. We stayed up and talked some more before Donna, our maid, made an old fashioned down home breakfast with fried chicken, grits and cheese for daddy, plain for me because I liked sugar and butter in mine, eggs, Canadian bacon, biscuits from scratch, fresh squeezed orange juice and jelly. It felt like home for once. I called Sharon the next day to get the ball rolling on charging that bastard.

Eighteen
Destiny

It had been a couple months since Elder Daniels started ministering to the youth at the church and I was on the welcoming committee. We had been out to eat a couple of times with the youth and I've shown him around town and even helped him prepare some of his sermons. So, when it was time for him to plan our church's youth day events I wasn't surprised he chose me to be his assistant. I just didn't expect my feelings for him to get in the way so easily.

He had never been married, has no children and was raised in the Bible Belt. Ideally, he would be perfect for me, but I didn't know if I liked him as a rebound or if my feelings were real. Shoot, every time he asked me to do something that involved us being alone, I'd freak out. I would try to get out of it and purposely cancel on him. It had gotten so bad that he made comments to Pastor who set up a meeting for the both of us in his office to find out what was really going on. I lied to Pastor about it and he basically told me he needed me to be there for our new minister and to be the best assistant I could be. He even said the church could pay me if that was the issue. I didn't deny the money because I needed it, but that just meant that now I had to be close to him all the time. The thing is, it didn't seem to matter to him. He said he wanted us to be close friends and just told me all kinds of stuff about himself. We were at dinner one night going over the plans for the event and he started asking me all these questions about myself. I was so flattered but tried to play it off the best way I could.

"So, Destiny. You grew up in Ohio in the cornfields," He tried to affirm.

"For your information, I grew up in the city, the capital to be correct," I said proudly.

"But I thought they still grew corn and they call it the cow town," He tried to make jokes.

"Just because we grow corn don't mean we're all country. It gets crunk in Columbus," I said and threw my hands up then shimmied a little bit.

"Crunk, girl I knew you had a bad girl side to you," He laughed at my antics.

"Well, I wouldn't say all that. But anyway, youth day is coming up quickly and we still have to plan out the day. Who are we going to fellowship with that afternoon Elder?" I asked.

"How many times do I have to tell you to call me Michael?" he asked and cocked his head to the side, obviously flirting.

"That's too personal and if I start calling you that by habit people will start to think something is going on between us," I said being serious.

"Oh really, I think you just don't want to let us be friends as God has clearly led us to be," he said, eating some of his shrimp.

"And how do you figure that?" I asked hoping he said something lame like being his assistant that way I don't have to think about my follow up remark.

"Do you realize you're the only person here who knows as much about me as you do? Even things Bishop don't know. And I appreciate that,"

"Well I'm just helping you get adjusted to the city and our church community, as he asked me to do," I said nonchalantly.

"Not all of this is about helping me out Dee Dee," he said and looked me in the eye. Trying to change the subject I looked away from his pretty brown eyes and I asked,

"How'd you know about my nickname?"

"I heard one of your girlfriends call you that one day and thought it was cute. It fits you too," He went back to eating the last of his dinner as I fidgeted from getting personal with him.

"Well I just think we need to stay as professional as possible so don't call me that and let's try to stick to strictly business," Because I couldn't handle too much more. And I left it at that until he brought up Stan.

"Oh, I get it. You don't want to get too close to any man now since one man did you wrong. Destiny don't let the enemy break up all your future relationships with men. Your husband is on the way and you will miss him by not trusting or believing in God to send the right man your way. I can feel it in my bones. I'm not a wolf baby, this I know. And I do believe that the Lord has set this thing up where we shall be close friends and confidants to one another," he professed.

"But I just don't want no more scandal to surround my name anymore Michael. I'm the biggest news that's hit the church in years," I reminded him.

"No baby, Jesus is and always has been. People are fickle, and one person's turmoil may interest them for a period of time only for another to show up and create something else for them to talk about. So, don't worry about it. I think the gossips are looking for new blood now," He tried to ease my concern. "It's okay to be friends with a man, even if I am a minister. Shoot, that's the best kind of friend to have really," He smiled as his eyes danced under the lights.

"Okay, well I guess it would be nice to have a preacher as my new best friend," I said and sipped on my Pepsi.

"I'm not just a preacher either, just remember that okay. I'm a man first, and right now this man wants some sweet potato pie." He motioned for the waiter to come and ordered our dessert and we continued to plow into the plans for youth day.

Δ

Today I would have been married. It felt so surreal. I mean last year I was happy as a butterfly fluttering around with Stan, not a care in the world. Shoot, I was all the way gone over him. I had lost a good forty pounds messing with him and this gym membership he got me for Valentine's day. I was a bit upset when he did that but when he also gave me tickets to Jamaica I couldn't help but be happy. He knew I wanted to look my best. Stan never really harped on me about my weight, even when I was about two hundred and fifty pounds. I was a big girl, but I still had it going on, thanks to Ashley Stewart, Lane Bryant, Catherine's, the Avenue and some select consignment shops. Lord I still can't believe it's over and I'm single again. I want to take all these pills, just get me some sleep and sleep all day for a couple of days.

I didn't go to work yesterday and the day before because I just didn't want to hear anything from anybody about this weekend. My boss was tripping too. She said if I took off another day like this she was going to have to write me up. I didn't realize my attendance had gotten so messed up over the past couple of months. I heard a loud knock on my front door. Okay, I knew they were going to do this even after I told them that I would be okay by myself this weekend.

"Hey girls." I opened the door expecting to see Niecey and Tracey only to find Stan disheveled and stinking drunk. I tried to close the door in his face. He pushed the door hard, almost knocking me over.

"How dare you leave me?" He demanded in such a tone I was scared for my life. I didn't know what he was going to do. His eyes were so dark and menacing even though they were bloodshot red.

"Stanley, look, you're drunk, let's not take this too far." I said in an even tone hoping to lighten him up a bit.

"So, what, you found you another man already, I knew you were too good to be true. All I wanted was to get married, have a couple of kids, my old life would be over, I only wanted you Karen." He moved into my space and smelled like he hadn't bathed in days.

"Stanley, I think you should leave." I was scared now.

"No, I'm not leaving. You're going to tell me why you left me. Is it somebody else?" He challenged me.

"Would that make it better, since you always had somebody else, another man." I stated defensively.

"Oh, here we go again. I'm not gay Karen. I'm always in charge in the bedroom, just like I would have been with you," He poked his chest out then looked me in the eye.

"Is that it, is that what you want? That's why you came here inebriated and funky. Don't do this Stan, leave with the little bit of respect you still have," I pleaded with him.

"Just tell me the truth!" He yelled and pointed at me almost falling over.

"I told you the truth. You just don't want to admit it to yourself. Now, I'm going to ask you to leave." I shouted back at him.

"Marry me baby, please, marry me." He grabbed me by the waist and fell to his knees. "We can still have it done today, nobody has to know about my past, it's all over with now. I need you." He stood up and started to try to kiss me in the mouth.

"No, you don't. You need help, the help I can't give you." I struggled to get loose from his grip.

"Oh, the help only Jesus can give me. How many times have I heard that? Karen, I need you to help me through this time in my life, only you can do this for me. We can have kids and it will all be over," He let me go and begged pitifully. "Please we can do this, I love you. Destiny, please."

"That's not the answer Stanley, marriage and children won't hide the fact that you like to sleep with men. I can't, I won't do that to myself and never to any children. Just leave, I wanted to get through today without any drama," My emotions started to take over and tears fell down my face.

"Drama free Destiny. Always drama free, yup that's you." He turned around and fumbled out of the doorway back to his car. I was a little worried, so I prayed that God would cover him in his car. God answered my prayers because the next day Stan was still sitting in the car in front of my apartment before I went to church. I crept by the car, so he didn't see me leave but when I got back he was gone. Maybe in another life and if he wasn't gay

Lord, I would be his wife.

Nineteen
Sharon
Summer

Months had gone by and I had been simultaneously dating two men who I believed to be the best candidates for my husband. Granted, I only had sex with Cornelius but that was because Marcus was still giving lip service to this "ain't no such thing as boyfriend/girlfriend" nonsense so he never gets too close and dare we stay alone for more than a couple of hours for dinner or lunch. But that was okay, just being that close to him made me more interested in God and the church. I knew I was a sinner, but I needed a husband and if I had to date both of them to catch one, I would. The only problem I had with Cornelius is he doesn't really know who I truly am on the inside. He was so captivated with my vitae and the like, that he rarely took the time to really get to know me like I wanted him to.

He was such a great man though. He understood my goals in life and appreciated my zeal for the law. He was just like me in a lot of regards. I didn't think he was totally monogamous though. I often heard him over the phone with someone who was clearly not a man and not business. But that was okay for now, he could have all his little freaks for all that nasty stuff he be trying to get me to do.

I had it all planned out. In about two months I would be engaged. I had put in enough work on this project to get three karats from either man and at this point I might get two offers. So now was the time to let my friends in on my shenanigans. They knew about both men, but they didn't know the whole story.

"Okay you guys, I need your help." I asked them as we sat in my living room sipping on Cordoba and eating pizza.

"You need us, Oh my God," Destiny said a little tipsy. She could never hold down quality wines or champagne.

"You're pregnant! I told you messing around with two men at one time would lead to pregnancy," Tracey said shaking her head nestled in my big comfy chair.

"Girl please, you do it all the time, one, two maybe even three or four and you have escaped pregnancy," Destiny said trying to sober up.

"Well what's up Niecey?" Tracey asked impatiently, ignoring Dee Dee.

"I gotta get rid of one of them," I said and sipped some more wine.

"Oh that's easy, Cornelius should go," Destiny said trying to balance her glass as she got up to go to the bathroom.

"Why him? He's my best choice," I yelled out to her.

"Because he knows nothing about you but what you make on paper and that you went to the best schools and would look good in the society papers when he runs for mayor," she hollered from the bathroom on the first floor near the kitchen of my condo.

"And, what's wrong with that? Shoot, that's the best part," I said as she sat back down with me on the floor. Tracey added her own two cents.

"He's fine on paper and y'all would make the perfect couple for the Black community but what do you really know about this man and what does he really know about you. You should marry for love not just fame and fortune. Wait, did that just come out of my mouth," Tracey said to herself feeling her head like she had a fever or something.

"Yes, it did," I assured her.

"I'm either getting old or losing my touch. Ever since that incident at Rob's with the Senator I've been changing," Tracey said scratching her head.

"For the better I say," Destiny said.

"Shut up heffa," Tracey stuck out her tongue at Destiny.

"Look y'all, he's not all that bad," I got back to the subject, me.

"I don't know why you're asking us anyway. We already know you're going to dump Marcus. He's too saved for you and he ain't playing the games you like to play. Plus, he's about $100,000 short from being worth your time," Destiny stated the facts. She knew me best since we were freshmen at Howard.

"Me and Marcus aren't really together, so he says. Shoot he's confusing with all this courting mess. I don't know if we are coming or going, but he has expressed the fact that he is looking for a wife and not some fly by night relationship," I said while painting my nails.

"And truth be told you love him," Destiny affirmed.

"No, I don't." I tried to deny my true feelings.

"Yes, you do. You've let that man get all up under your skin and with no limits. You are in love." Destiny continued to press.

"No, no I am not," I continued to lie. I had been falling for Marcus since I first smelled his Burberry cologne at mama's church on Valentine's day.

"You know what heffa, yes you are. Just look at the way you treat him. You actually take time with this man and listen to him. Y'all are dating, no matter what he says, shoot courting just like he said. And you've put yourself into this relationship unlike any other relationship we've ever seen. Either you love him or you're falling in love with him. Either way, he's the better man," Destiny ended her rant.

"Why can't she have both of them?" Tracey said out of nowhere.

"Shut up with your drunk butt," I told her and grabbed her glass because she had clearly had enough.

"For real, look she could have the booty and the mayor," She continued.

"The only thing is I don't know how the booty is with Marcus," I admitted.

"What!" They both yelled.

"You two haven't done it yet," Destiny asked.

"No love me long time with the choir boy hey," Tracey said, poking my arm. I pushed her away and admitted the faltering of my conquest of Marcus.

"Nope, and technically we've been friends for almost six months," I said, putting up quotations. "At least with Cornelius I know he wants me and we are compatible in the bedroom. Everything just adds up you know. I think I'm going to back off of Marcus and really just be his friend, no reason to string him along any further. Mrs. Daniels," I poked Destiny in the arm.

"What, where did that come from? Michael and I are just —" Destiny started to speak but Tracey cut her off.

"Michael, hmm first name basis. Now that's serious for you and the preacher," Tracey said.

"I mean Elder Daniels. We're just friends," She stated.

"Sure, y'all just friends," Tracey said sarcastically now combing through my hair.

"Uh, I thought we were talking about me," I protested.

"Okay heffa, hold on." Tracey poked me in the head with the comb.

"I know you ain't talking Ms. Videotape," I jabbed her in the thigh.

"Videotape?" Destiny asked, looking puzzled.

"Yeah, you didn't hear. Ms. Thang is the star in her own playboy movie that Rob sent to her daddy at the hospital demanding she stop the proceedings on Senator," I tuned her in laughing.

"I told you to quit taping yourself goofy," Destiny laughed Tracey.

"I can't help it, I look good on tape," Tracey said wiggling her butt like a belly dancer.

"You know we are all involved in some mess. You with the new preacher, you and the drug dealing pimp and me balancing two relationships. It must be summer in D.C," I admitted to everyone.

"True," they said in unison.

"So, what are you going to do Niecey?" Destiny asked.

"I'm going to put a little pressure on both of them to see who cracks. The first one to pop the question wins. And the first thing I'm going to do is use sex as a weapon. No more panties for Mr. Wynd and a whole lot of cuddling for Mr. Washington leading straight to my bedroom," The phone rang. "Speak of the devil, hello."

"Hey, you busy," Marcus asked.

"Just sitting here with the girls," I said.

"Well I was thinking why don't I cook us a little something later on tonight," He said.

"Okay, your house or mine?" I asked.

"Mine," he said.

"Sounds good to me." I said.

"See you around seven." he said.

"Okay." We hung up. "Well ladies, we must finish this discussion some other time. Actually, Tracey who is at the shop?" I started picking up the mess we made in my living room.

"Nobody you'd let touch your head." she said.

"You're right, I don't know what I was thinking. But I got to look good tonight. Operation marriage is in full affect and tonight is the perfect opportunity for me to see what Marcus is working with," I said and winded my hips. We laughed and started dancing like we were in a reggae music video.

"Look Niecey for real, choose wisely, and don't play with Marcus' feelings if you really don't want him. He deserves better than that and you know it. Marriage is serious and you never know, neither one of these guys has said anything concrete about marrying you," Destiny said.

"Not yet Dee, not yet." I said and put them out for the rest of the afternoon so I could get ready for my conquest.

Δ

That night I put on a nice tight fitting BCBG dress and

some stilettos. I have got to entice this man. He is becoming a challenge and I need to know what is really going on. I hated to admit it, but Destiny was right. I was falling for him, but I didn't know how to stop it or better yet if I wanted to stop it. Maybe if we had sex I would have my answer. I still couldn't believe he lived in such a nice neighborhood here in Baltimore. The landscaping at this place was so nice, he said he did it all himself with some coaching by his mother. I had the nerve to be nervous as I stepped out of my Benz. I walked up to his door and knocked.

"Hey." I smiled seductively when he opened the door.

"Wow. Um, well, are you just coming for dinner or should we go out?" He asked nervously.

"Just dinner," I said, trying to be sexy.

"I dunno if this is going to work." He looked perplexed.

"Why, I mean are you going to let me in," He had this look on this face like he was looking at a ghost or something.

"I'm sorry, where are my manners? Come in, come in. Take a seat," He took off his apron and just stared at me. I was getting all the right kind of responses, now I needed to just go for it. I walked up to him and pushed him against the door and kissed him passionately. He stopped me.

"Uh, um, hello. Have we met," He put my hands down to my side.

"Yes." I kissed him again, this time he didn't hold back and kissed me back pressing me closer to him. He wrapped his arms around me and was just about to grab my behind when the phone rang.

"Oh, oh. Um. Excuse me," He went to answer the phone. "Hello. I'm kinda busy right now sis. Yes, I have company," he looked over at me and smiled. "you'll meet her when the time is right. Okay, I'll call you back," He put down the phone and turned to look at me. He sighed hard and said, "I don't think we need to be alone tonight, so let's go out,"

"I don't want to go out Marcus. What's wrong with us spending some time together?" I pretended to pout.

"Nothing, but it's obvious if we stay here something is

going to happen and I don't want anything to happen like this," He said walking behind the couch trying to hide his fleshly excitement.

"Like what, we're both adults, and we can handle it," I moved closer to him. He looked up in the air, then back at me.

"Okay, what are you trying to pull?" He got serious suddenly, almost angry.

"What do you mean?" I asked, trying to play naïve.

"Don't play games with me girl. All this time you've been on this friend tip and now all of a sudden you come up in here like Dorothy Dandridge and try to put it on me. What's really going on Niecey?" He demanded.

"Fine, let's go. Where do you wanna go?" I said, still acting.

"No, let's talk about what's happening here," He sounded annoyed.

"What's happening here is I can't hide my feelings for you any longer," I got serious now.

"I never asked you to," He sounded concerned and sat on the arm of the couch.

"I want," I couldn't get it out. I wanted to tell him how I felt but that was not the right move right now.

"You want what." he asked and held my shoulders.

"Never mind, this is not going too well. I think I'm just going to leave," I turned and grabbed my purse and started to walk to the door. He walked up behind me and reached for my hand.

"It'll happen, just not like this sweetie," He turned me around, kissed me on my forehead and rested my head in his chest.

"I don't know if I can wait," I admitted seriously, not acting this time because I was overwhelmed by my emotions.

"Me either, but we will," He held my head in his hands.

"Love waits for no man," I tried to go back to hiding my feelings again.

"You don't say, you love me Sharon Denise Douglas?" He

lifted my head to see my eyes.

"You love me?" I asked him and looked him in the eye. I didn't let him answer then turned to walk out the door. Goal accomplished, the next time I am not going to take no for an answer.

Twenty
Destiny

Why was it that my case-kids were always the ones getting into trouble? Lord, I need your help. Antonio was only eleven years old and they were trying to put the boy in a jail for two years over nothing. Well, assault ain't nothing and I know the boy was bad but he's been through a lot in his short lifetime. His mother ain't about nothing and his father was already in jail, all of his brothers and sisters are on papers, and he has no one to look up to. I don't know if I want to have kids. Who is my next client? I swear you gotta have the right spirit to be a social worker in child and family services or you'll end up in the chair yourself. I heard my cell phone ringing in my purse as Sistah Big Bones played I knew it was either Sharon or Tracey. Lord it was Tracey.

"Okay now what do you want? I'm at work and I'm expecting Mr. Foyer anytime now." I answered the phone.

"That crazy man who keeps hitting on you with the ten kids and crackhead wife," Tracey said.

"Yeah. Dang, I tell you guys too much. So, what's up?" I asked annoyed.

"We have come to the conclusion that it's time for you to start dating again." Sharon said with excitement in her voice.

"Oh, here we go." I responded realizing they had me on a conference call.

"So, we have decided to hook you up with an up and coming commodities agent from New Jersey. Tracey please, run down his specs," Sharon said.

"Yes, ladies may I present to you Darnell Fisher age 37 from Newark, New Jersey. He is single with no children and lives in Silver Springs. He likes the outdoors, jazz and going to matinees. Right now, he is looking for a young woman who believes in God and is STD free. No drama and not a baby mama. So, what do you say girl. We'll have a threesome for old time's sake," Tracey said sounding too proud of herself.

"Ugh," Was all I could get out.

"Oh yeah right like I want to see either of y'all naked." Sharon mocked.

"Anyway, what do you think Dee Dee?" Tracey asked.

"I think you both are crazy. I'm not going out with anybody either of you hook me up with," I said.

"And why not?" Sharon asked.

"Because the last time I almost got a beat down from an ex-wife on steroids." I started remembering that horrid time they tried to hook me up with this guy named Troy again. We went out to dinner a couple of times and on the fourth time his ex-wife showed up and tried to pick a fight with me stating that he was still her man and if she couldn't have him, nobody could.

"You could've taken her," Tracey said laughing.

"Y'all just don't get it do you. I don't want to date right now. It's too soon and plus I'm busy." I stated not wanting to let in on the fact that I was falling for Elder Daniels.

"Busy with that preacher," Sharon said.

"Yeah Elder Daniels, your new man for real," Tracey added.

"It ain't even like that." I tried to explain even though I knew they were right.

"I can't tell. You spend more time with him and at the church than you do anywhere else," Sharon said sounding irritated.

"Well what else am I supposed to do?" I asked rhetorically because I could really care less what they thought. Being an active member at the church has kept me focused and off a psychologist chair.

"Live a little heffa," Tracey said, popping gum in the phone.

"Yeah, get out and explore the world. You're still young and beautiful. Just because Stan was a waste doesn't mean you have to give up on all men," said Sharon.

"I haven't given up on all men." I admitted.

"Oh, now I get it. You gave him some, I knew he was a freak," Tracey said nonchalantly.

"No, he's my friend. He's helped me get over my anger and he's been there for me," I tried to tell the two infidels.

"Tell the truth and shame the devil." Tracey was still trying to make something out of nothing. Now I was getting ticked off so I put the phone on my shoulder and went through some of my papers letting them go at each other over my life. I don't know why they think so little of Elder Daniels. Even though I hate to admit it, I have grown fond of the man, but I know how to keep my flesh under control. I want to date but I can't stand how my friends are presenting the subject to me like I'm desperate or in need of their dating services. I allowed them to continue bickering for a while then interrupted them.

"Don't you guys think I can find my own man." I finally asked.

"Yeah, of course, but it's more fun this way," Sharon responded.

"You know what, I gotta get back to work. I will talk to y'all later." I tried to end the conversation.

"But we haven't solidified your birthday weekend activities," Sharon interjected.

"Leave that to me, it is my birthday you know," I responded firmly.

"Just don't end up sitting at home watching TV or we will come over there with some strippers and make you dance booty hole naked with them." Tracey added her two cents.

"Shut up." I said then laughed at the thought.

"Bye." They said in unison.

Δ

Later in the week on my birthday Michael sent me a beautiful floral arrangement to the office. Everybody was asking questions and stuff, I felt so embarrassed but happy at the same time. He asked me out to dinner Saturday night, but I declined the offer because the girls talked me into the threesome with Darnell. Even though I wanted to go with Michael I knew it was best that I kept some distance between us. Mother Franklin thinks he has a crush on me and would like nothing better than for the two of us to get together. She said she was tired of the way all the single women kept throwing themselves at him. It was high time for him to settle down and I was the only woman she felt could handle him and his ministry.

It had been 8 months since the break-up with Stan and I have turned my life around with a lot of prayer and counseling. So, this 32nd birthday was going to be bittersweet. A new man to meet, good friends and not to mention all the attention I've been getting from this music producer. His name is Charles Bentley and he was with In His Spirit music company. He was visiting the church for our annual concert last month and heard me lead a couple of solos. He got in touch with Sister Shank and she set up a meeting with him for this Saturday morning. Well mama, my voice may be heard all over the world after all just like you prophesied. Now all I gotta do is get married and have some kids. I guess you could say I want it all, with good measure Lord.

Friday was crazy. It was like I was getting tried on every occasion. I went downtown with one of my clients to petition for paternity and the father showed up saying he wanted his kids back. The fool ain't seen them in four years. Then my little eleven-year-old terror cursed out the judge and got sent to juvy, which was better than where he said he was going to send him. My twin case kids were sick, and I was trying to leave early so my girls and I could go to the spa. The day in the life of a social worker, I swear. But it was all worth it because when I got back to my office Michael was sitting at my desk just as handsome as he wanted to be.

"Hi." I put a big ole' smile on my face.

"Hello Ms. Price." He smiled back.

"What brings you to the northwest?" I asked.

"Well I figured since I can't take you out for dinner tomorrow I would take you to a late lunch today. They said you've been busy, running around like a chicken with your head cut off. That's not good sister," He said as his eyes sparkled in the sunlight coming through my window.

"Okay, I guess I can't say no," I put down my work and sat for a second.

"No, that's not allowed." He laughed.

"So where are we going?" I asked.

"Downtown somewhere. Do you have any more clients to see today?" He asked.

"No, why?" I responded.

"Because it's 3:00 and I figured you might as well go for the day," He sat erect in his seat.

"Aww man, I forgot. Me and the girls have an appointment at the spa at 6:00." I wasn't about to miss my much needed spa day. Even though being with Michael would relax me just fine.

"That's fine that gives me about two and half hours of your company to celebrate with you. So, let's go missy." He grabbed my hand.

"Okay." I couldn't believe this man. I started to think Mother Franklin put him up to this, she was always meddling. I would have to remember to thank her for that. I grabbed my stuff and we walked out to his car and drove downtown. We chatted a bit and I just smiled mostly. We went to the Jefferson and it was nice there. I had never been in there and everybody was so well dressed.

"I don't have on the proper attire for this place," I said pulling at my skirt as my stockings slid down my thigh.

"Woman, you're beautiful and look fine to me. That's who you need to be worried about not anybody else. We have reservations anyway so there shouldn't be a wait." He reassured me and took my hand.

"Oh." The man had made reservations. He's probably had this planned all week. I started to giggle.

"What's so funny?" He squeezed my hand playfully.

"How long have you been planning this?" I really wanted to know.

"Since you told me no about dinner Saturday night," He admitted then grinned.

"You think you slick Elder," I tapped him on his shoulder.

"Oh, don't start that again Destiny. It's Michael for the rest of our time together okay. Can you handle that? we are not working together this is an outing," he retorted.

"A date?" I asked matter-of-factly.

"You said it, not me." He smiled real big showing off his pearly white teeth.

"I guess so." We sat and ate, talked and kept looking into each other's eyes. Suddenly I realized: "This is our first date." I accidentally said aloud.

"Yes, it is, is that a problem?" he asked.

"Well, I don't think so. It's just I didn't know you wanted to date me. We can't work together and date too," I affirmed, testing the waters, hoping not to get my face cracked.

"I know, that's why I have to tell you you're fired," he said as serious as he wanna be.

"What?" I asked dumbfounded.

"Yes, you have used your female charms to get me and now I can't handle it anymore. We must conclude our working relationship to work on our romantic one," he said with a straight face.

"Are you being serious?" I asked, now bewildered but liking it.

"Are you listening? Destiny I really like you and I want to see where this can go." He sounded so sincere.

"This is coming so all of sudden," I put my napkin on the table.

"It hasn't for me. I've been taken by you since the first day we met, but I knew you were still hurt over your past and couldn't try to tell you how I felt until you were healed and could trust again," he said.

"But I thought you said we would be best friends. This is more than that." I could distinctly remember the man saying that.

"Yeah, I know, I wasn't totally forth coming but I want to be now. Destiny, I think you are a wonderful person. I haven't met a woman like you ever in my life and I said if I met somebody like you I would make them mine and I can't just be your friend when I know I want more than that. Can you understand that?" He reached for my hand across the table. We looked into each other's eyes and it seemed like we were the only people in the room.

"Yes, but. This is too funny," I started to giggle.

"Why do you say that?" He smiled.

"Because, I've been hiding behind my true feelings too," I admitted.

"Mother Franklin know she know how to call them,"

"She put you up to this didn't she?" I asked.

"Nope, she just encouraged me at the right times," he responded.

"Okay, so what do we do now?" I wanted to know exactly what he had in mind.

"Well, we'll just get to know each other better and stop hiding our feelings from each other from now on." He bit his bottom lip like he always did when he was nervous.

"Well, I guess that means I don't need to go out with the girls tomorrow. They are sorta hooking me up," I said.

"Can I go?" he asked cheerfully.

"You know what, that sounds like a good idea. Maybe then they will get off my back about you." A group of people sang happy birthday to one of the restaurant patrons.

"Get off your back." He looked confused and leaned over to hear me better.

"It's a long story. But it's almost 5:30, where's the waiter at I want a doggie bag." I said.

"You are so cute." He kissed my hand then motioned for the waiter. We got our bags and headed to the spa. I told him I'd call him with the particulars for tomorrow night. Surprisingly he didn't try to kiss me. I was a little disappointed but remembered we had the next night and possibly forever to enjoy each other's kisses.

Twenty One
Tracey

"What am I supposed to do? This fool has a darned video of me having sex and has been threatening me he'd plaster it all over the net and send it to the papers if I don't back down off of Senator Keeley." I told the girls as we steamed at the Four Seasons hotel.

"This is how war works. Just let me handle it. He can't deny medical reports from the doctors after the incident. It's a good thing your father talked you into going to the hospital to get checked out and have a rape kit done. He can't deny those pictures and the drugs in your system." Sharon tried to reassure me.

"Yeah, but he's playing dirty. I've been seeing those thugs ride by my shop at night when only a couple of us are working. I had to do a celebrity's hair and one of the fools walked in asking for braids," I gave them the run down.

"Why didn't you lock the doors knowing you've been seeing them riding around?" Destiny asked, sounding concerned.

"Don't you start too. Anyway, Mo had some security with her, so they got the braids then left. But I don't know what that fool is planning. And Chucky wants to be Superman now. He thinks he is a gangster or something. What am I going to do?" I asked rhetorically.

"Pray and keep praying and pray some more because you are truly in a mess that you started because God didn't tell you to date that man. And." Destiny started her ranting about the Lord, but I tuned her out because I just didn't want to hear that from her right now. I needed to know what I should do. Daddy says just keep the shop locked at all times and get some security. Niecey talking about this is how "war" is supposed to go. And I just don't know. Plus, my period is late, but that could just be stress because Lord knows I don't need any babies right now.

"Dee Dee you done yet girl, come up for some air, we'll let you go and get that minister's license if you want one," I said then Sharon started laughing. Destiny just sighed and then said something explicit which was something I would never thought I'd hear that heffa say. We all just fell out laughing then. My girls were always there for me no matter what was going on in my life.

Even though I knew at times they got tired of my antics and I knew for a fact that Sharon thought I was two-faced, they loved me just the same. I'm going to get Dee Dee something really nice for her birthday. She deserves it for everything she has been going through. And I know she is right about God and prayer. I just got to get serious about my Christian walk and live right. I've been through so much stuff over the past couple of years and I know it's only by the grace of God that I don't have AIDS and I'm still alive with no children. Children? What if I am pregnant? What if the baby is Rob's? Oh my God what have I done?

"Girls you're going to have to tell Darnell that he won't be needed tomorrow night." Destiny said as we walked into the locker room.

"Why?" Sharon asked, pushing her into me.

"Because, Michael is coming instead. We had a date today," she said joyfully.

"I knew you were messing around with that preacha-man," I said, trying to act like myself again.

"We just decided to date today. He fired me and everything." She dried off her hair and smiled.

"He fired you. Oh, I guess he is serious then. Well it's about time. Dang, I thought I was going to have to start taking profiles for you too," Sharon stated.

"Oh, I don't need your dating services ma'am, just be the lawyer we know you to be. Anyway, he's been liking me all this time and I didn't even know it," she said.

"Oh, heffa I could have told you that. He spends all his free time with you and tells you everything. He better be liking you or he's just weird and lonely." I cracked up laughing.

"Don't start. So, after the meeting with Mr. Bentley at In His Word I'll see you guys at dinner, right," She asked.

"That's right, tomorrow we will finally see if Ms. Price will be the singing sensation we always knew she would be," Sharon hugged us.

"Yup, just make sure I get my 5% off the top because I've been doing your hair for years and I expect to be well compensated for doing the new gospel diva's hair and makeup, shoot your whole look. Because you know you are going to need a new look. And you're dating a preacher now. Well, that's an extra couple of hundred because those first lady dresses are hard to come by," I joked.

"You know you are something else. But, of course you will be doing my look. Aww man, I'm 32. Just think, I would be married by now." Destiny started to realize where she was in life.

"To a fool if it had not been for the Lord intervening when He did. He does show up and show out." I finally admitted to her.

"Wait a minute, Tracey was that you girl. Hold on, let me feel your head, you okay baby. You need some water." Destiny acted like she was taking my temperature placing her hand on my forehead.

"No but I might need a pregnancy test," I finally let it go and let God.

"Wait, are you being serious?" Destiny sat down with me. Sharon walked over to me and held on to my shoulders.

"I think I'm pregnant y'all. But I don't know who the daddy is. It's been two months since my last period and I just don't know what to do." I started to cry.

"Do you want a child Tracey?" Destiny asked.

"To be honest, I think it's the only thing that's going to finally make me grow up and be real about my life. Y'all know I'm not all the way right, look at some of the stuff I still do and I'm almost thirty-seven years old. This whole mess with Rob is ridiculous to say the least and all the men I've slept with. I'm a whore Destiny." Tears streamed down my face as reality hit me all at once. "a true hoe from hell and I play like I'm a real Christian. Even though I really do want to be more like Christ. I really do. I figure if this is my punishment for all the stuff I've done in my life then I deserve it, pregnant and unmarried. I don't even think Chucky would forgive me for this," I expressed my innermost feelings.

"How do you know it's not his?" Sharon asked.

"Because I can't remember who I had sex with during that time. What should I do?" I asked them with great concern.

"Let's get dressed and go get you a test first before we do anything," Sharon said after a long silence.

"Tracey, can we pray?" Destiny asked holding onto my hand as I cried.

"Sure." I hugged her.

Δ

We went back to my house since I lived the closest to the spa and the store. I bought a First Response kit and let Destiny pray one more time, I don't know why because if I'm pregnant then I'm just pregnant. I prayed by myself in the bathroom after I took the test and then went to wait with them in my bedroom. I started to wonder about the baby and me being a mother. I hope I'm better at it than my mom. What am I going to tell my parents? And Chucky, Chucky is going to flip out. He will probably want to get married as soon as possible though. What am I talking about? This ain't his baby. I hope it is though, because I don't think I can handle it if it's Rob's. I don't want anything else to do with that man. But it will be just my luck that it is his and then I will have another thug to worry about, especially if it's a boy, a little boy, Jesus. The timer went off on my phone and I knew it was time to check the test results.

"Well ladies, I guess y'all gonna have to go shopping as

aunties. The test says I'm pregnant." I told them the news.

"Are you okay?" Destiny looked at me.

"Yeah, it's time I settle down anyway. Maybe now I can answer Chucky about getting married," I said.

"Wait, when did he ask you to marry him and why didn't you tell us?" She asked and smiled.

"He asked a couple of days after the Senator Keeley incident. But I wouldn't answer him because I knew he was only asking because he felt threatened. He always needs something to light his match before he gets afire about something, even marrying me. I dunno," I said.

"Go talk to Mother Franklin about it first before you do anything and just be real with her." Destiny gave me some advice.

"That's your girl Dee. I can't be telling her all my business, she already thinks I'm some kind of a harlot. I'll just be reaffirming what she already thinks of me," I stated.

"Tracey, this is so unlike you. You never talk down about yourself and even though I know this is heavy, you are so serious. I think as a psychologist Mother Franklin would be good to talk to right now before you make any rash decisions," Destiny said.

"We'll see. What do you think, Niecey?" I asked.

"I just can't believe your crazy heffa butt is pregnant, and before me." She tried to lighten up the air in the room. "You still need to go see your OB though, just to make sure."

"Girl, that's the third test I've taken this week. Each said the same thang. Heffa, you pregnant." We laughed.

"Well, I hate to leave but I got to get prepared for tomorrow morning. I would stay with you and, I don't know, think of baby names or something." Destiny interjected.

"Oh, don't worry girl, I already know what I'm going to name her if it's a girl," I said.

"What's that?" They asked in unison grinning.

"Destiny Denise," I answered.

"Aww, Tracey," Destiny cried.

"   Tracey," Sharon said as they both hugged me.

"If it's a boy I'm naming him after my father, unless I marry Chucky,"

"Just wait on that, you don't want to rush into a marriage just because you're pregnant and want a father for your baby," Destiny adds, still being an old wise maid.

"I know, but I do love the man, just haven't always been monogamous and loyal to him. Plus, I always thought he was a punk. But he has really manned up since this whole rape thing. It's amazing what men will do when they feel threatened or you mess with their woman. Too bad I had to find out how good of a man he is this way, huh." I admitted.

"Yeah," They said.

"Well go on now, both of y'all, mama needs her rest. I gotta be at that darn shop tomorrow; the Queen is in the city for something at H.U. And I have got to be fierce no matter what this little darling does to this ole body," I said.

"You ain't old yet girlie." Sharon said.

"Yeah, but I'm older than the both of y'all. And Dee Dee don't worry about not being married yet, he's coming sooner than you think," I said.

"Okay, yeah this baby is changing you because now you are prophesying into my life and I ain't mad at it." she said.

"What about me?" Sharon asked pouting.

"You just quit playing chess with people's lives and you'll be alright," I affirmed.

"Whew we, wait till I tell Mother Franklin. You can always rededicate your life to Christ Tracey. Don't wait till tomorrow, it's not promised," Destiny said excited.

"I'll be okay," I said.

"Okay," Destiny grabbed her purse.

"I love you," I told her.

"I love you too," She said.

"Aww, I love both of y'all. Give me a hug." We all hugged each other and cried. Later that night I took Destiny's advice and asked for forgiveness of my sins and for God to come back into my life again. I admitted that Jesus was Lord and He did die for my sins and rose on the third day. I feel so much better knowing that not another day will go by without me truly being a believer and doer of the word of God.

Twenty Two
Sharon

This case with Tracey was becoming cumbersome. Since the girl turned state's evidence on Robert and decided to file attempted rape charges on Senator Keeley the partners wanted me to take care of this case only. It was a good thing too because now I could concentrate more on getting that Negro locked up for a decent amount of time. He didn't even know she was pregnant but I think it's better that way because if he knew he would surely try to harm her and I didn't want that on my conscience. Tonight Cornelius and I were going out for the Fireman's Ball.

It should be wonderful. I hadn't been to one of those since I was at Howard and was dating James Houston, Mayor Jeffrey's nephew. I think he might ask me to marry him soon. He asked me just the other day how I would feel about marriage. I toyed with him and said it depends on who's asking. Then he tried to grab me for a quickie and I swiftly told him I couldn't be his pussycat forever. We talked some more about marriage and what it would look like. He even tried to guess my ring size. Then he asked me about going to the Bahamas or maybe Brazil just to get away.

You see, that's what I'm talking about with this man. He had all the assets he needed to handle a woman like me. Taking a trip to Brazil in the fall sounded terrific. By then this case may be over and I'd be engaged. But, what about poor Marcus? What about poor Marcus was right, poor Marcus. How could he even think he could take good care of me? He didn't even have a portfolio, just a money market savings account with about fifteen thousand in it. I mean, I did basically admit to the man I love him, but that's a part of the game right. Who am I kidding?

Lord, what in the world am I doing? Well, I did say I

would get two rings and my plan has been fool proof thus far. So what I don't love Cornelius, he would keep me in the lifestyle I wanted and deserved. Marcus would help me to grow though, especially spiritually. But shouldn't I be doing that on my own. I needed some advice but who should I talk to who's not going to judge me and basically tell me what I wanted to hear, marry Mr. Wynd. But I do love Marcus.

"Ms. Douglas you have the district attorney's office on line one." Alex interrupted my private thoughts.

"Send it through," I said.

"Sharon," Isaac Milburn said.

"Isaac, how are you?" I replied.

"I'm fine, I have some news you might be interested in," he stated.

"I'm all ears," I said eagerly because I wanted something to break in this case with the senator.

"We just picked up a Mr. Robert Thrasher on a drug bust in the southeast about five hours ago," he said.

"Five hours, why am I just hearing about it now. You know he's involved with my case. What do you have on him?" I asked.

"Enough to put him away for at least fifteen if not more. You still have your case against him right," he affirmed.

"Of course I do," I said.

"Well I think you need to get to my office as soon as possible don't you think. And don't worry, I don't think we will need Ms. Simmons testimony after all, we also have charges pending on tax evasion separate from his dealings with her. Now I don't know where that puts you with Senator Keeley, but it might look favorably if you think about settling. The real criminals will be locked up for a very long time," he declared sounding too proud of himself.

"Aww, now it wouldn't be right if I didn't consult my client on the matter now would it. And the last I checked attempted rape is still a crime," I reminded him.

"Well at least you've come down from the rape and assault counselor," he stated.

"I bet he was happy about that," I said.

"I don't care what the bastard is happy about, I just want the whole thing out of my hair."

"See you on Monday Isaac," I tried to end the conversation because he was getting on my nerves.

"Make it around ten."

"You have a good evening." I said.

"You too Sis." he said. Great, now I could really let loose tonight. I had my green gown from Versace. He ordered it especially for me with the shoes to match. The limo was picking me up at seven thirty and then I would be whisked away with my prince for the evening.

Δ

"Oh, darling you look wonderful. I knew that gown would put your body to shame, you look flawless." Cornelius kissed me on the cheek and helped me into the ballroom door.

"This old thing." I giggled and flirted with my beau.

"Girl we might have to break those heels in later." He whispered in my ear from behind putting his hands on my butt.

"Behave." I snapped at him trying to be elegant tonight. Too many of the right people would be here and I had to be at my best at all times. Now that I think about it this would be the ideal place for him to pop the question, but I couldn't be too ready especially if it was supposed to be a surprise. I even practiced my surprise faces before I left in the bathroom mirror. He called from the limo and said tonight will be a night I would never forget. So, I guessed my dream would come true. Finally, Lord, thank you. I deserve this so much and then some. He's the right man for me. I'll grow to love him, and he'll grow to love me, we'll be fine.

We started to mingle throughout the room and shook hands with city officials and other high ranking people in the metro area. Everyone was dressed to the nines in tuxedos and ballroom gowns. You could tell they paid good money for their Jimmy Choos, Christian Louboutin, Vera Wang, Giorgio Armani and Dolce & Gabbana. The band played some of the jams and even tried to do some hip hop.

We danced a bit and they served dinner and that's when it happened. He stood up and waited until it was a short silence in the room and started to move towards the dance floor to the band. He grabbed the microphone from the lead singer and asked me to join him in the middle of the dance floor. He then got down on one knee and said:

"Sharon Denise Douglas, you are my air. Without you I cannot breathe and with you I am a whole man. I hope that you would give me the privilege of being your husband for the rest of my life. I am asking you, my friend, will you be my wife?"

I was ecstatic, I didn't have to fake it I just said yes and hugged him. The band started playing "A Ribbon in the Sky" by Stevie Wonder and we danced and then others met us on the dance floor. A couple of print magazines and newspapers took our picture. He introduced me to Mayor Collins.

"Mayor Collins I would like you to meet my fiancé, Sharon Douglas." Cornelius said as I just stood there dumbfounded. Did he just call me his fiancé? "Sharon, sweetie. She's still a bit flushed,"

"Oh, how wonderful. I hope you have all the happiness in the world." His wife said then shook my hand.

"You picked a winner, Wynd. I would be happy to give up my seat to a man of your caliber knowing you'll be taken care of by a woman such as she." Mayor Collins said. And then the night was a blur, until we got back into the limo and headed home. I was laying my head on his shoulder and he was rubbing my knee with his head back. I was admiring my ring when he said,

"I know about Marcus."

"Huh?" Astounded I replied.

"Look, don't deny it, I have proof. I always knew you were dating someone else and that your mother lives in Baltimore, not on the north side either and that your biological father is in jail, not dead. I know everything about you Sharon. That's why I need you to sign this before we go to Brazil because when we get back I'm going to put in my plans to run for mayor. I need you to be ready for that too, so you have to break this thing off between you and him," he said without any emotion.

"What about you and her?" I asked not backing down.

"I don't love her, she's just somebody I do when I want certain things you can't or won't give me. I'm glad you understand how this is going to be. You will be a good partner and I knew it the first time I got profiled by you. You really need to sharpen your skills though, Mr. Washington is too beneath you," he stated. I looked down at my five-karat diamond engagement ring and wanted to throw it at him. Instead I just moved away from him. "Oh, you have feelings for him," he asked, sounding a bit jealous and concerned but not concerned enough to be angry.

"That's none of your business," I was defensive.

"Just read the pre-nup, I don't care if you have your little flings because I know I'm going to have my own, just don't fall in love with nobody but me, whenever that happens." he said. Stunned I asked.

"You know I don't love you,"

"I know I don't love you. But it's time for me to get married and you are the best candidate out there who is worth the time and money for this race I'm about to run and my future goals. We've only known each other for a few months or so anyway, it'll come in time and if it doesn't oh well. I found a wife, and you got the husband of your dreams. I respect you and I won't hurt you on purpose that I promise, but as far as you loving this other man I can't have that. You are my woman and he can't compare anyway." He stated the facts. For the first time I hated him, but I still wouldn't give the ring back. I worked too hard for it. I did everything you're supposed to do to get a ring like this. Wasn't this what my mom's pastor prophesied about, me having the husband of my dreams. Even Marcus said you don't have to be in love to get married. We didn't speak anymore until we got to my house. He let himself into the house and I guess you could say we broke in my new heels. Lord what have I done?

Twenty Three
Destiny

I am nervous as heck. They better have my key right. Listen to me sounding like a diva already. Charles said he wanted me, no needed me to lay the vocals on this song so he could shop it to the other managers. The managers, how appealing was that? I couldn't wait to hear it. The melody was easy enough. Shoot, I could sing anything, just tell me what it was once, and it was on. That's why he said he had to get me signed before somebody else swooped me up. He said he had heard my name around for a long time and had to take a look for himself and what he heard was amazing. I think he was just trying to soup my head up though. I was on my way to the studio and thinking about everything that was going on in my life. Driving always gave me time to reflect.

There was a big scandal surrounding Stanley at the church now. That man who kept pestering me at choir rehearsal, turned out to be one of Stan's old lovers. He found out about us and joined the church just to start some stuff. He finally got his revenge though. He outed Stan at some big time accountant's convention. Some way the fool got pictures of Stan in a compromising position and plastered flyers of it all over the conventions site. Then he had the nerve to send out a massive email to a bunch of Stan's people by hacking into his email address book. The boy even had the nerve to print up some church fans with the mess on it, but only a few people got those. Bishop had a fit but couldn't help but laugh. Mother Franklin said she bet he'll stop now.

Still though, the most awesome thing was my friend got saved. Tracey came back into the arms of the Lord the Sunday after we got the results from her pregnancy test. I fell out. God is awesome. My job was going fine, stressful as ever though. I was going to be a recorded gospel singer, and I had a man. Michael is wonderful. Sends me flowers every Friday, just because. We're taking it slow, which is a good thing because I did just get out of something and didn't want no more drama. I finally made it to the studio. It is always buzzing in here.

"Hey Ms. Price," Some woman behind the desk said. "Charles is in studio two, take the elevator to the third floor, it's to the right."

"Thank you," I'm so nervous, Lord, but why though. I got this. Lord give me strength. Once I stepped out of the elevator I could see Charles and a couple of other people in the studio behind some big desk with gadgets all over it and then I looked to my right and there it was, the microphone. Wow, here I go Lord I whispered aloud.

"Hello Charles." I hugged him.

"Ah, Destiny, how are you. Looking good girl, God has been good to you I can tell," He took a step back and looked me over.

"He always has and always will be," I grinned.

"Well you ready to get started?" he asked.

"Yeah, but can we pray first?" I placed my purse in a chair.

"Of course, we always start off all our sessions going before the Lord in prayer. This is Taqi, Chareese, Cherelle and Senora. Taqi Shemalri is my right-hand man in here and these lovely ladies will be laying down the background vocals for you today. You'll be seeing Chareese Miller a lot though because she's one of our new artists as well. I hope you two become good friends." The dark-skinned girl with a gap tooth grinned at me like a goofball. "Now, let us go to the Lord. Auspicious and all wise Father God we come to you today first giving you all the honor and all the praise. We come to you humbly dear Lord asking that you have your way with us in this ministry of music today. Let our voices be lifted up only to worship and praise your name dear Lord and not out of form and fashion. Because we know that through praise and worship we please you and we ask nothing more than that you be edified in our works. These and all other blessings we ask in your son Jesus name we pray. Amen. Amen everybody." He ends the prayer.

"Amen." We all say in unison.

"I've heard a lot about you Sis." Chareese said and gave me a big bear hug.

"Thank you, are you from DC?" I asked because she had a country drawl.

"Oh no, I'm from Dallas, can't you tell?" She responded and did this annoying laugh.

"Uh, yeah," I patted her on the shoulder to make sure she was okay. The other girls looked past me and smirked, one of them whispered something to the other and they laughed. Here we go again, no doubt, more catty women.

"Okay girls, everyone in the box. Destiny take the lead mike, the rest of you, you know your places. Let's get to work." Charles directed us and we followed his orders. The session lasted for about three hours and I did fine, once I got the willies out. The song was written by Tanner Cornell out of Memphis. He was a gifted song writer. Charles said I would meet him next weekend.

Now all I had to do was go do this one last home visit that I couldn't get in yesterday. Levert, my oldest case-kid was never at home and he was starting to really worry me because I knew he be out there doing Lord knows what in the streets. Gosh it was beautiful out here, I loved the month of August. The air wasn't too dry and sun still peered out even through the cloudiness. If I ever get married I want to get married in August Lord. I pulled my Camry up to up outside Levert's foster home. I hoped Ms. Tucker was there too, they both be trying to get ghost when they knew I was coming over here. I couldn't stand southeast DC, it's full of so much degradation. Aha, speak of the devil.

"Levert, I'm over here." I motioned to him and he started to cross the street. I saw two other guys walking towards him from behind with hoodies on. He ran up to the grass. The guys behind him pulled out guns and started shooting in our direction. I dropped to the ground and tried to crawl towards him. He had fallen close to me and I knew he was hit by the string of bullets. The guys came and shoot him again but ignored me. I didn't know what happened next because when I woke up, I was in the Howard University mental health wing.

Twenty Four
Tracey
FALL

Lord, I couldn't take no more of this. It had been almost forty five days, and she still didn't seem no better. Last month, Destiny was doing a routine home visit when she witnessed her case-kid get shot right in her face. She must have blacked it out or something because the police found her walking around in southeast DC disheveled with blood all over her. She had been walking around for two days, hadn't eaten or anything. Somebody called the police when she walked into Popeye's and tried to order some food for free.

We were at Howard University Hospital talking to the doctor about her condition. When they found her, she was talking gibberish and wouldn't let anybody touch her. They said they had to restrain her in order to take her here. Sharon and I had been worried sick since.

"So, what you're saying is she had a nervous breakdown." Sharon asked Doctor Sweets.

"Well yes, you could say that. She has created a world where no pain exists. She has gone into her world and has not found the exit doors, so to speak. The shooting triggered something in her mind and to protect herself it has decided to create its own world," he tried to explain her state of mind.

We sat there in silence for a moment and I let out a heavy sigh. Destiny had been through so much already with Stan last year and now this. Lord, why do you put us through so many trials and tribulations?

"How long will she be like this? She doesn't even recognize her own sister." I asked, holding Danielle's hands which were shaking. It took the heffa long enough to get down here after we finally found her and told her that her sister was in the hospital. I didn't know why they were not close, but this girl got some issues. I thought I had issues but this heffa took the case. We finally found her after Sharon looked up her nursing license after reading through some of Destiny's things to find out her occupation. The girl came home when their mother died but then left Ohio without telling her family where she was going.

"Doctor, what are you diagnosing her with again?" Danielle said something finally.

"At first glance we believe it to be bipolar disorder," Doctor Sweets responded.

"My aunt had that stuff. Dee Dee used to suffer from depression and Mama was just crazy," Danielle admitted to the room sounding dog-tired, like the news just took every breath left out of her.

"Danielle don't say that about Mrs. Price. She was your mother," Sharon scolded.

"Who was crazy," She looked at Sharon in disgust. "I need a cigarette. I'll be back." She got up and left us there.

"Well, how long do you think she will need to be here, doctor?" Elder Daniels asked. He had been here almost every day mostly being quiet and listening to her rant and rave. I dunno, but that man must be in love or something because I knew for a fact that clueless Stan would have never stayed after taking one look at her with her hair all over the place, drooling and shaking.

"Well, until we can get this medicine to work properly she will need to stay here. There is no magic number of days I can tell you right now. So far, she is responding well to what we have her on now, which is good because at first we had a lot of problems," Doctor Sweets said reminding us of how Destiny would walk around the hospital naked thinking she was a god and other crazy stuff. One day she took a shower like every half-hour, so they had to lock her down because she was scrubbing her skin off. I just couldn't believe this was happening to her, she was so full of life and had everything going for her.

"So, what should we do doc," I asked as my stomach

started to churn, the baby was hungry.

"What you could do now is continue to visit with her and try to get her to stay focused. Right now, as you can see she's doing pretty well. This is a good day for her. Elder Daniels has seen a lot of what she's been going through and she's used to him. I don't know how she will react if her sister continues to visit though. That has been upsetting her," he started writing notes on her chart.

"But she or we can't tell her she should stop coming," Sharon interjected.

"It might be better for her right now until she's better. From what I understand she hasn't seen her sister in almost five years," Elder Daniels said.

"That's not Destiny's fault," I said, a little annoyed at what he's trying to suggest.

"I'm not saying it is, but for right now we need to be concentrating on getting Destiny healthy again, not reconciling an estranged relationship with her sister. That's just too much right now. Am I right Doctor Sweets?" he turned to face the doctor again.

"Yes, Destiny's health is the number one focus right now. Here at Howard we are sensitive to the needs of our patients first and foremost. Reconciliation is not high on the priority list right now." The doctor affirmed. We all sat in silence and watched Destiny coloring another picture. She seemed so focused on that little Mickey Mouse picture, like she was a kid again. I wanted to hug her and tell her everything is going to be okay, probably like her Mama would if she were alive. Now that I thought about it we should have seen the signs that something like this was bound to happen to her. She had been through so much in the last three years it was a wonder she hadn't broken sooner. I mean it was nobody's fault her Mama died, but this stuff with Stan could've been avoided. I could have probably saved her from a whole year of pain.

"Destiny, do you want to say something to your friends?" Doctor Sweets asked.

"Yeah, have y'all seen my neon crayon?" She asked oblivious to what is going on in her life right now.

Δ

Chucky and I decided to get married next May. By then the baby would be born and at least I wouldn't be fat anymore. I started counseling with Mother Franklin, but I haven't told her about the whole marriage thing. Daddy was pissed to say the least, but only because he thought we should wait to have children. I just didn't have the heart to tell him the baby may not be Chucky's, he would probably have a heart attack for real. Mother was excited about the whole thing. Although she didn't want to be a grandmother yet, she couldn't wait to have this little one in her arms.

I was more focused on my walk with the Lord now, even reading more of the Bible. I liked the book of Ruth. She got her man and really didn't do nothing but stay busy going to work and tending to her widowed mother in law. But I know I was a Jezebel for real. I also knew I had issues like Gomer in the book of Hosea. She had some issues too and used her body to get what she wanted from any man all the time. I always thought that was supposed to be the thing though. In this day and age, being a diva or a vixen was the hip thing to do. If you ain't a dime piece, shoot girl you ain't too much of nothing because men like a woman they can show off. And you better know how to work some magic in that bedroom or you were doomed to be by yourself. I had been in enough relationships to know: sex was a weapon. But now, when I look back, the only person it had been killing was me. And now I was pregnant by a pimp no less. I could have AIDS though, so I guess I had the best judgement there was for me, if this was really a judgement from God. It seemed more like a blessing in disguise to me.

I mean look at my life now. I was going to church and being real in my Christian walk, betrothed to a good man, and going to have a lovely child soon. I hoped I did have a boy though, I was going to name him after daddy too. Shoot, we all started off last year talking about wanting to get married. Looks like at least two thirds of the group would be jumping the broom. But I didn't know if Sharon was really going to marry Wynd. He gave her this crazy prenuptial agreement and she was all upset about it. I didn't know why though. She knew he was a republican.

"Ooo-la-la," I spoke into my cell phone.

"Hello, Ooo-la-la Salon, this is Trina, how may I help you?" Trina answered the phone.

"Hey girl," I said.

"Hey. How's Ms. Destiny?" she asked.

"She's doing a lot better. Soon they will be able to do some real counseling with her. She's opening up and at least responds to us now, especially Elder Daniels." I told her.

"You know that's her husband," she said.

"I don't know nothing yet, but if he is I ain't mad at her because that man has been there in the trenches through all of this mess," I swung left onto Thirteenth Avenue.

"We should give her a coming home party when she gets out,"

"Yeah, that would be nice. She would appreciate that. Look into that for me," I said.

"Okay, but what's up with you Mama Tee?"

"Oh, girl, don't start. I just wanted to see if any of my clients showed up yet?" I beeped my horn at some crazy kids running across the street.

"Well Ms. Maggie is here, but you know she'll wait for you. Shasta called in sick again."

"I must have a heart of gold or something because I should have fired her early this year. All she gotta do is shampoo." I weaved onto Georgia.

"And she don't hardly do that right," She started to laugh.

"Well I'm on my way in." I waited for the light to turn green drumming my fingers on the steering wheel.

"Okay," She said then we hung up the phone. I headed

down Georgia Avenue to the shop and finally got there within ten minutes from hanging up with Tina. It was packed as usual for a Friday, plus school just started a couple of weeks ago. Danielle was coming in to get her nails done and something done to her head. She looked terrible after the meeting with the psychiatrist. She almost broke down when we told her she shouldn't visit until they got Destiny healthier. Elder Daniels drove her back to the apartment and got her something to eat. I knew she shouldn't be alone, but I just don't have the strength to be with her right now, not after what she had done.

When Destiny's mother died Danielle was still estranged from the family. She had gotten married to some big time preacher and basically shunned her family, said they were beneath her. Well about two years after marrying this so-called preacher he left the church in a state of bankruptcy and her there to clean up the mess and a baby. She still wouldn't come back home though. We heard stories from Dee Dee about how her mom would reach out to her and beg her to come back home, but she just would not do it. Then their mom started having all these mental health problems and it was believed she was really schizophrenic. But they never found out the real deal because she over dosed on some sleeping pills one day. So, we weren't surprised when the heffa showed up to the funeral late. Now that I thought about it, Destiny Karen Price had been through hell and back, and you know what, she was going to get through this too.

I know she will, I pray she does. *Lord bless my friend, make her whole again. Renew her mind and refresh her spirit Jesus. The enemy was getting really busy in her life right now, but I know you above all things are a healer, Jehovah Rapha, I've heard other saints say. Heal her broken mind and spirit. I love you and I know you can do all the things that I ask. In Jesus' precious name I pray. Amen.*

Twenty Five
Sharon

Okay, I was mad now. No, I was pissed. This fool knew my best friend was in the hospital, but he still wanted to go to Brazil. And to top it off this outrageous prenup has gotten on my last nerve. I missed Marcus. I hadn't seen him in almost a month and we hadn't had a real conversation in a while either. You know what, I'm not even going to front no more. I love Marcus. I want Marcus. I have to tell him the truth, the full truth.

"Can you come here please?" I dialed my assistant.

"Yes ma'am," Alex answered then walked into my office.

"I need you to set up a dinner for two for me and Mr. Washington for tonight,"

"Ma'am, it's 4:43 p.m." he said frankly.

"I know what time it is, but I also know you know how to get things done around here Alex." I tried to stroke his ego, so he would do me this favor right before he left for the day.

"Oh, you think so," He started to grin.

"Yes, I know so. Just make it somewhere inexpensive and close to Chevy Chase. It can be late tonight too," I kept up the act.

"Okay, Sharon." he said and walked back to his desk.

"Okay, Alex," I decided to let that slide, it's not every day he got a compliment from me. I started to get back to my case when Alex walked back into my office.

"I got you something at Adriactico's. Does that sound okay?"

"Yeah, what time?" I asked.

"Around 7:30, do you want me to contact Mr. Washington?" He handed me some papers.

"Yes, and make it sound like an emergency, something really important," I took the forms and gave him my coffee mug so he could put it in the kitchenette.

"Okay," he said.

"Thanks," I said.

"I'm going to go after that, okay boss?"

"That's fine. You worked hard today." I stated the truth. We had been working on the new case and he had kept up with all of my demands throughout the day. If he kept that up I would have to give him a good holiday bonus.

Δ

I got to the restaurant and saw Marcus' new car parked near the front. Well Lord, if this is going to work I need your help. I walked into the restaurant where only a few couples were left for the day. I asked for him and they sat me at his table.

"Well hello," he said, smelling good.

"Hi," I said trying to hide my nervousness.

"Sharon. What's going on? I know about Destiny and everything, but I expect there is something else going on that you are not being up front with me about." he asked abruptly. He sounded like he was not going to take any crap off of me.

"Can we get something to drink first?" I tried to stall.

"No. Stop playing and tell me the truth." He raised his voice. I cringed and dropped my head. He was not going to put up with any of my shenanigans.

"Okay, okay, okay," I sighed heavily. "Marcus, a man asked me to marry him." I looked at him to see if I should go on or what.

"I'm listening." He sat back in his seat and crossed his arms. I watched his body language to try to figure out the right words to say. The next words that came out of my mouth could end our delicate relationship. I had to be totally honest with him if I had any chance to keep him in my life.

"He's everything I thought I wanted in a man, except," I

tried to explain.

"Except what." He looked me dead in the eye.

"I don't love him." I finally admitted it.

"And," he said, unconvinced, placing his hands on the table.

"I love you," I told him and tried to grab his hands.

"No, you don't. You can't," he said annoyed, pulling away his hands.

"How could you say that?" Defeated, I slouched in my seat.

"Because you've been playing this game since we met, and I just fell for it like a fool. You're a trip," he said and shook his head crossing his arms again.

"Marcus," I was taken aback because he had never talked to me in such a tone. Tears started to form as I willed them not to fall.

"You're just like all those other women I've dated, only out for themselves and wondering when they are going to get a ring. Well, here," He slammed a ring box on the table, got up, glared at me and walked out. I grabbed the box and ran after him yelling his name.

"Marcus." He pushed the lock to his car. "Marcus." I grabbed his arm.

"Get off me!" He yelled and pushed me away.

"We can work this out. I told you, I said no to him." I begged as the tears escaped and ran down my cheeks. My stomach turned as I realized I was going to lose him.

"No, you didn't. I know you, you played the numbers and I came up short. Why? Because my profile isn't as swanky as his, because I don't drive a Maybach or work for some big law firm. I saw the pictures in the Post, congratulations!" He shouted angrily.

"You knew all this time," I asked dumbfounded.

"I'm not stupid Sharon. I didn't know you were dating the both of us at the same time but I kind of figured that out after I saw the paper. I read the Post daily on my bus route. You are so selfish. I was going to propose to you the same weekend. Had it all planned out and everything. Just couldn't take the ring back. I wanted you to see it. To see what I would do to take care of you." He sounded exasperated.

"I want to accept the proposal," I said, trying to get back into the niche.

"News flash you phony Jezebel, that wasn't a proposal." He got in his car and left me standing there with the box in my hand. I walked to my car crying with people looking at me. Now what was I going to do? I got two rings but the man that I wanted just drove out of my life. I should have listened to Destiny.

I needed to talk to Mama; she would know what to do. If he saw it then I know she did and that's probably why I hadn't heard from her in weeks. She was probably mad too. Cornelius just had to make a spectacle of the whole proposal. But that was what I expected him to do. I didn't expect to fall in love with Marcus though. Well, since I was batting a thousand I might as well tell this fool I was not signing those papers and I was not going to Brazil and I was not marrying him. If I couldn't have who I wanted I didn't need to be with him. My phone started ringing in my purse shaking me from my inner thoughts.

"Hello," I answered, still bewildered.

"So, did he give you the ring?" Someone asked me.

"Mama" I said confused because she didn't sound like herself.

"Yes, Sharon Denise Douglas, this is your mama. When were you going to tell me you've been prancing around DC with some man who wants to be the next mayor? Better yet, why did you lead Marcus on all this time? Who are you Sharon Denise Douglas? Are you that devoid of character that you would do whatever you have to do in order to deceive and keep a man? Will you do anything to get married, and marry anybody? That man loved you, it was hard for him to admit but he did, and he would have done anything to care for you. And you played a dirty game with his heart. After he told you he was only after one thing you still played with him like you were in court or something." She chastised me.

"Mama, I know but." I tried to get two words in.

"But nothing. I didn't raise you to be this desperate. To be a fake harlot, living a double life. Where is my child?"

"I'm right here mama. I'm right here." I told her desperately.

"No, no, you can't be my child. My child knows better. Give him back his dignity; give him back the ring Sharon. That's the least you could do,"

"Mama, I want to be with him. I'm breaking it off with this other man, I don't want to be with him." I explained to her the truth, so she would forgive me.

"You don't have a choice anymore Sharon. He doesn't want anything else to do with you." She uttered to my disappointment.

"Have you talked to him?" I asked.

"Yes," she said.

"Where is he now?" I pleaded.

"I'm not telling you anything, you don't have to worry about me helping you anymore either. You know how to catch the right bait all by yourself." She hung up the phone. My mama hung up on me. He had been talking to her all this time too. *What have I done Lord. I don't pray like I should, I know I don't, but can you please help me please. And this time it's not to get him to marry me or anything like that I just want him to forgive me.*

Lord will you please forgive me. My Mama called me a fake harlot, a hoe. I'm a hoe. He called me a phony Jezebel, am I all these things. I was just trying to be the right kind of woman for the right kind of man. That's it that's all. I want to get married and have a husband that loves me. I don't want this fake stuff. I don't want this mess I've created with Cornelius. Show me what to do, how to make this right. Show me how to be real with you and everybody else.

I'm tired Jesus. My friend is at the mental health ward at Howard because she was at the wrong place at the wrong time, and because she has been stretched so thin. My other friend is pregnant by a low down dirty bastard. I don't want to end up like that. Maybe I do have a problem. I know I have issues with my daddy but Lord, I don't know what to do. Make me right Lord. Make me right. I sat in my car crying out to the Lord for what seemed like hours. When I finally made it home I tried to call Marcus, but he refused to answer my calls. I knew then, I had lost the love of my life.

Twenty Six
Destiny

It was raining outside and the sign to the Howard University Hospital was dripping wet as I watched it from the fifth floor window. They kept moving the purple, flowering orchid plant. I've told them time and time again to leave this orchid alone. It was such a pretty contrast to everything that was going on in here. Lord, should I tell this fool that the dang on TV ain't on. How long have I been up here? These people were nuts. I didn't have no clothes here, I'm tired of these drawings and I want to see my friend. He usually comes up here around this time, but I think that stupid heffa wanted to talk to me today.

"It's group time everyone." the nurse announced standing in front of the therapy room. Lord knows I didn't want to go to no doggone group, but I knew if I didn't go they would keep me till Jesus came and I was ready to take a bath in my own tub.

"Destiny, you coming to the group today? I think you will like this one." The nurse asked.

"I guess so. How long have I been here?" I responded.

"Oh, just a little while." she lied.

"When can I go home?" I asked annoyed.

"Just a little while longer." she lied again. About four of us filed into a room and sat at the desks. Somebody started acting up outside the room as the therapist closed the door. I was tired already, sweet Jesus.

"Good morning everyone. How is everyone today?" she asked.

"Fine." I said.

"Hello, and what is your name?" A woman asked wearing smelly pink painted pig pajamas.

"Destiny," I replied.

"Say hello to Destiny everyone." Everyone said hello and some skinny girl came up to me and gave me a hug.

"You'll be alright." The girl said and sat back down. The troublemaker outside came to the group.

"Hi Jovan." the nurse said as he entered the room.

"I'm here today Shirley. You tell them I came here today." the man pleaded.

"Alright, have a seat and let's get started." she motioned for him to sit down. The next half an hour went by like molasses. We talked about anger and how it affected us. She had given us an assignment and told us to write about why we felt angry. My anger diary was full of stuff. It seemed like I was angry with everyone, especially my sister and Mama. How was Danielle gonna come up here and act like ain't nothing happened in all these years. Like she really cared. And why did my Mama leave me. And who in the hell shot Levert and why did they have to do it in front of me.

Why was God angry with me all a sudden? I didn't do anything to deserve all of this. I prayed daily, I went to church sometimes three times a week, I was a good girl. First that fat bastard put his hands on me when I was little, then that faggot lied to me. Wait till I saw Stan's behind again. I had some words for him, going through all that counseling, through the motions really.

After the session I went back to my room to just sit and think. I stared out the window.

"Hey there girl." A familiar voice filled my room. I turned around to face him. It was Michael. I started to cry. "That's okay, let it out," He hugged me, then we walked to the visiting room.

"Michael, I've been lying to myself for a long time. I'm mad at the world," I announced.

He held my hand as we sat on the couch. I loved the fact that he had been coming to visit me since this whole thing started. Even when they gave me my diagnosis, bipolar disorder with psychotic features, he didn't stop coming. That was honorable. "Okay. Why are you mad?" he asked, rubbing my arm.

"Because everybody is always messing with me. My Mama left me, well she killed herself. My sister just doesn't care. Stan, well he's a liar. And that man touched me," I spilled my guts.

"Who touched you, Destiny?" he asked, sounding very concerned.

"My teacher, back in fourth grade. I thought I told you that," I said matter-of-factly.

"No, Destiny, remember it's me Elder Daniels. You haven't told me a lot of things. But I know you are upset with somebody else. What happened to your father Michael Price?" he asked, squeezing my hand.

"I don't know," Just then Doctor Sweets came into the room and took a seat.

"Hello Destiny. You remember who I am?" he asked.

"Yes, you're the doctor. When can I go home?" I asked, releasing Michael's hand and crossing my arms in defiance.

"Just as soon as we get some other things straight. Do you mind if I sit in here with you and Elder Daniels?" he asked another question.

"No," I responded watching him take notes.

"Can I ask you a question?" The doctor asked.

"Yeah, why not that's all y'all do around here," They both smiled a little.

"Do you remember when you were a little girl and your father died?" He asked. I didn't respond. I just sat there and thought about that day, the day the whole world turned black and cold. The day I never wanted to remember, but I couldn't get out of my head because it was just so horrible. The day my mother killed my father.

A few moments went by and I started to speak. But I wasn't speaking to them, I was talking to somebody else, somebody who would finally listen to me and believe me. When I was ten years old I came home to find my Mama and Daddy fighting again. Danielle was already home and was in the kitchen eating some cereal. I just acted like everything was normal. But then the fight got ugly and Mama ran into the kitchen.

"Get up and go next door." She told us in a panic.

"But Mama I gotta do my homework." I protested.

"Girl, get your butt up and do what I said." She demanded. I looked at her and she had blood running down her head. Daddy was in the other room calling her all kinds of names and stuff. He was high as a kite. I looked at her again. Her eyes looked like they were on fire, something that I had never seen before. This would be the last time he ever hit her again, but he didn't know it. I got up and started packing my book-bag as she fiddled with a locked drawer.

"Forget that bag girl and do what I say!" She yelled. Danielle had already ran out the door. I turned to go out the door but hesitated when I got on the back porch. I went back inside the house and into the front room. POP. My ears started to hurt. Daddy fell to the floor. The blood was so red and smelled like old wet copper pennies. I stood there and watched him take his last breath. Mama told me to promise to never tell anybody what happened. I never broke our promise until now.

Δ

Four days went by and I was beginning to actually like the group. Jovan is off the hook and my meds were starting to work for me. I had been in the hospital for seven weeks and they said I may be discharged soon. I couldn't go back to work though, not for another six weeks or so. But I didn't care. I needed a break. Some detectives finally came up here and asked me some questions about the shooting. I told them what I could remember, but it wasn't much. It happened so fast.

I had to start calling Michael, Elder Daniels again because I kept thinking that he was my father while my meds were being calibrated. My sister was staying at my house still; she didn't go back to Michigan running scared like she always did. Sharon and Tracey were coming up here today and Mother Franklin was up here yesterday. She told me I was calling her Mama every time she came to see me, so she stopped for a while just until they got my meds right. Tracey was going to bring me some clothes.

"Jovan the TV is not on yet. It'll be on in about fifteen minutes," I told him.

"Judge Judy is on." He responded and started picking at a sore on his arm again.

"Not yet Jovan, not yet," I said, in vain mostly because I know he's just going to sit there and stare at the TV until they finally turned it on for the day. I couldn't believe I finally told someone about my parents. Seeing my mother shoot my father had always haunted me, but I didn't tell anybody just like she said. Plus, I guess it was self-defense. He was beating her, been beating her for years and we had gotten so used to it we would just go in the kitchen or go next door until the fireworks were over. Mama said no more that day though. I didn't blame her though. I knew if she could have had it any other way, we wouldn't live like that. That's why I always make sure my case-kids are not surrounded by danger at home. Too bad Levert was out in the streets like that.

I couldn't believe Elder Daniels had been up here every day to see me. He brushed my hair yesterday, said I was looking like Alfalfa. He made me laugh, something normal in this crazy place. I gotta give it to Howard University Hospital though. They try to take care of you, no matter what you did to them because they said it was a couple times I was acting up. Throwing stuff and hitting people, just tripping out. All out of anger built up over the years. Now I had bipolar disorder, but I would be healed in Jesus name.

"Destiny your guests are here," a nurse said.

"Okay," I left the TV area to go to the visiting room. There I saw Tracey and Sharon.

"Hey boo." They gave me a hug and a kiss on the cheek.

"Got something for ya," Tracey handed me an overnight bag. "They took your sharpeners, thought you might want to put on some makeup for Elder Daniels," She said.

"Girl stop," I tapped her on her arm. She looked puffy a bit. That baby would be here sooner than later. I had the best girlfriends a woman could have. They were always in my corner and never judged me about any of my issues. I thanked God all of the time for them, they were real troopers.

"Now, sit down here and let me do something to that head." she said, picking me with the comb.

"How are you today, Dee Dee?" Sharon asked.

"I'm doing a whole lot better. Group is doing me some justice and me and Doctor Sweets are getting somewhere," I explained.

"That's good to hear." she said, smiling politely. They were looking at me funny. I knew something was up, but I dared not ask. I just wanted to have a good visit with my friends.

"Um, we need to talk to you about something." Tracey said.

"What's up?" I asked, trying to keep an open mind.

"Your sister wants to come up here again," Sharon said shifting in her seat. Tracey rushed to say something.

"Now you don't have to say yes, we just thought it might be alright now since you're doing better," Tracey pulled at my shoulders, so I could turn to face her.

"I think that would be okay. Plus, I would like to get somethings off my chest in session," I leaned my head over as she brushed my long locks.

"Okay good, is tomorrow okay?" She asked.

"Yeah," I responded. A short silence filled the room. "What is that Sharon?" A diamond ring glistened on her finger.

"Oh, it's my engagement ring," She said.

"When did you get engaged?" I asked, still not remembering anything yet.

"About the same time as the shooting, but then I got unengaged and now, well now things are complicated." She lowered her head.

"Complicated. What do you mean?" I asked. She told me the story about her and her two conquests. Although I was not at all surprised, I was a little upset with her about Marcus. He was a good God-fearing man and she should have never led him on. He would make a wonderful husband for anybody who valued his love. Sharon didn't seem like the kind of woman who could value true love from any man. She just had too many issues for that and loved to be in control.

"So, what are you planning to do?" I crossed my arms. Sharon looked up at me and Tracey then let out a long sigh.

"Well we haven't spoken for about almost six weeks now. I wanted to still give him some time to calm down first. Now I plan to visit him and talk this out," she said, taking out some stuff from my bag.

"You better talk like your life depended on it," Tracey said, shaking her head. I sat there between her legs shaking my head too.

"And then some." I added.

"Oh, forget y'all heffas," We laughed a good laugh. "Girl, let me see your feet," Sharon asked.

I took off my socks. They looked horrible, like I had been stomping in flour and salt. She took out some foot sloughing lotion from her purse and got up and went to get a pan of warm water. My girls pampered me for about two hours until Dr. Sweets came in and broke us up. I then went to the group and ate. I waited patiently for Elder Daniels to come and like clockwork he was there around seven.

"Hey sweetie," he gave me a hug and handed me a bear.

"Hey, thank you," I responded then kissed him on his cheek.

"Whoa, there Missy," he was taken aback and moved his head out of the way.   Embarrassed, I said.

"Oops, I'm sorry. I forgot myself." He smiled at me and pinched my cheek.

"No, it's okay, just didn't expect it. You're looking good today. I see you got some of your clothes and your hair looks nice," He said and ran his hand over my braids.

"Thank you," I fixed his tie.

"How was your day?" he asked so I started to rattle off the day's events. I even told him about Sharon and her relationship woes.

He sat back and crossed his arms listening intently. I knew he was about to preach one of his mini sermons. He did that sometimes, especially when he heard me about to give up. I could always count on him to give me a good sound word and encouragement at the right time.

"Sounds to me like she missed a few sermons on what singleness is supposed to be about and how it's not a women's job to find a husband. She also missed rule number one, love thy neighbor as thyself. Hopefully, the young man will listen to her and hear what she has to say, but I doubt very seriously if he will want to marry her still," he stated.

"You don't think so," I chewed my bottom lip concerned because I really wanted it to work out for her even though I knew she was dead wrong.

"No, I wouldn't. Especially after she cheated on me and got engaged to another man," he said and chuckled.

"She's living in a dream world huh?" I chuckled right along with him.

"Pretty much but hasn't she always." he declared.

"Pretty much." We laughed and then started to play cards. He visited for about an hour and then I attended a wrap up group and headed to my room for the night. I started another journal and tried to write in it every night. Tonight, I wanted to list everything I want to tell my sister and why I had been so angry with her all these years.

Twenty Seven
Tracey

We were at the bridal boutique on third and Chucky was as happy as a little boy who just got the new G.I. Joe with the Kung Fu grip. We already picked out the invitations, the seating decorations and now we were about to discuss the cake. He wanted chocolate; I don't care as long as it doesn't show up on my thighs later. Ms. Yvonne was nice, a bit dim-witty if you asked me, but she's helped countless other brides and grooms with their weddings and each went off without a hitch. Of course, Mother suggested her, and I couldn't say no. Daddy just sat there as usual with his hands in his pockets.

"So, we could have like a chocolate swirl cake right." Chucky asked Ms. Yvonne.

"Yes, and we could combine it with any other flavor that you want Tracey." She told me trying to get me to engage in their two-person conversation that was supposed to include me, the bride.

"I really don't know, chocolate seems like enough for me." I said then excused myself to go to the bathroom. This morning sickness was a trip. Mother followed me but waited outside the stall before saying anything.

"Darling, you don't seem like yourself today. What's wrong?" She felt my cheek like she used to do when I was a little girl and she knew I wasn't feeling well.

"Ma, I'm just not up to it today that's all." I replied hiding the fact that I really didn't want to be there. She was on cloud nine though so I masked my feelings to get through it.

"Well we could reschedule and come back when you're feeling better. We've made a lot of progress and it is only late September. We already know where the wedding will take place, who will officiate and where the reception is going to be, so the hard parts are over. Now you and Chucky can have fun picking the little stuff that you will most remember. I want you to enjoy planning your big day baby," she said and gave me a hug. I went back into the stall and sat there for a second, mostly to avoid talking to her anymore. Thoughts of our upcoming meeting with our marriage counselor started to cloud my thoughts.

I told Mother Franklin about Chucky and she basically said I ain't ready to get married. I knew she was going to say that, so I didn't know why I even bothered to tell her. But she did say she would still counsel us. I dunno, maybe I really ain't ready which was why I'm not at all thrilled about planning this thing. My ring was the bomb though. He went all out with it. It had a four-carat emerald cut diamond surrounded by eight round diamonds along the sides. It sparkled even when the sun wasn't shining.

"So, baby I'm going to go back out here with them, try to talk to your father some more about this. He's interested to know what's going on and thinks you still need to keep the charges going against that horrid man," She said.

"I'll talk to him." My dad was a man of honor and he would like nothing more than to make sure Senator Keeley met his maker in court. This whole thing had been bothersome to him to say the least, but he's being a soldier about it.

I couldn't believe he showed up today. This must mean he was softening up to the idea that I was having a kid and getting married. After the meeting with the wedding planner we would meet with Mother Franklin. This should be interesting to say the least. Although the Bishop was not going to be officiating, I still wanted to go through the counseling they had at my church. I knew it was a long shot that she would ever say we were ready, but I had already made my decision, I was marrying Chucky. He would be a good father to my baby and he loves me. I loved him too for the most part. I finally got out of the bathroom and headed back out with the others. Ms. Yvonne made an appointment to see us in three weeks. Chucky and I got in his car to head over to the church.

"Chucky, whatever she says, just listen first before you say anything," I said as we drove over.

"Why do you say that lovey?" he asked.

"Because Mother Franklin don't play when it comes to marriage and she knows everything about our situation. She even knows that this baby may not be yours," I explained.

"Well, she can't stop us from marrying one another, especially if we want to get married. We'll see, it will all work itself out. Okay." He patted me on the knee. We drove in silence the rest of the way there then parked and went inside. "Wow, this is nice boo. I've never been here but I bet y'all have church going on in here." he said walking through the corridors of the church down to the administration wing. The glass walls made the chandeliers shine as we walked. Plush purple carpeting cushioned our shoes as we finally made it to our destination. The secretary seated us and called Mother Franklin on the overhead. He looked at a picture of the first family. "She's your first lady, dang, I know he's a happy man." I pinched him on the arm as the secretary looked at him with disdain. I just smiled at her.

"Ah, Sister Simmons, this must be Mr. Charles Pryor. How do you do and welcome to First Metropolitan. I'll be with you in one second." Mother Franklin said and went into her office. She returned and motioned for us to come in.

"So how have you been Tracey?" she asked.

"Oh, I'm fine, been a little sick lately but that's just the baby." I said smiling.

"And you Charles," she asked.

"Call me Chucky, my father is the only one who still calls me Charles," he admitted.

"Okay, Chucky. Let us look to the Lord." We prayed and then she asked, "So you guys want to get married. Why?" Her demeanor changed from the sweet Mother Franklin to Dr. Patricia Franklin, the psychologist. I could tell Chucky was taken aback, so I answered first.

"Well, we've been together for a while now and we love

each and decided that now would be the best time to get married. Plus, I am pregnant, which is not an issue, so we think it's the best time," I said definitively then smiled like I was trying to impress my first grade teacher for the first time.

"And what do you have to say Chucky," she asked.

"Well like lovey says, we love each other and it's time to take the next step in our relationship. I don't want to be with anyone else except her and I'm ready to settle down," he said proudly then grabbed my hand and kissed it.

"What does settling down mean?" she asked then started taking notes.

"Well getting married. The end of being out there single," he responded.

"That's not what marriage means though. What does marriage mean to you?" She asked both of us. Just then I felt him tense up, let go of my hand and sat up on the edge of the couch.

"It means that two people, who are in love, get together and commit to one another, until death due they part," he responded then looked over to me. I shook my head in agreement.

"Does that mean you forgive her for sleeping with another man? And having a baby by another man, because she loves you now, but she didn't stay committed. What about that?" she asked. He sat back, I fidgeted. I knew this was going to be hard, but this was murder.

"Can I say something?" I chimed in and patted Chucky's knee.

"Sure, go right ahead this is your session too." She folded her hands across her desk.

"Well the whole cheating thing was just me trying to keep control of my heart. I wanted to stay in a relationship but still play the field just in case I got hurt. Even though I really love Chucky I just couldn't let the relationship control me." I told her the truth as I saw it.

"Well you do know that once you get married you will lose even more control. So how is that going to stop you from going out and getting with another man when the going gets rough in this marriage and it will?" she asked and looked in my eyes. We looked at each and smiled awkwardly. "This is what I want you two to do. I want you to find out from each other what marriage means to you and what it would look like. Who's going to pay the bills? Who's going to feed the baby and go get her diapers? Who's going to cook and clean? But I want you to really sit down with one another and figure out what marriage means to you? Is it a ministry or just something to do when you come to an eclipse in the relationship? Be honest and frank. I want to see you again in about three weeks. We will do about eight sessions and I will try to get you prepared for the road ahead that you are both so gung-ho about going through with." She wrote something down on her notepad.

Chucky huffed and sat up on the edge of the couch again. "Why do you say it like that Mrs. Franklin?" he asked.

"Well, I'm not one to hold my tongue, especially when it comes to this subject. But to be frank, I don't think you two need to get married. I think you're doing it for all the wrong reasons and if you do that not only will you mess up your lives but the life of that innocent child," she said matter-of-factly.

"Well, we got eight sessions to get through first, so we'll just see about that. Are you ready Tracey?" He got up and headed for the door.

"We need to pray before you depart from here Brother Pryor." She told him and stood to her feet. He walked back towards the middle of her office and we formed another prayer circle. We held hands and prayed, but you could cut the air with a knife. He didn't say anything until we got into the car.

"Who the hell is she to tell us we are not ready to get married?" he said, annoyed.

"Baby, I told you she is up front and to the point. Maybe we do need to slow down a bit," I said trying to smooth things over.

"Look, all you have to do is just take care of my baby. That's my baby. I don't care what anybody says, especially not her." He put the car in drive then sped off out of the parking lot. We didn't say anything else until he dropped me off at home. He kissed me on the cheek and sped off again. I said a quick prayer watching him zoom down the street. *Lord, I don't know what you want me to do, but I really think we might be doing the wrong thing at the wrong time. Please, show me your will in this thing.*

Twenty Eight
Sharon

Cornelius went to Brazil with his other woman. I gave him back his ring and everything he had ever given me. He told me I was the most asinine woman he had ever met. I told him he was the most ostentatious bastard I'd ever met. All in all, me breaking up with him was the wisest choice I had made in years. Yeah, he seemed like the king I'd been waiting for, but he would never treat me right and there would always be a condition attached to the feelings we had for one another, if we ever really had any in the first place.

Marcus agreed to meet me at the park today. I finally got him to meet me so we could talk. For October, the weather was still pretty nice out. The leaves were starting to turn and I loved the different color hues you could see on all the trees. There was a cool breeze and the sun was out. I hoped he listened to me and heard what I had to say. I couldn't deny that I was cheating on him, but to be totally honest, he never really said we were in a monogamous relationship. That was my best argument when I called him. He said he would give me a chance to explain. So, we would see. There he was sitting on the bench under an old oak tree.

"Hello Marcus." I said, waiting for him to stand and acknowledge my presence. He didn't move an inch.

"Hello Sharon. Have a seat." He sounded like he was going to make this hard for me. Lord, give me strength.

"It's a beautiful day out don't you think/" I tried to lighten the air between us.

"Yeah, considering." he stated and finally turned towards me.

"Considering what?" I asked.

He shook his head, tisked and sat on the edge of the bench. "Look, don't start with the small talk, say what you have to say so I can go back to my life." he said sternly.

"Marcus, you have to know that I didn't mean to hurt you." I plead my case in front of the worst jury I had ever faced. He was not falling for any of it though.

"No, you just meant to lead me on after I told you I was only after one thing." he stated.

"But you kept being skeptical about if that was me or not. I'm not a mind reader." I said.

"What about the time I told you that I loved you?" He stood up.

"You didn't exactly tell me that remember. I asked you after you asked me, and I didn't give you a chance to tell me before I left. I didn't want to get my face cracked." I looked up to him looking down on me.

"Oh, stop splitting hairs. That doesn't mean I don't love you, just because you were playing games doesn't mean I was," He said and looked away.

"It wasn't a game," I stood and got in his space.

"Oh, it wasn't, then explain to me why you played me the way you did?" He faced me.

"Let me just say this. I made some wrong decisions Marcus. I realized too late that I should have never split my time between you and a man who could never really love me for who I am. I didn't know what I had until I lost it and I want it back," I told the truth and tried to reach for his hand.

He pushed my hand away. "What makes you think I want you back? See this is what I'm talking about with you. You think that you are the best thing smoking since hot-links but you are not. You fall short in so many ways, but that never bothered me until I found out the type of woman you really are. You profiled me and discovered that I didn't measure up to all your requirements, but then something unexpected happened. You fell in love with me. And now you're fighting like hell to try to get back something that you never really put very much value in. You don't value the love we have Sharon. The only thing you value is what you can measure on paper and I just don't think that's enough for me," He moved away from me, upset.

"Marcus, let me say something." I shifted my weight in my heels.

With little patience he uttered. "What? What do you want to say that you think will change my mind?"

"I want to tell you that you are right." I placed my hand on his shoulder. "I do value things that you can measure. However, now that I know that there is such a thing as true love that you can't measure in pennies, pounds, or anything else. I want to cultivate it and make it last forever. Please, don't take away the only thing that has ever meant something to me. At least give me the chance to start over and make it right." A long silence ensued between us. It was torture standing there waiting for him to say something, anything.

"I don't know if I should." he finally said exasperated.

"Pray about it first," I begged.

He laughs at me mockingly. "You are asking me to pray about something. You are really going all out on a limb ain't you?"

"What is that supposed to mean?" I asked, not happy with what he is insinuating.

"I'm not even going to get on you about your Christian walk, but since we are being real let me start. You only go to church to show off and because you think you are supposed to, but what do you really get out of it? Do you really have a relationship with the Lord? I thought you did, you had me fooled. Seeing what you could do to me, knowing how I feel about you made me believe otherwise. I will tell you this though, you can lie to me if you want to, but God knows your heart for real. How do I know you are only saying all of this to keep that two-karat diamond engagement ring? I just don't think you are really ready to be with me and be loved Sharon. You wear a mask, and I finally got to see you take it off and I don't like what I see. I doubt if the Lord likes it either." He took a couple of steps backward.

In that moment I knew I had to take my pride out of this

if I was going to get him back. I tried another tactic. "So that's it. You're just going to leave me and the love I have for you. You don't want to at least try to make this work. Marcus don't punish me for not knowing the difference between something real and something perceived. Honestly sweetie, I didn't know I could love like this." I said and tried to hug him.

"Since when is your love so strong Sharon. Is it because I don't want you anymore? Or is it because you don't have any control over this situation? I gotta go." He pulled himself out from my grasp.

"Wait, wait a minute." I grabbed him by the arm and faced him. I couldn't believe I was begging and chasing after this man again. But if I let him go now, I knew I would regret it for the rest of my life.

"I am a work in progress Marcus. You are right about so many things but that does not change the fact that I love you and there is something between us that we should not let just die. I don't give up on something I want, and I never give up on something that I need. I need you Marcus and you cannot tell me that you don't feel anything for me anymore. I am sorry that I hurt you and that I let you down. But if you would just find it in your heart to give me a chance to make it up to you I promise I will be the best woman I can be for you," I pleaded. Tears started forming in my eyes, but I held them back.

He stood there and studied me. I didn't think he was going to say anything else because he turned away for a second. He faced me in apprehension and opened his mouth almost stuttering, "H—, how about you just be the best woman you can be for yourself. Before we can even start over again Sharon you have some issues you need to deal with first. Stop being this person you've made up and be the person God made you to be. That would help the situation a whole lot. If you can't do that, then there is no way I would even consider giving you another chance," he said to my astonishment.

I grinned like a kid in a candy store. "So, what are you saying?" I couldn't hide my exhilaration.

He couldn't deny his feelings anymore. "I do love you Sharon and it's been hard for me to get over you, mostly because I don't know if I really want to. You are the one, but you don't value that, and I don't think I can handle it."

"I do value it." I smiled at him. I was about to get him back, finally. Yes Lord.

"How could you when you were dating both of us and said yes to his proposal?" he asked, stepping back again. I stood to look him in the eye the best that I could.

"I honestly can't answer that other than to say I thought the life I've always seen other prestigious people have was the life that I wanted. I thought that I wanted a man who had a lot of clout and money and fame, but when it got right down to it, I just wanted a man that loves me for me. And Marcus, you are the only person other than my mother and my girlfriends who knows who I really am. I intentionally let my hair down with you and was myself because you made me feel like a real woman. A person to be adored, a person who doesn't need to wear a mask and hide behind a bunch of letters behind her name. You make me feel real, and I can't go back to being the old Sharon, the lawyer who only dates prominent men in the right areas because that is what she grew up fantasizing about. You are real, and I can't go back to being fake, I won't." I relinquished myself.

He pulled away from me again. I started to panic again because he wasn't believing me pouring my heart out to him. "Sharon Denise Douglas, what you got to realize is that you need be real for yourself and God. Not for me or anybody else. Just be because you are. Look, I gotta go, but the lines of communication are open. I might regret this later, but my spirit is telling me that I won't. Don't let me down for talking to you again. This doesn't mean we are together, as a matter of fact, I want my ring back." He held out his hand and I handed it over. That was painful, but I knew it was the right thing to do. He said goodbye and left me standing there. For the first time in decades I thought I was going to faint. I remembered when the judge gave Daddy his sentence and I lost it. I felt like that all over again and now I had to live in that reality.

The reality that I almost pushed this great man out of my life because I was being greedy and selfish. I didn't really know what it meant to be like Esther, Ruth, or the Proverbs 31 woman my mother said I needed to strive to be. I sat down and started to ponder over my life. In less than one year I dated two remarkable men and was proposed to by both. Still though, I was nowhere near my goal of getting married than what I was New Year's Eve. What a difference a year makes.

I had come to the conclusion about something, however. I needed to stop acting like someone I was not and just be real with myself and everybody else. And the first person I was going to start with is the Lord, Jesus Christ. I knew He already knew who I was and what I was capable of, but I would say I scared myself sometimes.

To think I was willing to pander and hustle myself out in a relationship with an up and coming politician just to say I had him on my arm really got to me. Mama was right, I forgot myself and settled. The silly thing about all this was he was doing the same thing and I knew without a shadow of a doubt we would never love one another. That relationship would be predicated on means and ends or supply and demand, a noose around my neck for the rest of my life and for what. Just so I can still wear Prada and Dolce and Gabbana. I could still dress fashionable with Marcus. I would just be on a budget. I could still have the nice house, cars, and everything I am accustomed to, I would just be more of the breadwinner than he would. And that wouldn't stop him from providing for me the best way he knew how. Shoot, he already got a house all by himself and on his own salary, there is no telling what he would've done to make sure we made out okay. It could still work.

Lord, I'm looking for a miracle, but first I gotta work on me. What is my purpose in life Lord? What would you have me to do with or without a husband? Am I really supposed to get married, or I am gifted with singleness? I hope not because Lord you know I can't contain, plus I want to have children. I was going to take the time and get these questions answered for real. I knew I had issues, but I didn't think I had them bad enough that I needed to see a psychologist. I wasn't crazy or anything, but I had my issues. Lord, please just don't give up on me, Niecey Walker is still here inside this shell. I need you to help me break it Lord. Don't give up on me.

Twenty Nine
Destiny

It had been about two weeks since I got home and my sister was getting on my last nerve. She was so messy. I mean I knew they said I had obsessive compulsive disorder features but this heffa was just plain nasty. Put the dishes in the dishwasher after you are finished with them and stop leaving cups all over the house, dangit. I went to get me some milk and couldn't find one clean cup.

I needed to decide when I was going to go back to church. I knew I had nothing to be embarrassed about, but still people talk. I knew that it was all over the news and other clergy came to see me other than Bishop, Mother Franklin and Elder Daniels. Some were really genuine in their interests; others just wanted to solidify the rumors that I finally tripped out over all the stuff that has happened to me this year.

So what, I never told anybody I saw my mother shoot my daddy and that she just might be schizophrenic. I had my reasons. I didn't want anybody to know that I could have the same issues. There was this one time when I was in undergrad when I was walking around the Quad with some pajamas on in January and no shoes talking gibberish. But that was a one-time incident. I didn't know that wasn't the first time I had been in the psych ward at Howard. It wasn't until the doctors told me they saw me before after this latest episode that it dawned on me that I really had problems.

Still though, there were those times when I'd get really depressed. When I was in high school I tried to take some sleeping pills but got caught with them in the school's bathroom. I really wasn't trying to kill myself, at least I didn't think I was. Let me quit lying, I was. Shoot, there had been a couple times I got so depressed I'd think about just ending it. When Stan and I broke up I bought a whole bottle of pills and just sat there with them in my hand for hours crying. Matter of fact, where were those darn pills.

"Danny." I walked into the guest bedroom opening the door without knocking.

"Yes." She answered not looking up from her phone.

"Girl, turn down that music. Have you seen a bottle of sleeping pills in my room?" I asked.

"Yeah, I needed something to help me sleep a couple of times, why. You don't need any of them, they got you on something to help you sleep, remember." She stated.

"I just wanted to know where they were at." I said.

"Oh, I got them." She said and turned back over on the bed. She was ignoring me.

"So, what are you going to do today?" I asked trying to hold out an olive branch and really communicate. She was my flesh and blood and sooner or later we needed to reconcile our relationship.

"I thought about going shopping or to a movie." She said.

"Did you want to go together?" I asked.

"Well, I dunno, do you feel up to it." She got up and started combing her hair.

"Yeah, I gotta get out of this house." I found a rubber band on the dresser and handed it to her.

"Humph. I didn't think you would want to hang out with me after all you said to Dr. Sweets." She started our candid bickering.

"Here we go again. Are you ready to talk about this or are you just going to make different hints and then leave like you always do?" I stated not falling for her antics.

"I don't want to start nothing in your fragile state. I know this must all be hard for you right now." She said with disdain rolling her eyes to the top of her head.

"Yeah it is hard, but I can't and won't keep stuff bottled up anymore. That's what started me down this road in the first place and you were part of the problem." I crossed my arms.

"You know I could just go home." She crossed hers.

"Ain't nobody stopping you." I told her and waited for her to take another jab at me. That was how we talked. We didn't discuss anything; we talked at each other and argued until she made her final point, then exit stage right which should be in one, two, and three. "That's right, just leave, you could never face the reality of things especially when it's staring you right in the face." I was too tired of her mess.

She turned around and walked right up to me. "You're full of crap! You ain't all this helpless and need all this help. You had it all. Mama always looked after you. I was the one who had to do everything on my own. So what, now you got bipolar disorder, that doesn't give you the right to throw stuff up in people's faces." She stood right in my face. I didn't know where all her anger was coming from all of a sudden, nor did I care. I knew one thing though, she had better back up off of me because I was not going to take any of her bull crap anymore.

"Like what Danny? What have I told you about yourself that was not the truth." I yelled at her angrily.

"That I run from my problems. I always face my problems. I came down here, didn't I?" She continued to be in my face, but I wasn't going to back off until she did.

"What about Mama's funeral Danielle? How long did it take you to finally bring your tail back from Detroit and face the fact that your own Mama killed herself? What about at Daddy's funeral, you got sick. You weren't sick, you just didn't want to be there for—," I started to express my true feelings, but she cut me off. It really hurt me growing up when she refused to be around whenever there was trouble in the family. I wasn't quite ready to tell her everything though.

"Who? Be there for you? You ain't never there for me," She screamed.

"You always put your friends before me, even when you almost got killed in that car accident when you were sixteen, you leaned on your friends more than anything even though me and

Mama were there wiping your butt and cooking you soup all the time. We did that, but you treat us like step-family," I said.

"Y'all always had a bond that I could never penetrate. It was like she loved you more or something," She sounded hurt.

"No, that is far from the truth. All I ever heard was I wish Danielle was home or would call me or come to see me. When you went away for school you didn't come home until you graduated. We didn't see you for almost five years." I told her now trying to put some space in between us.

"At least I was in the same state." She cornered me again.

"And what about your son." I swung the most hurtful words I could at her.

"Oh hell no, don't you even go there. It's not like you've been saved and satisfied all your darn life." She swung back.

Not letting her get the upper hand over me. "Where is Tommy Danielle?"

"He's with his daddy's family." She backed off a bit.

"You didn't even let us get to know the boy. We saw him once, and that was by accident, you weren't even going to tell Mama about him. What is wrong with you? Do you want to be alone for the rest of your life? Your friends haven't even called down here looking for you, and don't say they call your cell phone because it's turned off, I checked." I made my point.

"Why are you all up in my business. Look, I'm leaving this weekend. You're at home now and it looks to me like you don't need any of my help, you got enough people prancing around here helping out. Even got the old reverend doctor wrapped around your finger." She jabbed again with her words.

I walked up in her face now. "What the hell is that supposed to mean. You know what, you right; it is time for you to leave. I'm tired of arguing with you every day and looking at my house all messed up with your crap everywhere. I just hope you at least keep in touch this time, so it won't take so much time trying to reach you. You should at least keep your number published, you know we don't speak a lot." I was so emotional now and almost started to cry as my voice cracked.

"Like you really want to talk about something other than yourself and how good life is for you. Ooo, I got a recording contract. Ooo, I'm engaged to an accountant, too bad he swung both ways." That was it, without hesitation I slapped her. She smacked me back. We started to tussle and fought each other like we were little girls again. Except this time, nobody was around to break us up. The next thing I knew I heard a knock at the door. It was the police.

"Open up, it's the police!" The officer said banging with his flashlight no doubt.

"Hold on a minute." I pulled my shirt down and got up off the floor. Danny was still sprawled out but started to get up as I got closer to the door. "Yes." I tried to smile as they looked passed me through the door of my townhouse.

"We were called, is there a problem here? The neighbors say they heard a disturbance going on, like someone was fighting." He said with his partner standing behind him and Mrs. Stradley standing behind him with her dog. That was one nosey old woman.

"No, we're fine over here, everything is okay." I lied.

"How did you get that mark on your face?" He asked. She marked my face, I was gonna kill that heffa. "Umm, I scratched myself, I just got out of the hospital though so, ain't no telling."

"Where is your husband?" he asked, flashing his flashlight between Danny and I.

"Oh, I'm not married. My sister is here, she has been staying with me since I was sick." I said, still catching my breath.

"Ma'am could you come here please." I looked at her and she had a busted lip and scratch on her face too.

"Okay Ladies, do you want to tell the truth now or am I going to have to take the both of you downtown?" He asked not buying my innocent act.

"Sir" Danielle said. "Yes, we had an altercation, but she did just get out of the mental health hospital. Everything's okay now though, I'm about to go to a hotel and someone will be over here to stay with her to keep her safe. If that's okay, nobody needs to go downtown or anything, we are both a little scratched up."

"Do you agree ma'am or should I take you to the crisis center." He asked me. I almost copped an attitude but realized that would just feed the fire.

"I'm okay sir. She just needs to leave my house." I said.

"We can wait here while she gets her things." He said.

"No, no that won't be necessary. I'm leaving for sure." She said.

"That's up to you Ma'am." His partner stated.

"No, it's okay, I'll be okay she's not going to touch me and I'm not going to touch her. Thanks though." They left, and I closed the door.

Danielle started packing her stuff and I called Niecey to see if I could go stay with her or vice versa for a while because I felt awful. I got off the phone and let her call a cab and make hotel reservations. We stayed in separate rooms until her cab came. I went to tell her goodbye and to apologize but she left without saying a word. I broke down and cried like a baby.

Lord knows I didn't want to alienate my sister. She was just about the only family that I had left but we couldn't get along to save our own lives. Still though, she never wanted to face the reality that she was never there for me or mama when we really needed her to be. Anytime stuff got hard she got ghost, and that hurt like hell.

One time I had the horrid task of putting mama in the psych ward, I think it was the first time, I didn't know what I was doing, and I needed her to be there to help me at least so we could cry together. But not her, she had to go out with her boyfriend. Danielle had some demons she needed to face. Maybe this fight was something that was bound to happen; maybe now she would face the man in the mirror. I dunno, but I couldn't be her doormat anymore.

She was dead wrong for bringing up Stan, especially after what her ex-husband did to her. I never put that in her face, how dare she. Good, Niecey was knocking on my door. She must have been flying over here because I lived in northwest DC and she stayed in Chevy Chase, Maryland.

"Hey girl." I let her in.

She walked right past me because she saw the place was a mess. "What the hell happened here, Dee Dee?"

"We had a fight. The police came and everything." I told her.

"A fight, y'all too old for that and you know it. Did you beat her tail?" She said smiling.

"Yeah." I gave her the hands up.

"She probably deserved it." She slapped my hand.

"Yeah." We laughed a bit more.

"Come here, give me a hug." She gave me a big bear hug. "Troubles don't last always remember."

"Yeah, but they seem like they do. How have you been?" I asked.

"Fine. I talked to Marcus, we had a serious discussion about the relationship." She walked into the kitchen looking for a glass.

"Well?" I handed her the one I washed out earlier.

"Well, he asked for the ring back." She sounded hurt.

"Aww." I was displeased. I hoped he wouldn't do that.

"But the lines of communication are open again. He says he doesn't know if he will be able to trust me again. Also said something about me not valuing our love," She poured herself some water from the fridge.

I washed out another glass and got some water too. "Well, do you?"

"Why you ask me that girl?" She asked.

"Because you didn't act like it, that's why heffa. But before we get into your love life can I finish telling you about Danielle?" I said.

"Oh, I'm sorry. Look at you, taking the doctor's orders to be about yourself first and other people second," She said.

"He don't have to tell me twice. Anyway, she threw Stan up in my face and kept bringing up what we talked about with

Dr. Sweets. So. I pulled her card and slapped her, she had no right to even try to throw him up in my face," I told her.

"But why slap her Dee Dee? That ain't even like you," She said.

"I guess you could say I've been wanting to hit her for a long time and she finally opened an opportunity for me to do it without me feeling too bad about it," I admitted the truth.

"But still though, you said the police were here and look at your face. Don't let this disorder change who you are. You are still saved, sanctified, and set-free. The enemy wants you to take on this angry woman persona, but you and I both know that you are not that angry with everyone and everything that has happened to you. You had the shock of your life and wigged out, so what, that could happen to anybody. I mean I know you and your sister have had a strained relationship for many years, but that still does not excuse your behavior." She was right.

"I know, but it felt good to hit back for once. Now it's out of my system. She just doesn't want to admit that she should have been there during those trying times in our lives, with mama dying like that and then when we were coming up and she kept getting "sick". I gestured quotation marks. "She makes it seem like it's my entire fault that I should have been strong enough to deal with it by myself. I wasn't, not at sixteen and eighteen years old. I know she is younger than I am, but I would have liked to see that she was at least concerned about what was going on. I love my sister Niecey, I really do, but she has got to start opening up, so we can talk and put all this stuff behind us. I want to go to counseling," I stated.

"Well you know after this it will be like pulling teeth to get her to even come back down here, no less go see a counselor. Just work on you boo. Let all this other stuff work itself out in God's time. I know you love your sister, but she has her own cross to bear right now and maybe she doesn't want to talk about it because she is hurting too," She said.

"Oh, I know she is. She opened up a little bit to Dr. Sweets and said she is angry that mama was sick and that I seemed weak to her for always wanting her to be around for everything even though I'm the oldest and therefore it's my duty to do so. She said she should have never been subject to a lot of the stuff that went on in our family at such an early age. She blames mama for a lot of stuff that mama couldn't control and with me. Well she says I act like I'm strong, but I'm really weak and it shows because now I have a mental health disease that could have been avoided if I dealt with stuff back then rather than push it to the side for later. Dr. Sweets quickly corrected her about that. I cannot be blamed for my disorder, to say the least I was born with it, and it has been a blessing that I never showed any manic episodes before with as much stuff I've been through over the years. I mean yeah, situational circumstances brought out the disorder, but I had to already have the predisposition to even get this far." I finally ended my spiel.

"Well it doesn't matter because by His stripes you are healed. Just take your medicine every day and take advantage of your counselors and you will be okay. Have you talked to Elder Daniels lately?" She asked.

"Yes, he has been a God send. I haven't talked to him today though, because he had some meetings to go to and is going out of town with the youth this weekend. You know I am really starting to like this man. He was there for me and didn't have to be. I mean when I heard that he came every day and endured me mistaking him for Michael, my dad, I was like whoa. What a friend I have found in him. We are taking it slow, but you know what, I wouldn't be surprised if he turned out to be the one for real." I got ahead of myself.

"That's what me and Tracey have been saying because he sure didn't have to do what he did. Most men would exit stage right after finding out the girl they like has some mental health issues." She went back into the kitchen to get some chips.

"Yeah, but not a real man of God." I grabbed some popcorn for myself.

"I've lost mine for all intents and purposes." She sounded down and out.

"For right now, just give him his space. Time will tell and if this is really what God wants for you it will happen in due season." I cheered her up.

"He said I was wearing a mask and he finally saw what was under it and doesn't like what he sees. I had to admit to him that I am fake, I gotta be." She finally admitted something I've known since we met. She knew how to put on airs all the time rarely taking down the front, even in front of me and Tracey.

"No, you don't. You're not with us." I said.

"I have been though, and worse I've been faking my Christian walk acting like I'm all saved and stuff when in my heart I know that I'm not. I mean I believe in Jesus and everything, but I only started going to church because mama made me. I was eight years old when I first joined, and I haven't really been true since then. Yeah, I joined the Metro on my Christian experience but as far as being baptized as an adult and declaring that Jesus is Lord of my life. Destiny I am sorry to say that I haven't done that. And Marcus helped me realize that I need to be truthful and real to myself and to God. So, I'm going to get baptized and declare what is right, be saved for real and stop faking the funk." She declared.

"Aww boo, you've made me so happy." We hugged and I said a small prayer of thanksgiving for my sister in Christ.

"Thanks for the prayer. I know that it is because of you I can be a Proverbs 31 virtuous woman myself." She said.

"Just take your time girl and be a Proverbs 31 virtuous woman for Jesus, let Him be the man in your life until He connects you with the man you should marry. I'm not saying that Marcus isn't the one, but right now you are embarking on a whole new thing in your life. You are a new Christian and as a novice you need to be open to God's will in your life. Who knows what He has in store for you, but you first have to be there for Him in all things personal, occupational, spiritual, etcetera. So, you're going to re-dedicate yourself this week." I asked.

"Yeah, no time like the present right. To think it took a man to push me back into the arms of the Lord." Sharon ate some chips and sipped some water as I looked for my pills.

"Well ain't nothing wrong with that. It was the right push though, right." I said.

"Right." She said.

"Hey, I got a book for you that could help you right about now. It's called What to do until love finds you: getting ready for Mr. Right. It's by Michelle Hammond, it's pretty good and will give you some things to ponder over what's happened and what will happen on this road to being married." I went to my bookshelf in the dining room, found it and handed it to her.

"I guess the man finding the wife is really real." She said.

"Girl that's a word, straight from the book. I tried to tell you that, anytime you try to counter what the word says you get into trouble. But at least you've admitted that you were wrong and are willing to be made right for the right reasons. I mean don't do this if you think it's going to get you closer to your goal of getting married Sharon. I know the kind of opportunist you can be at times." I cautioned.

"No big Sis in Christ. This is definitely for real and about God and me. I could care less if Marcus stays in my life or not. Right now, I am more interested in getting right with God. That's more important than anything I've done in my life today, tomorrow and yesterday." She affirmed.

"And that is the truth." I gave her another hug and we started talking about Tracey and the baby. We made some more popcorn and then watched a movie and my sister actually called. She apologized and said she would make sure to call before she left this weekend. I was really surprised. I thought I would never hear from her again, but God is good. I took my meds and planned to take them in the morning too. I had to take this stuff four times a day. I couldn't wait to go to church this Sunday. Everything was going to be alright. I could finally see the light at the end of the tunnel.

Thirty
Tracey

I finally got rid of that crazy shampoo girl. She tried that "I'm sick" routine at the wrong time this time. Now that I was pregnant I wasn't taking crap off of people anymore. She had to go, my other employees were getting ticked off and kept trying to do some of her same antics. Now I had to hire somebody else before the holidays got here. We could manage but having a shampoo girl made the whole experience here a little more extravagant. Plus, I didn't like shampooing people's heads, you never knew how long it had been since some of these heffas had washed their hair not alone their tail.

Mama got all upset after Chucky told her about our first meeting with Mother Franklin. She said we didn't need anybody trying to tell us if we are ready to get married or not. The assignment she gave us was a mess. We talked about it for hours until we came to the conclusion that we both had some seriously different viewpoints about what marriage means and looks like.

He actually thought I should stop working after the baby was born and hire a manager for the shop. He didn't realize this shop was my first born, I had to be there for her. Then he said something that truly tripped me out. He wanted a prenuptial agreement. Who in the hell did he think he was? He ain't CAP Sr. with the real paper. I went off on his tail, but he said he put that down to see what I would say.

He wanted us to go to his church, but I was starting to really enjoy my fellowship at the Metro especially since I rededicated my life to Christ. I just didn't want to leave there and go to his church. Now that I thought about it, I had never been to his church. It could be one of those dry hymnal-singing churches where the preacher speaks all monotones and the choir only sings the old spirituals or something. I mean I didn't mind the fact that he wanted his pastor to do the ceremony and the ceremony to be at his church, but I was not moving from the Metro.

Then there were these duties he wanted me to commit to. We had to have sex at least four times a week. Now, that's a lot even though I did like me a good roll in the hay. I had to cook and clean because he believed in all those old fashioned wifely duties. He should be the head of household and I tended to the children and the house.

Please, I was gonna be a new millennium wife with a career who had a nanny to help me take care of this baby. Didn't he realize that it's already going to be crazy for me with a new baby? I dunno, Lord were we really ready to do this? I thought we needed to wait, but he was so gung-ho about going through with this thing. It's not that I didn't love him, I did, but there were just some things we needed to really consider before we took such a big step.

I mean I always had the notion that I wanted it all, the single life and the married life. But now I knew I could only have one or the other and that the other takes a lot of work. I did want a father for my child, but the Lord will supply all of my needs, with or without a man. Lord show me the way because I really didn't know if I was doing the right thing right now. I had about three heads to do today, so the day should be easy. I needed to get off my feet soon because my ankles were starting to swell. I should find out who was next and get the day over with already.

"Trina, who is on my books today?" I asked.

"Just the girls and Ms. Maggie." Trina said while looking at the appointment book.

"Where's Ms. Maggie at, she's running late." I noticed.

"Uh-oh, that's five dollars towards the jar." Lamar said.

"You know Ms. Maggie is the only one who doesn't have to pay fines in my shop. She's been my customer for the longest."

"That's true, speaking of which here she comes." Ms. Maggie walked in slowly with her cane. She had a concerned look on her face.

"Hello Ms. Maggie, you alright this morning?" I asked.

"Yeah baby, just slow this morning that's all. I want my regular stuff. Where's the shampoo girl?" She asked.

"Oh, I had to fire that heffa Ms. Maggie. She didn't like to come to work."

"Well if you don't want to come to work, then you don't deserve a job." She said.

"You're right about that. Come on over here and let me wash your hair." I sat her at the sink and started shampooing her hair. She asked me something.

"So, when are you getting married?" She asked.

"What did you say Ms. Maggie?" I tried to act like I didn't hear her.

"When are you getting married? I see that stomach pouting out and I know your Mama taught you better." She said.

"Well if you must know it will be in May. And you are definitely invited." I started to massage her scalp as the conditioner settled on her wet hair.

"Are you sure you're ready?" She asked and looked up at me dead in the face.

"Why do you ask me that Ms. Maggie?" I smiled uncomfortably.

She huffed and rolled her eyes, which is something I've never seen her do, well at least at me and at the same time. "Because you just don't strike me as the marrying type chile. You are so full of life and like to be in the spotlight doing your own thing all the time. And this business is your life, you wouldn't know how to slow down and be with one man and raise a family."

"It's funny you should say that because I've been thinking a lot about that these past couple of weeks. We have to go see my Pastor's wife for counseling next week. She gave us an assignment to find out what each of us think marriage really means and to say the least it's been an eye opener." I admitted.

"Well marriage ain't nothing to take lightly, and you might be a little bit more interested in it now that I see you're in premarital counseling. Still though, that doesn't mean you're ready. Take your time and definitely don't do it because you're gonna have a baby. It used to be that a lady needed to have a husband to have a baby but y'all young people done changed thangs so much these days. You can be single and raise your child, just be sure to keep the father apart of their life." She said and relaxed more in her seat.

"You make a lot of sense Ms. Maggie. Just keep me in your prayers okay." I finished washing her hair and in came Sharon with one of her bad suits on. Destiny came in right after her with this scratch on her face.

"Heffa, what happened to you?" I asked Destiny.

"Me and Danny got into a fist fight." She said.

"Baby, you're too big to be fighting." Ms. Maggie said, shaking her head.

"Right, what is up with you girl. Them happy pills are making you nuts." I joked.

"Shut up Tracey. She just got on my last nerve and brought up the wrong thing at the wrong time and I did the go off." She said.

"Not the go off." I laughed.

"Yup, the go off." She and Sharon both laughed with me.

"Well, I bet you're happy she's not staying there anymore." I stated.

"Yeah, she's leaving this weekend. But guess who's rededicating their life to Christ on Sunday." She stated.

"Who?" I asked her flabbergasted.

"Me." Sharon said proudly.

"What, but I thought everything was everything with you and Jesus girl." I asked because Sharon has been going to church for years. She ain't like me, I knew full well I wasn't saved and had no problem telling the Lord I was a sinner and needed his help sometimes. But not Sharon, she praised the Lord and everything. Um, you just could never tell these days when it comes to Christianity. I mean I knew she could be fake in other ways, but not when it came to God.

"Yeah, well not really. I've been faking the funk for a long time and decided it is time to stop being phony and be honest with myself and the Lord." She admitted.

"You finally took off that mask Niecey. I never understood why you liked to hide your true self from everybody and just let your hair down and be down to earth like you really are." I said.

"Yeah, but it's more about being real with God though. I've been hiding for so long that I forgot myself and who God is and should represent in my life. Now I want to be the woman of God I know I can be and the first place to start is by re-dedicating my life to Christ and getting baptized. This will be my first time." She said.

"What, even I, the true whore from hell herself, have been baptized before. I didn't get re-baptized when I recently rededicated because I believe I don't have to, but for you to be doing this for the first time that's fantastic." I responded.

"Well I'm just glad that this year is coming to an end and both of my friends have their lives on the right track with the Lord. Now we can all go to bible study and different seminars and services together and I won't feel like I'm dragging y'all there in vain." Destiny said.

"Aww, we weren't that bad. Were we?" Sharon asked.

"Yes, especially Tracey. Always showing up considerably late and sometimes not even at all. But now it should be well with your soul to hear the word and live by the word every day." She stated as I started to massage Ms. Maggie's temples.

"Wait, every day." I asked jokingly.

"Every day heffa, don't act like you didn't know." She cocked her head and put her hands on her hips.

"I'm just playing." I said as I started to dry Ms. Maggie's head with a towel.

"Umm, Tracey, where is the shampoo girl?" Sharon asked, changing the subject.

"She fired her." Ms. Maggie answered for me.

"Why'd you do that?" Destiny asked.

"That heffa didn't like to come to work and I think she might really be sickly." I told her as I directed Ms. Maggie to one of the hair dryers. Sharon sat in my chair and I started to scratch out her scalp. Destiny sat in the chair across from us and started a conversation with Lamar. He'd been changing here lately too. Said he found out his lover was HIV positive and he was concerned about his own health. He was scared to take the test, but I told him I would go with him to get it done to help settle his nerves. I was going to take one too, even though I took one right when I found out I was pregnant for sure.

Am I settling by marrying Chucky just because I'm pregnant? I mean the baby ain't even his, I'm sure of it. Still though, he was a good man, and I do have love for him, shoot he's always been there for me no matter what. And he really loves and adores me. He'd drink an ounce of my bath water everyday if he could. I had all of these thoughts just running through my head when Sharon's grabbed my arm.

"What, what's wrong?" I asked her, startled.

"That is my head you know, not a record or something. What are you thinking about?" She asked.

"Nothing girl, I'm sorry." I told her.

"Nope, tell me what's up because you ain't touching my head again till you get whatever it is off your chest." She said and got up out of my chair. I looked at her, rolled my eyes, huffed, then plopped down in the chair and finally opened up.

"Okay. Do you think I should marry Chucky?" I said plainly.

"Uh, I don't think I'm the right person to ask that question. Ask Dee Dee." She said shying away from the conversation.

"Dee Dee, let me ask you something?"

"Hold on Lamar, yeah girl what's up?" She responded.

"Do you think I should marry Chucky?"

"I think you need to really pray about it and make sure you're doing it for all the right reasons and not settling for him because you know he would take care of the baby. You can do that yourself; you don't need a man to do that, even though it would be nice. Plus, didn't you say it's not his. I mean, I don't want to sound negative. I just know marriage is a serious ministry that you need to be ready for and not just something to resolve to do. Have you talked to Mother Franklin about it?" She asked.

"You know what, I have, and we are actually in couple's counseling now." I replied.

"Oh, so how is that going?"

I paused and tilted my head to figure out what to say. "It's going. She gave us a homework assignment and asked us to define marriage to ourselves and one another."

"Well, did you do it?" She questioned.

"Yeah, and basically we got some issues to work on before we jump the broom."

"Like what?" she asked.

"Like him wanting me to stop working and get a manager for the shop when the baby is born."

"Okay, what's wrong with that?" She stated and shrugged. Sharon chuckled.

"I can't leave my shop to nobody else, it's my baby." I told them both and got a little attitude because they both were acting a bit condescending.

"No, your child is your baby and she will need you more than this shop for the first months of her life. I don't think he's asking for too much there. Plus, you hardly even work here anymore." She said.

"You sho don't. We're good to see you on Fridays and you only got a good six clients you do regularly besides the rich and famous." Lamar added.

"Boy, stay out of grown folks business." Sharon interjected.

"Hey, it's not my fault y'all women always want to have these kinds of conversations at my place of employment. I just want to hear the juicy details anyway, so I'll be quiet." He said giggling.

"We'll talk more about this later." I told Destiny.

"Okay." She said.

"Okay." Sharon agreed. I got up and let her sit down to finish scratching her scalp. I was going to talk to Chucky some more about our plans to marry. I wasn't totally settled on the idea that we needed to get married right now. He should be understanding. He loved me, right?

Thirty One
Sharon

It's Sunday morning again at the Metro and the Lord was surely in the house. I felt so anxious. I just wanted the Bishop to get to the call to discipleship so I could do this thing. Good thing I wore my favorite suit, one of the first ones I bought when I got my raise last fall. We were all sitting together today. Destiny said she would start back singing next year. She had to put off making the song with Tanner Cornell too, at least until they could get him to come back to DC. Bishop was about to come to the podium, good.

"Good morning First Metropolitan." He said.
"Good morning" We responded.
"God is good." He said.
"All the time" We responded happily.
"All the time," He said grinning.
"God is good. Hug your neighbor and tell them you love them today." He paused and hugged Elder Tim White then went back to the podium. He said "We are going to go to a popular reading in the word this morning. It has come to my attention that some of our sisters need to be reminded of just how much they mean to the Lord and that they do not have to settle for second best when He is the best thing to ever happen to them in their lives. Folks turn to Proverbs 31 verse 10. And let's read together."

"Who can find a virtuous woman? For her price is far above rubies." We all said together with our Pastor. He cleared his throat and sipped some juice then stated.

"How much are you worth?" That was the title of his sermon. He prayed and we listened intently. Some of the things he said really got to me because I thought I knew how much I was worth, but I guess I never looked at it from God's perspective. He clenched to the women of God because we are so resourceful, our being was so vital to the ministry that he had to create us for Adam or he would have gone mad. He only gave us to Adam after He noticed that it was not good for him to be alone, to be lonely. Although we were made to be a partner to Adam, women have been dear and near to the Lord from the beginning. We are his daughters and He wanted us to understand that we meant the world to him. If not He would have made it possible for men to have babies and give men the emotions and empathy that we have for ourselves, our families, loved ones and friends.

Being a virtuous woman of God was critical to the kingdom of God and we should all strive to be virtuous. Our price was such a high price and we are highly favored which is why we can't just deal with any man who comes our way. God wanted us to be faithful to Him first and foremost because He was the only one who understands and treasures our worth for what it's truly worth unconditionally. I had to cry when he said that. Destiny squeezed my hand and gave me a tissue. I always thought that this passage was just about how to be a good wife, but it's about so much more than that.

Bishop continued on and then he did the call to discipleship. I took the long walk up the aisle to a new life in Christ. Of course people started looking at me crazy because I've been here all this time, what's my problem. I just smiled and kept my head up because I knew what I was doing. The girls and I went to dinner after church and started discussing the sermon.

"So really and truly you have to be all these things before you can even be considered ready to get married. That's too much." Tracey said sipping on her juice.

"No, not at all, not really." Destiny said. "Basically a woman needs to work at these things in order to be considered virtuous and that has nothing to do with getting married so to speak. You should want to be virtuous just because it is a good thing and it's immeasurable to the man who will one day find you and know that he wants you to be his wife." She stated while eating a piece of pie.

"I got something more out of it too." I interjected.

"What did you get out of it Niecey?" Tracey asked.

"That God's virtuous women are rare and precious. That all of us who want to be Proverbs 31 women may not measure up in the beginning but we should always try to be. That God's virtuous women are the ones He knows he could leave in charge of many ministries and the church because of our character, not just our families. It was just nice to hear we need to strive to be like that not just to get married but for Christ sake. Now I understand why Stan kept telling you that all the time." I explained.

"Yeah, but he couldn't pay the price now could he." Destiny responded.

"Do you think that Elder Daniels will?" Tracey asked, eating some of her pie.

"I dunno, I try not to think about him like that. That gets you in trouble most times. It would be nice though. Have you thought anymore about you and Chucky?" Destiny asked Tracey.

"I've decided to talk to him about it some more and take this real slow. I definitely don't want to get married next May though, that's too soon. So, I don't know how he's going to react to that news. I know Mother is going to have a cow though, but I can't marry to please her either. The only person who might be happy about all this is Daddy. To my surprise he might shout about it." She laughed.

"I think that's a good decision for right now." I put in my two cents.

"Oh, you did have something to say about it. Surprise, surprise, surprise." Tracey said.

"Forget you Tracey." I told her.

"You would never. Yall, I'm gaining weight and I don't like it. I can't fit my "gimme some" jeans." She said.

"You need to throw out them jeans anyway. I thought you had turned a new leaf." Destiny said.

"I was just trying on some stuff to see if I could still get in them. By the time this is all over I will probably have gained thirty pounds or so." Tracey told us.

"That's good though." I said.

"No it aint, speak for yourself when you have your first child. She better be pretty too." Tracey responded.

"How do you know it's a she?" Destiny asked eating some of her ice cream.

"I don't think the Lord would give me a boy, ain't no telling what I would do to him. Plus I figure since I really do want a boy I'll use reverse psychology on myself so I will have a boy." Tracey explained her backward plan.

"Girl, you got issues." Destiny laughed at Tracey.

We sat there going over some notes of the day's preaching. What I can't fathom was how I took the whole passage out of context for a long while always thinking it's for wives only. Destiny explained very well some other notes she had on the subject. They really had me look at myself hard. Shoot, I started truly feeling like a Delilah exposed after the whole talk. I got some issues, everybody does, but I had some that I never thought I had.

I mean, mirror mirror on the wall who's the most pattes de velours of them all. I think I am going to see a psychologist and just work on me and why I feel the need to hide who I am from everyone. What am I hiding from? Why won't I let myself be myself for myself and not others? Why haven't I seen any of my nieces and nephews or ever talk to anybody about my childhood? Am I that embarrassed about where and how I grew up? Why do I refuse to discuss my father or go to see him? It's not like other African American families had my kind of upbringing, living in the hood, from foot to root, sometimes taking the law into your own hands.

Daddy, isn't that bad. He was there for us and he did marry Mama, which most die-hard gangster drug-dealers don't do. He was proud of us, proud of me. Maybe I should contact him and go home for the holidays, both of them. Oh Lord, soul searching was going to be a hard thing for me to do.

"Hey what do you guys think about going home for the

holidays, well at least for me?" I asked.

"I think it's a wonderful idea Niecey. You should go home and see everybody and make up with your Mom." Destiny said.

"Yeah, and you know you haven't met any of your brother's and sister's kids. It would be nice. The only thing is you can't come in there empty handed." Tracey said rubbing her full belly.

"Why I gotta bring them something." I asked dumbfounded.

"Because if you don't you'll look like a total, well for lack of a better word, jackass." Tracey said giggling.

"Did you just call me a jackass?" I said trying my hardest not to get upset.

"Yeah, he-haw, he-haw." She laughed at herself making noises like a donkey.

"Yeah, you might want to bring at least the kids something. And just take it slow, if they act a fool, don't react like a fool. Be open and start to feel them out. It's about time you started to really get to know your family. They are the only one you have." Destiny said.

"I just realized I am all alone in this world and if I don't get close to someone other than you guys I will stay all alone." I said almost in tears.

"Oh, don't beat yourself up boo. You are never totally alone. You are one of God's precious creatures and you are even more dear to him now as a restored Saint." Destiny said and went on to say how much better I've been acting since I finally turned my life around and how the new me will be welcomed with open arms. It sounded good but she doesn't know my family, they can be rough when they want to be. It will all work out though.

I'll call Mama and ask her if I could come there for Thanksgiving and spend the night, unless somebody else was coming by and doing the same. I'm kinda looking forward to seeing everyone again. Shoot, Lakeya just had another baby not too long ago. And now that I think about it Hollis still owes me money from when I represented him. That boy knows he can owe a bill forever. I knew it would be a stretch to ask Marcus to come, so I'm not going to. I will send him a card and maybe a basket for his mother. That's not too forward.

Thirty Two
Destiny

I couldn't believe I was having Thanksgiving at Bishop's house with his family, Elder Daniels and some other clergy members. When Mother Franklin asked me, I was like I dunno, but she said she doesn't think I should be alone for the holidays especially with everything that has happened this year. It would be nice to be amongst fellow Saints of God this holiday season. She said not to make any plans for Christmas but I think me and the girls are going to go to Florida. Tracey doesn't want to fly so it will be a nice long drive. We haven't done one of those trips since college.

Danny called me this morning. She said she will be here and would like to come to dinner too if that was okay. I guess a good knock about was all we needed to be closer. Still though, we're too old to be fighting like that and I don't ever want that to happen again. Mama was probably rolling over in her grave. I'm picking her up from the airport now.

I'm making some progress in counseling. I didn't realize how much baggage I had on me. My psychologist, Dr. Smithies said most of it has transformed into excess weight all over my body and if I started to deal with it maybe I could begin to lose the weight as well. I never really put the two together, but now I gotta deal with the Depakote putting more weight on me which was one of its major side effects. I'm just glad I finally found an African American female psychologist, I was surely surprised when they sent me to some white man first. I was like no offense sir, but you don't know a thing about the Black experience. There's Danny, why did she have that big ole bag and who is that?

"Hey girl, let me pop the trunk." I said looking at a young man who was the spitting image of Daddy. He went and put his bag in the trunk too and then opened the back door. Am I seeing who I think this is?

"Hello, and who are you?" I asked the little boy.

"I'm Tommy." He said and took out a Gameboy from his backpack.

"Well if your Tommy, I'm your Auntie, Destiny. You can call me Auntie Dee Dee."

"Yes Ma'am." He said nervously.

"Hey girl, you meet your nephew." Danny asked.

"Yeah, what a big surprise." I reached over to hug her.

"Yeah, well I only get him on major holidays, but that's going to change isn't it Thomas." She smiled looking back at him.

"Yeah, that is going to change." He said and smiled for the first time. We all got to talking and catching up. I found out the boy is six years old and has been living with his father's mother and father. He liked it but misses his mom. Danny lived a couple blocks over from him. They don't live together because she lost custody to his father in the divorce and then he didn't even want to take him so he left him with his parents just to spite her. The things people do in divorce just to hurt each other.

All of this could have been avoided if Danny would have listened to our Grandmother who said Tommy looked like some backwoods wanton preacher. But she just had to have him and his pretty green eyes and a big wedding with all the trimmings that come with it. She got pregnant two years later and then found out he had a couple different women on the side, one of which was pregnant too. He left her right after she had little Thomas and moved to Chicago to build another church with the other girl who he got pregnant. The only good thing to come out of the marriage was little Tommy who loved his Mommy.

"Mommy, can we listen to Kirk Franklin?" He asked Danny.

"Yeah baby, hand me the c.d. Is that okay Dee Dee?" She asked me.

"Oh, Kirk gets played in here all the time, I bet you I already got the c.d. up here."

"I like Stomp." He shouted and danced.

"Okay, you got it kid." I played the music and we drove home to my apartment. The next day was Thanksgiving and for once I'm spending it with my sister. Mama has been gone for about three years and this was the first time her girls have been together since her passing. It was also the first time her grandson has been with any immediate family ever. God was so merciful.

∆

Thanksgiving was wonderful. Tommy helped us make some greens and he even made a cheesecake almost by himself. He wanted raisins on it though. We couldn't talk him out of it so we put half raisins and half cherries. Michael said the raisins were a splendid treat. After dinner we all went to the movies. It was funny seeing Bishop and Mother Franklin together outside of church and just cuddled together with each other. I mean I've been to dinner with them before, but not at their home with their family. They knew they loved one another just by the way they would look into each other's eyes. Everything was going well until Bishop up and asked Michael.

"So son, when are you gonna make a move?" When he said that I knew he was talking about him getting married and as much as I wanted him to say something about me, I was kinda dreading his response.

"Oh, I'm taking my time sir, good things come to those who wait." Michael explained smiling.

"Good answer. But you know, sometimes God gives us treasures that we have to grab quickly and hold on to dearly or they will pass you by." Bishop told him.

"Well, I guess I'll have to consult him to find out where my treasure lies." He said to the Bishop.

"I guess you do young man, I guess you do." Bishop

responded.

The movie was nice and afterwards Danny, Tommy and I went downtown DC to look at some of the lights and stuff. Tommy was amazed at the size of the Capitol building as he tried to take pictures of it. We parked and let him climb the steps. Danny and I talked some more about plans for the holidays. She said she was going to take Tommy to Jamaica for Christmas for a week and didn't care what Thomas had to say about it. She hasn't even told them she was going out of town yet. I told her to be careful since she was trying to get custody again. She blamed her youth and being stupid and in love on losing her son. She also said I really touched a nerve when I brought him up the last time she was here. I apologized again for the whole incident and we promised one another we would never hit each other like that again. Then we started to talk about Mama.

"How did you deal with putting all the stuff together for her funeral?" She asked me playing in Tommy's hair in the backseat.

"Through a lot of prayer and Granny Mae helped me with a lot of it and Auntie Juanita. They let me do it because I was determined to make her proud." I said.

"How did you get the church to have it there." She asked.

"Mostly because we had been members there for so long and I was still on the roll as a member even though I've been living in DC for years. Mama still went but she didn't go like she used to when we were young." I told her.

"What do you think was going through her head those last days." She sounded a little depressed.

"Same thing that probably goes through my head some days. Just tired and wanting rest from everything and everybody, not wanting to go on because life seems too hard. She truly believed there was no other reason for her to live no more." I stated and remembered the pain of depression.

"Was my Granny mad at me because she only saw me when I was a baby?" Tommy asked.

"Oh no baby, she loved you most of all. She would ask me

about you all the time and prayed for you. She loved her only grandbaby. You know Dee Dee what gives me peace about the whole thing." Danny says.

"What?" I asked.

"The fact that she's not tormented no more. Is that wrong?" She stated.

"Naw, it's human. Mama went through a lot of stuff and her diagnosis was heavy on everybody. Let me ask you this though, why you take so long getting home?" I asked her turning down seventh.

"I thought that if I didn't go, she would still be alive. Just like I thought if I didn't come down here you wouldn't be sick. I got issues, Sis. I'm a runner, always have been. Can't stand to be in pain, don't like to show emotion." She said rubbing Tommy as he slept in her lap. The phone rang and I picked up. Michael was calling to say goodnight and mentioned how much fun he had with me. He asked if we wanted to go shopping tomorrow. Danny said of course, the early bird catches the worm. We drove home and talked some more about Mama and Daddy.

It felt good talking to my sister instead of talking at her. This was the first real conversation we had had in a very long time. And all it took was a six-year old boy to come in between us, divine intervention I say. Niecey called and said dinner at her Mom's was a mess. Everybody just looked at her like she was a ghost then her second oldest brother said the prodigal daughter returned and gave her a hug. She had to be introduced to all the kids who were all asking who is that? She said It felt good to hold a baby. Her sister said some things to her but she was polite. One thing I forgot about Niecey was how much she liked and needed to be accepted by people. She was the middle child. One day she'll get over that. We called Tracey on three way to see what she was up to.

She picked today of all days to tell Chucky she wanted to postpone the wedding for a later date. She said her Daddy almost shouted for joy. Her mother was mad at her and Chucky stormed out of the house leaving his parents there by themselves. I told her she could've picked a better time to do that but I forgot who I was talking to. Her response was.

"Heffa, you know me, gotta put a stamp on it."

Thirty-Three
Tracey

I just couldn't take it. We had been at odds about everything and the final straw was when he said he was not going to have his seed being raised by no other woman but their mother. This was after I told him I grew up with a nanny who became our family maid but was more like my Godmother. He was not trying to hear it and so I waited until I saw him on Thanksgiving to tell him we needed to slow down. Then he got all crazy, so I called off the darn thing.

He couldn't change my mind either. He was being unfair and didn't want to even consider what I was trying to say. The nanny would only be for a couple of years but he said that would be like a replacement when all I had to do was have someone else manage the shop so I could be home for our family. This ain't the fifties and I ain't Mammy.

When he started getting loud at my parent's house I had had enough. I was trying to just give us more time maybe until next May maybe, but since he was acting like a caveman he could be alone in his cave. I could take care of this baby myself. It was a new day and single mothers had been taking care of children for decades now. Plus, the Lord is my shepherd and I shall not want.

That's right me and Jesus got this. There was no way in the world that I would give up my career to be a stay at home mom just so he could scratch his ego. His mother might have been cool with staying home raising him and his brother, but I am not that type of woman. Nobody was going to put me in a box, not even the man I love.

So now I had to get used to my decision. I would still go on ahead and hire another shampoo girl and get another stylist to help with the new traffic of clients. That way I could take days off when I needed to be there for my son. Mother should be able to help as much as I needed her to, she was about to retire anyway. This was all going to work out.

Still though, I wanted Chucky to be there for our child. Who was I kidding though, he was not the father. I knew in my heart of hearts it's Robert's child. I just didn't want to give that fool any kind of foot end in my life. My money was all screwed up because of that meanderer. Now I needed to prove to the government where all this money came from and there was no way I was going to be able to admit that he was a drug dealer and a pimp. How in the world did I get myself into all of this mess?

Δ

It was a week before Christmas and I still had not heard a word from Chucky. Even though I broke his heart, I was sure he would beg for me to take him back at least once. I hadn't heard from him since that night he left my parent's house, but I refused to call him. I was starting to get worried, but I just know he was going to do something for Christmas. He always did. He could at least call a heffa though.

Things at the shop have been getting crazy. The first girl I got to shampoo had water all over my floor in less than a half hour. I had to fire her quickly. Then I found another girl who was about to graduate from hair school. She was working out fine except sometimes I think she tried to give clients her card like she was a real hair stylist. She still got six months to go before I would even attempt to let her really do hair.

My new hire stylist was working out okay I guess. She was older and really laid back, but she kept up with the latest trends and was a beast at sew-ins. When she did her first one at my shop she charged over four hundred dollars. When her client got out of her chair though, she looked like a brand new woman. I had to tell Ms. Jackie, girl if she kept this up I was going to have to charge a diva tax and get a piece of that.

Now I was waiting on Mother to give me the last piece to

the Christmas tree. Every year since I was three years old I had to put the star on top of the tree. Daddy loved it and always took pictures while filming it. Then we would sit in front of the tree and sip cocoa while he read the story of Christ being born in a manger. I couldn't get into it at all this time and must have gotten him worried because he stopped in the middle of the story to ask.

"What's the matter Strawberry?" I looked at him then busted out laughing because he hadn't called me my childhood nickname since I was twenty two. He started calling me that because I would beg for a whole bowl of fresh strawberries, eat them and have juice all over the place including my hair.

"I'm just thinking about my future. Chucky hasn't contacted me since we broke up." I explained.

"I always knew that boy was a coward. If he was a real man he would fight for you and not give up so easily. You don't need no man like that in your life, not as no husband at least." He said.

"Well she didn't give him no choice. You practically pushed him out of your life by acting like a child. Who cares about that darn shop, you need a father for my grand baby." Mother added.

"See I knew I should have kept my thoughts to myself." I got up off the floor and started towards the closet to get my coat.

"Where do you think you're going? We still need you to help us get this house together for the party tomorrow night." She huffed.

"I'm taking my fat butt home. I don't need to hear any negativity about my decision. If you were really concerned you wouldn't throw that up in my face Mother. Daddy thanks for listening and at least trying to make me feel better. I will be late for the party, but I will be there when I feel like showing up." I didn't even let her finish her words and just walked out the house.

I didn't want to re-think my decision. This was the best thing for me for right now. If God really wanted us to be together He would make a way but by the way Chucky was acting, so non-responsive, it's safe to say that our relationship was really over.

Thirty-Four
Sharon

So now it's Christmas and I was all alone. I will not break down and cry today no matter what. I made my bed now I gotta lay in it. Dee Dee said she would try to stop by later on so we could exchange gifts. I would go to Baltimore to see Mama, but I didn't want to bring everybody down with my mood.

I really wanted to call Marcus. If I could just talk to him one more time everything would start to turn around, I just knew it. I wanted to invite him to our annual New Year's Eve party. I'm going to call him, gotta show some courage for love's sake right.

"Merry Christmas, may I speak to Marcus?" I asked the woman who answered the phone. My heart sank as I waited in anticipation for him to pick up the phone.

"Merry Christmas, this is Marcus." He exclaimed joyfully.

"Hello Marcus." I said shyly.

"Oh, wow hello Sharon." He sounded surprised.

"Merry Christmas. How have you been?" I asked, trying to feel him out.

"Merry Christmas to you too. It's good to hear your voice. I'm doing a lot better, how about you?" He really sounded concerned and sincere.

"Oh, I'm making due. I didn't want too much just to invite you to our New Year's Eve party this year. Would you like to attend?" I asked, being hopeful.

"Sure, that would be nice. Can I bring someone?" He asked. Immediately I was depressed again and sulked on the phone.

"Yeah, you can bring your new boo." I sulked. I couldn't believe he had moved on already.

"Oh, there's no new woman in my life. And I like how you tried to fish around
to find out. It's nice to know that you still care. I still care Sharon." He said.

"Do you really?" I asked with glee.

"Yes, I fell in love with you and that is something that hasn't changed. But I don't want to be rude to my company. Send me an email for the party and I'll be there with bells on." He said rushing me off of the phone. I was smiling from ear to ear and just told him I'd see him soon.

"Oh Lord, was there really a chance still for me? I knew I didn't deserve it, but I would love a second chance. And God if you gave me another chance, I would do everything I could to keep Marcus and make him my husband. I know it was going to take some time, but Lord have mercy on me." I admitted out loud full of hope now. I knew it was going to take a miracle but after all the changes I had made over the past couple of months I knew anything was possible with God.

Δ

It had been three days since I spoke to Marcus and I was acting like a crackhead that needed another fix. I didn't know what I was thinking while I was dating the both of them knowing full well that I had fallen in love with Marcus. Cornelius kept calling and trying to come over because he wanted some sex. He had the nerve to still take that stripper on our vacation. I don't know what I saw in that man.

I knew what it was. He had everything on my profile list of the kind of man that would be a good husband for me. The only problem with that was I never once sincerely prayed and asked God if he was the man He wanted me to marry. It was all in His will now even the break up with Marcus.

Everything was going to work out though I just knew it would. Marcus was coming to the party and I was going to make sure that I was stunning. He would be hard pressed to even look at another woman over me. I had been praying earnestly about who God wanted me to marry. Of course, my vote was for Marcus for obvious reasons, but the major reason was because he was the only man that I ever dated that pushed me closer to God.

He did everything he could do to make me face the music. He never settled for me to just be behind the mask and not stand up to how I was feeling. He prayed for me and with me. I never did that before with any of my suitors. He made me want to be a better woman of God and take my relationship with God seriously.

Marcus was the kind of man that any woman would be proud to have on their arm. That was why I had to get over the fact that he was just a bus driver. The man still earned over forty thousand dollars a year and even though he didn't have to, he still manages to take care of his mother. That was more than what I could say for Cornelius. That clown put his mother in a nursing home as soon as he got the opportunity.

When God blessed me with my husband I was going to do everything that was needed to be the wife he needed. I will be his helpmeet and help him reach the goals that God will set before him every day. All I ask Lord is that you make me into the woman of God you need me to be before I become the wife you need me to be for my husband. It's no longer just about what Sharon wanted. If I wanted to be Marcus's wife I had to start actively waiting in patience. I had to really get prepared in my heart. On paper I was a great catch, but I knew my heart needed to change in order to be what he will need me to be. Lord that was all I had to ask.

Thirty-Five
Destiny

The girls and I decided to get in the car a drive down to Florida for a couple of days after New Year's. The drive down here was a mess because we kept making stops to let Tracey use the bathroom. After finally making it to St. Petersburg we went straight to the hotel and slept before going out to dinner. The beach was breathtaking at dawn. We got up early and ate breakfast in the sand. Most of the discussion this morning was on our love lives or lack thereof.

I don't know what Tracey was thinking by breaking up with Chucky but she was a strong woman, so I knew everything was going to work out just fine. Niecey got the courage to call Marcus Christmas day and he agreed to come to our New Year's Eve party. They had a lot of fun too. Now I was sitting here writing in my diary reminiscing over the last year or so.

I still couldn't believe I was single again, but I had a new friend. Michael was a good change from Stanley. Even though we have decided to just be friends again because of everything that happened lately, I sometimes found myself daydreaming about more. I don't know what the Lord had in store for us, but I just wanted to make sure I didn't make the same mistake again.

My sister Danny and I have really gotten closer and we had so much fun while she was here over the Thanksgiving holiday. I was so glad we reconciled our relationship and decided that life was too short to stay angry with each other over the past. She was going to need support in the next couple of months as she fights for custody of my nephew. The good thing that happened was her ex-husband was caught stealing from his new church and this time the board decided to press charges.

All in all, life was good and I could not complain. I mean

yeah, I was not one man's wife but nevertheless I truly understand the meaning of how to be a virtuous woman of God as described in the Bible. Everybody says just read Proverbs thirty-one ten though thirty-one and you will understand what that means. But applying it in everyday life, without being a wife, was something that was hard to do. Still though, every chance I get I will be measuring my walk against the word of God daily.

Not just so I would be prepared for a husband here on earth but so I could be the woman of God he would have me to be for the kingdom. There was nothing like the present to do what God said to do with my life and walk in my purpose. That was why I would be at the music studio with bells on next month ready to sing God's praises.

Whatever may come between Michael and I will be by God's timing. I was really falling for him, but I needed more time to get to know him and understand the man that he is. When I get back I hope to have dinner with him and maybe get better acquainted. Who knows, he may be looking for a wife soon and I may be in his sights. Who was I kidding? I was betting on it.

I sat there pondering over the things that had taken place then I prayed for Stanley and his ways. *Father I ask that you help me to totally forgive him and get over this entire situation. I know I say I forgive him but sometimes I get a twinge of anger that comes out of nowhere. I wanted to be able to trust a man again with my heart, to truly trust him. Stanley's betrayal was one that I didn't think I could survive. However, your grace has been sufficient Lord, and I thank you.*

Now all I had to do was walk in my purpose. Love would be there to find me at the appointed time but for now Destiny, girl just walk in your purpose. Like Mother Franklin said "A day walking in purpose is a day the devil doesn't have any control over". I have been doing well though. I've been taking my medicine every day and have even been doing some much needed walking. My health was not going to get the best of me because God is my Jehovah Rapha. With that being said I shall be healed in the name of Jesus.

The beach was absolutely breathtaking. I loved the fact that the sun was shining and the water was so peaceful. It wasn't a bunch of people out here though only a few couples sprayed about. Looking out across the water reminded me of the peace that was God's and the fullness thereof. When it all boiled down to it we each had to remember that his grace was sufficient and his mercy everlasting and that whatever good and perfect gift he has for us will be ours, in due season.

∆

Today I was meeting with my new manager Meek Turnbull. He said he would be able to get me the recording contract that I was worth. His boss who I met with last year said he would be the best guy for me to work with as a newbie. I didn't care just as long as he was about his business and wouldn't lead me astray. I saw a tall lanky Black man walk in with a nice leather coat on. He walked straight to my table.

"Hello, Destiny Price?" He held out his hand.

"Yes, Meek Turnbull?" I stood to greet him and shook his hand. We said our introductions then got right down to business. He said the next few months were critical in developing my sound and finding music for my debut album. He was saying so much I had a hard time wrapping my head around everything.

"So, wait let me get this straight. When do you expect me to have my debut album released?" I was confused.

"If we make this a full court press we should be able to have you ready by 2010." He said with so much assurance. I sat there in total disbelief. I could not believe that I would really be a recorded gospel artist in a little over two years. This was simply amazing, but I still was a little confused.

"But I don't have a contract yet how can I have the album ready without a contract?" I asked and waited for him to somehow let me down.

"Oh, that's no big problem. I thought they had sent you the letters already. You should receive one in the mail soon. We will all meet and hash out the particulars. Don't worry baby girl, you will be signed and singing His praises in front of millions before it is all said and done." Meek said and started packing up. We said our goodbyes but not before setting up a time to meet in the studio with everyone.

This was it. I was going to be singing God's praises in front of millions just like I dreamed as a little girl. I couldn't believe it, but I was so happy. Even though my health had taken a hit and I am no longer engaged to be married, I had no complaints. To God be the glory.

Now all I gotta do was show out at the studio and let them hear who I am as a singer. This should be easy. I was born to sing. Michael was going to be so proud of me. He knew I was meeting with my manager today and that I was so scared. He prayed for me over the phone before I left then told me to go in peace. I really like that man. *"Lord if you find in your heart let us take a journey together that you want us to take and be the man and woman of God that you need us to be. I promise I will give you all the honor and all the praise."* I prayed aloud.

How many times have I prayed that prayer? This time though I felt more convicted in my spirit about it. I wasn't just saying the words without understanding the meaning and the repercussions. As God answers this prayer let our lives be manifested into what is needed for the kingdom. After it was all said and done, I shall be one man's wife.

Epilogue

As the year started to get on its way we all had one thing in common: we were still single. Tracey no longer believed that being some man's coin, a dime piece, was what a real woman needed to be. Now that she was carrying a child she had to become the woman of God her child would need and that meant growing up and leaving the players alone. Hopefully this year she would finally realize that love was already in her midst.

Sharon finally took off her mask. Profiling as a woman that didn't need anybody was something she had to come to grips with. It cost her the love of her life but if restoration was really the season she was in there was no boundaries on what lay ahead for her. Love would be there when God says it's time for her to receive it.

And me, well let's just say being a wife wasn't something that was supposed to happen last year. Escaping the snarls of the devil has brought me closer to my dream. Still though, one day I would be able to tell the world: I am one man's wife. Destiny Karen Price would be that Proverbs thirty-one woman, no matter what the cost. I could also attest that my best friends would be that woman in today's world too.

Books By This Author

Love Without A Limit: Dimes, Profiles And Wives Book 2

The second book in the series for Dimes, Profiles and Wives.

To Say I Do: Dimes, Profiles And Wives Book 3

The third and final book in the series for Dimes, Profiles and Wives.

Fool For Love: The Devil In Disguise

A short story based on actual events.

Thank you for Reading

Please be ever so kind and leave a review and share your thoughts with others about this work.

Always,

Toya Raylonn Vickers

Made in the USA
Middletown, DE
16 October 2023

40891008R00146